WHEN THE ONLY WAY OUT IS OUTER SPACE

Time is running out for Alfons Anton, otherwise known as the wild beast of Saucer Hill. The Sadoos are after him, the Second Coming is about to come, and Alfons is going to stand trial—for triple murder!

Even as the oxygen shortage gets shorter and the list of catastrophes gets longer, Alfons refuses to give up hope that the alien Azydians will bring Bianca back to him. But little does he realize how much more zany life will be when the aliens finally do come back.

SAUCER HILL

PAUL ADLER

AVON
PUBLISHERS OF BARD, CAMELOT AND DISCUS BOOKS

SAUCER HILL is an original publication of Avon
Books. This work has never before appeared in book
form.

AVON BOOKS
A division of
The Hearst Corporation
959 Eighth Avenue
New York, New York 10019

First Avon Printing, October, 1979

AVON TRADEMARK REG. U.S. PAT. OFF. AND IN
OTHER COUNTRIES, MARCA REGISTRADA, HECHO EN
U.S.A.

Printed in the U.S.A.

J'annonce vérité simplement et sans pompe,
Et mon présage vrai nullement ne me trompe.

Nostradamus

• One •

I don't mind having killed them. They didn't seem to, much, either. I'll kill more if necessary.

For them it was probably the fulfillment of a dream, a vision, a prophecy. It may have coincided with their idea of the future. Certainly it was necessary for my own.

I've strung them up, robes and all, at strategic points below the top of the hill: one to the northwest, one to the northeast, and one approximately to the south. Three American Sadoos, seekers after wisdom, walkers in the path of peace!

They serve as a warning to trespassers: Beware of Man. Watch out for the wild beast of Saucer Hill!

Most of those who venture into the wilderness that still belongs to Primitivo Populi—even though Pops is long gone, the fences broken down along with the law that once protected them—most of those who come here are like the three pendulous young sages with their bulging eyes and rotting mouths: meek, intent on inheriting the earth. They smile insanely. They roll their eyes when they see me. They turn up their palms and chant. Within minutes after dying, an evil wind breaks from their orifices, the stench they have held back through their holy lives. Once you have smelled that stench even those who still walk cease to be human!

They came up from Port Creole early in the morning. They had either camped at the foot of the hill, which is unlikely because I would have heard them if I had not seen them, or else they spent the night in one of the adjoining valleys, and started up at dawn. They came with the sun, bells chiming, hairbands fluttering. And they kept climbing: through the eucalyptus grove, chanting and stopping every now and then to touch the grass with their foreheads.

I let myself down from the fort and watched them come up the hill seeking salvation, a pathetic procession. The sun was engaged in its useless struggle with the brownish veils of smog that hung in layers over the landscape. Here and there the distant columns of San Francisco shone through, dull and unreal. Mount Tamalpais crouched rough and defiant to the southwest. But close to me, all around me, there was still birdcall and leaf, and the giant eucalyptus at the edge of the summit platform, surrounded by grey-bearded California oaks and the tangle of shrubbery that yields blackberries twice a year.

The hawks still survey this country. They are aloof to all. Gliding, circling. In five years since I built the fort atop the tree I have not seen them flap their wings more than a hundred times. At dawn or dusk they will deign me with their proximity high up in the eucalyptus. Sometimes in rain or wind they ride out the weather on a top branch. They may be waiting like myself. They may be waiting for my departure.

I stood squarely on the little summit meadow when they panted and heaved into sight, led by a tall, bony scarecrow; one destined to shed what little remained of his flesh and skin. As soon as they saw me they halted and gave obeisance, bent low, touched their foreheads to the ground and remained transfixed on their knees for a long time. At last the scarecrow pulled himself up and approached.

He carried a long staff, using it more like a crutch than a symbol of his caste. His face was powdered white, but streaked with dirt. He had tried to paint a bright red cloverleaf on his forehead. This had now smudged, though its outline was still visible. The lipstick red had mingled with the white powder. His forehead was dirty pink. His hair hung in greasy strands to the shoulders, his beard was matted. I was about to lift my hand, when he stopped, ten feet away. I noticed that his fingernails were long, as a witch's; filthy, cracked and broken.

"Humble pardons for intrusion, Master," he mumbled piously, "we come in peace and do not wish to disturb your meditations, seeking solitude ourselves and refuge from the noisy marketplace with its multitudes . . ."

"Shut up!" I said roughly.

He bowed his head and stood like that while his companions began to chant again, prostrating themselves, raising their heads from time to time, eyes closed. Their robes were filthy, but their faces not as offensively decorated as that of their leader. They were his disciples.

"Shut up!" I screamed, and the chanting stopped. I took two long steps, seized the scarecrow's staff and stepped back.

"This is my hill," I told them. "I live here. This is my territory. You can rest for an hour, then you go!"

"We have vowed to start our monthly Silence, Master," said the leader. "We will start at noon, and will not speak again for three days. No man may order otherwise. Grant us this time. The Divine Mother will reward you beyond your greatest hopes. We will pray for you as we merge with the ocean of bliss that is the Divine Mother!"

"One hour!" I said.

He reached mutely for his staff. I crouched and broke it in two over one knee. I handed him back one of the pieces. I told him that I would keep the other half until they left. I said that the Divine Mother had no authority on this hill. I repeated that this was my territory and that I wanted no one here besides myself. Meekly, he shuffled back to his friends. Then, together, they advanced to the center of the meadow and squatted there. After a while they assumed yogic positions, turning their faces to the sun. Opening their hands to the light.

They sat like that through the day. In the evening they made a fire, and took turns keeping it alive. I killed them in the pale light of dawn. I came down from the fort and slipped my knife between their ribs, one after the other. They offered no resistance. Only one of them, not the scarecrow, had his eyes open. He looked at me with love and forgiveness in his gaze until the light went out of it.

I had to tie a piece of cloth around my nose and mouth. I broke and rubbed eucalyptus leaves between the heels of my hands and stuffed the mixture in behind the cloth, then I dragged them down the hill and strung them up by their own belts and prayer shawls. They were light as feathers, but they stank like tons of rotten flesh.

A week has passed and they stink worse than ever. Even in the bitter taste of fumes that drenches everything here, their stench is distinctive. I don't mind it. It doesn't matter. I think of it as holy incense for the Divine Mother.

• TWO •

I saw Captain Mahoney's tiny Ford, unmarked, wind its way in and out of the forest down in the valley. It crossed the bridge at the end of the stow lake, moving steadily up toward the broken-down gate to the Populi lands.

Carefully I opened the black-and-gold box with my playing cards and began to shuffle them. They have an old-fashioned apple printed on their backs: golden dots on a maroon base, dots in neat rows, seventeen little dots in each row, twenty-seven rows on each card, most of them blocked out by the outline of the stylized apple. It's presented in silhouette with a commercially psychedelic design of flowers, teardrops, leaves, spirals and curlicues in gold, yellow, green, candy-pink, sky-blue, light-blue, red and white, and common orange.

To describe it well I have to use my memory as much as my eyesight. The colours have faded and the diamonds on the Diamond-2 are no longer diamonds. Time has made triangles and torn tents out of them. Next I turn up Diamond Jack whose mutilated double-image gazes out this way and that, never at me, always away from me at perhaps a thirty degree angle, but not as though he were looking into the distance. Flaking though they are, his eyes are soulful and his mouth holds still the touch of a smile: sweet, sad, innocent, sensual.

Then the Jack of Hearts, his dapper brother, in profile, with a meticulously kept mustache that curls perfectly at the tip. A more audacious ladies' man, in his left hand he holds the perfect flower with emphasis on the stamen, symbol of virility, fertility. Then the Queen of Spades, a somber lady. These cards need shuffling, and I shuffle while Tim Mahoney approaches.

Down by the burnt-out ruin of Primitivo Populi's once-proud estate, he parks the Ford and starts on the long walk up. Tim is in his sixties now. He keeps himself in shape. He looks to me like a young man with closely cropped grey hair. He moves steadily, without haste, leaning forward as he enters the eucalyptus grove, and even more steeply when he emerges.

I keep these cards mainly for shuffling. I've lost one of the two Jokers. The other one shows a black-and-white engraving of Capitol Hill and the words: Congress, Congress. The first Congress is printed into the sky above the dome, the second is its reflection in the white sea of shiny playing card surface now dulling, thinning from use. Every week or so I put them in perfect sequence, and it takes me at least a week to shuffle them into acceptable condition for a meaningful drawing and interpretation.

Tim is coming up the main path to the south and he passes one of the three Sadoos on his way up. I expected him to stay longer at the site, but he barely breaks his stride. I can't see the hanging corpse, but by now I have a good feel of Tim's rhythm and the time between clearings is just right for him to have walked right on through, maybe just glancing at my stinking sentry.

He is still wearing his surgical mask as he comes up over the edge and makes it onto the plateau. He takes off the mask, folds it as he approaches and puts it in his pocket. A neat man, a bachelor serving the law, Captain Timothy Lance Mahoney.

"Whew!" He raises his eyebrows. "Good exercise!"

"Be my guest!"

We shake hands. He isn't smiling. It's hot in the muggy sunlight and mosquitoes are out, so we walk over into the eucalyptus shade. We sit down. He takes out a pack of cigarettes, taps one out and offers it to me. Then he takes one out for himself and lights them with his lighter. Beads of sweat are on his forehead. And wrinkles.

"This is a bad thing, Al," he says, puffing smoke.

"Yeah," I say, "it stinks!"

He looks very serious, his face is perfectly straight. His baby blue-green eyes are wide open here in the shade and I can see that he hasn't come up here for an explanation. He wants to talk business.

"I'm trying to find a way around it," he says thoughtfully, "but I can't see it. The Chief is gonna want to bring you in."

"They were trespassing!"

He just keeps looking at me.

"They attacked me!"

He shrugs his shoulders.

"With what, Al, with what?"

I show him the broken staff. He shakes his head.

"That's silly, Al. Look at yourself. You're a big, healthy man. Who's gonna believe it?"

"This is my hill. I own this hill and three valleys right up to the county lands and Mount Tam!"

"Not legally you don't. Pops never adopted you, you're not his son, and he left no will. Technically it's Bianca who owns it."

"Bianca is my wife!"

"Is she? She's been gone for twenty years, Al. That's not gonna cut any cake."

"I have a daughter with her, and I don't care where she is."

"You don't have a marriage certificate do you?"

"No," I say. "I don't have any papers at all. You know that. I have a deck of cards, that's all the paper I need. Hell, Tim, I use grass to wipe my ass!"

"Sure," he says. He is just holding his cigarette and it burns away between his fingers. Before it gets to the filter, he heaves a big sigh and says: "Gee, it's nice up here!"

The hawks are out, four, five of them, gliding above and below, and a couple of seagulls are winging over from Mount Tam down to the lake. His nostrils flare as if he is taking a deep breath, his chest heaves, then he coughs and grimaces.

"Look, Al," he says, "there's only one way to get through this. I've thought about it, and there's only *one* way. It'll mean that you have to leave here. You'll go in somewhere for a year or two, no more, I'm sure. Maybe then you'll be allowed to come back!"

He pauses and lets his eyes roam freely across the soiled places, the thumbling, dilapidated wilderness.

"You got to plead Insanity," he says at last. "It's the only way. It's simple, it's easy. You'll have no trouble. Couple of years they'll let you go, I guarantee you. You got a history in this county, Al. You know and I know that there's a lot of people, a lot of the oldtimers, and they think you're nuts. You know it. Everybody's gonna say: Sure, he blew his knot. I knew he would, yes sir, it had to happen!"

Then I had a flash of what was happening and I could see that this was the thing with which they would force me to go all the way. This was nothing to get out of, it was what it came down to, all of it.

"How many murders this month so far, Tim?" I asked, getting up.

He lit another cigarette, apparently determined to stay.

"Plead Insanity, Al. Make it easy on yourself!"

"How many murders?"

"Thirty-seven."

"And last month's total in the county?"

"Seventy-three."

"How many suicides?"

"Ah, come on," he said, puffing, "lotsa suicides. You know what it looks like down there."

"So there are three more suicides up here. You get your crew up here, cut them down. They're religious fanatics. They committed suicide."

"With *your* knife?"

So he had stopped and looked at the bodies. He must have done it quickly and expertly. I pulled out the knife and handed it to him.

"Why not?" I said. "I did them a favor!"

"None of this will work. The Chief wants you to come in. He wants you to come in tomorrow!"

He, too, got up, toying with the knife. He held it up and made it gleam in a spot of dull sunlight. He weighed it in his hand. Then he gave it back to me.

"How'd they get up on the trees when they were dead?" he asked.

"I put them there. When I found them dead, I used their bodies, that's all. Who cares!"

He shook his head, walking out into the light.

"What if I don't come in?"

"We'll have to come back and get you."

"I'll be up in the fort," I said.

"We still have enough fuel to run a couple of chain-saws, Al. We'll bring your tree down. You can ride it to the ground. Maybe you're lucky and break your neck!"

He walked out across the meadow and I followed him. This was the first time I had seen Tim mad at me. He stopped.

"Hey," he said, turning. Now there was a smile on his face. It was a grim smile, as if he himself were determined to see this through, as if he were me up here, waiting, waiting through the years while the world was going to pieces. He smiled grimly as if he understood all of this and envied me my position. But also he smiled disdainfully, because I was a sap, and a crazy man.

"You still waitin' for that saucer of yours?" he asked, pulling his surgical mask out of the pocket.

"Yes sir, Captain Mahoney," I said cheerfully. "Any day now!"

I watched him going down the hill. Once he slipped, floundered, but recovered his balance. Turning, he waved back up at me, as if he had known I was watching. Later that day, as the hills were rising to meet the sun in the turn and swing of the earth, a van labored up the steep grades, and in the failing light of dusk they cut the corpses down and took them away.

• Three •

I shuffle the cards and the King of Spades comes up. Could be Tim. Maybe Tim of twenty-two years ago, just after Bianca disappeared. A younger Tim Mahoney, Lieutenant, Missing Persons, Port Creole Police Department. I shuffle cards, memory pictures, snatches of conversation.

"And when was she last seen?"

"Kinda hard to tell," said Primitivo Populi. Or

maybe: "Can you recall, Mr. Populi, when your daughter was last seen in these parts?"

No, even then Tim was informal, more intimate. The King of Spades with the confident look of authority, in the unfolding of his maturity, forty years old, on his way up to the post of Chief of Police of the City of Port Creole, California.

"It's hard to say," Pops, then around seventy, may have said.

Tim Mahoney stirred his coffee, looking appreciatively around the enormous ground floor of the barn, remodeled to make a giant living room. Pops liked community, dinner conversation, wanted his workers to sit at his own table. He knew what was comfortable, he had taste, and he loved to show his rough side.

Old, comfortable furniture was arranged in casual groups and clusters, random constellations which were shifted around from time to time. Whenever anybody sat down or got up, dust wafted through the muted sunlight that came through patches of milky plastic in the roof.

"Maybe you could try," suggested Tim.

"Sure," said Pops, "you're not pressed for time, are you?"

"No, sir. As long as it takes!"

"Oh, well," Pops grinned deviously, "nice to see a man who enjoys serving the community!" Or something like that. And then Tim may have said, politely: "I don't mind telling you that I like my job."

Tim has always been a good police officer. He listened to everybody. He took his time. He didn't rush. On the other hand, he knew just when to get up and leave. Even then he had learned that patience was the key word in his business. A man didn't have to run all the time. What counted was that he ran when it counted.

He listened impassively. He did not interfere, nor did he encourage the talker by nodding. He wasted no energy listening. He sat behind his cup of coffee, perfectly relaxed, spending easy time with eccentric Primitivo Populi, the old man of the hills.

Even then a lot of people were disappearing. It was nothing special. Some were found dead, some crawled away from a rape with bashed-in heads, some never showed up again. An astute observer of the scene had called it a "subliminal civil war" or at least the beginnings of such a war.

Port Creole still maintained the glitter of its special historical position. Its inhabitants had been preparing for months for the Port Creole Bicentennial, in celebration of the arrival of the Threemaster *Liberté* manned by mutinous French soldiers and almost two hundred natives, male and female, from the East Coast of Africa, in the Year of Our Lord, 1777.

Every year a full-scale replica of the *Liberté* carrying every inch of available sail blew into San Francisco Bay, negotiated channels and shallows and dropped anchor a stone's throw off the Port Creole Old Town. Crew and passengers, happily united through the perils and hardships of a two-year voyage, rowed to shore and the celebration began.

Port Creole had maintained its status as a Free Town in Free Territory and all of Creole County even now, at least in theory, has the right not to renew its pledge to the Union of the American States which is made every year on the occasion of this celebration. From where I sit I can see the Creole County Civic Center, the vast dome of its once-golden roof now faded and cracked. The solid-gold model of the *Liberté* that sailed proudly through the Fifties and Sixties and Seventies, atop its spire was sawed off and melted down during the riots of '84, when the starving mob stormed it demanding money and food.

But then, when Pops Populi's spread was still a fine estate, and the Civic Center sparkled and gleamed visible to the highest orbiting space station, then there was still some order, some hope for finding Bianca, for making this a special case. And Tim Mahoney was the man to do it.

He looked at his folded hands while Pops talked.

"Bianca likes to be alone. She takes long walks by herself, and she does this all the time. Sometimes she takes a sleeping bag and spends a night in the woods. I pay no attention to her leaving. I know she left Friday, but I don't even know if she left early or late. Maybe early afternoon. Certainly on Friday. It's hard to say."

Tim leaned forward and rested his elbows on his thighs. He looked like an athlete on the bench.

"She's a strong girl, even though you couldn't tell it by looking at her. She'll walk through all that land clear to the bay sometimes, all the way to Creole. I gave her a break, you know. Couple of times she stayed out, so I figured maybe she left late on Friday, so by late Saturday she would be back. Even Sunday morning I figured. The nights are still cold, so she wouldn't spend more than one night, maybe two at the most, that makes it Sunday. Monday morning I call you for sure. Now it's Tuesday. Took you a whole day!"

Tim didn't move.

"I came as fast as I could," he said, "we're understaffed."

Bianca had probably decided to leave at last. It didn't surprise anybody on the spread, not even me, and I had only been there for a year. She never gave the feeling of permanency, of home, even though she was thirty-one years old and had always lived with her father. Her absence was natural. She was often away and even though these were always short periods, they were absolute. When she left, she was gone for good, and when she came back it was like a homecoming. I was always happy when she came back.

"Don't get me wrong, sir," said Lieutenant Mahoney, "but did your daughter have a friend, a lover, somebody who might be jealous?"

Pops was not in the least embarrassed.

"What do you think?" he asked the younger man. "It's not the same as it was when I was a kid. Yeah, sure she did. But she'd never pick a jealous type, not Bianca. Pierre Brasseur, for one, if you keep it to yourself."

"The fighter?"

"Around here we call him the Champ!" said Pops, smiling.

Tim slowly looked around at us. Nothing seemed to escape him.

"This is Alfons," Pops said toward me, "he's the youngest. He's sixteen."

"Seventeen," I said.

"Lost his dad in Vietnam, mother offed herself. I picked him up in town last year. He's a bright kid. And

17

talking of lovers, I think he's head over heels for Bianca, aren't you?"

It was not true. I adored Bianca. She had taken me through the Populi lands. She ran like a goddess of hunting. She knew every glen and burrow in the five-thousand-acre wilderness. I wanted to be like her. How could I have fallen in love with my idol!

"What do you think happened to her?" Tim asked me.

I was flattered by his attention.

"Oh, it's okay," I said, trying not to giggle, "I mean she's okay. This is nothing. You don't know Bianca. Nobody, no nothing surprises her, I mean you can't catch her by surprise. She can sense a bobcat half a mile across the valley."

"But she may have gone to Port Creole," he said.

"No bobcats in Creole," I smiled.

Lieutenant Mahoney got up, thanked Pops for the coffee and told him that he would think it over. He'd go and see the Champ, of course. He would look at all the information and let us know what he came up with. He shook hands with Pops, waved at me and took a long slow walk across the barn floor to the big front door which Pops had shipped from Italy. It had religious figures carved on it, local saints, the Holy Virgin, the Infant, and on each corner protruding prominently, the ancient Roman fasces. Tim walked out into the sun and I followed him.

He got into his old unmarked Ford with its oversized antenna that still seemed to be swaying. He took off without looking at me, driving slowly, with a minimum of dust raised.

I ran up behind the barn, through the oaks and along to the lookout where I sat down and waited while he wound his way down toward the valley floor among the trees. At last he came out into the open and bumped through the gate onto the asphalted, county-maintained road, accelerating just slightly.

He wasn't in a hurry then, he's not in a hurry now. If they come up here to get me it won't be any different. He'll leave his men down by the ruins and climb up alone. He'll bring me in by himself, peacefully, for old time's sake. He doesn't understand that I can't leave here, that

I'll fight, not for my freedom or for my life, but for time. If I have to kill him to gain half an hour I'll do it.

It's been twenty-two years, but it might just as well have happened twenty-two minutes ago and I remember every moment of it. The saucer could not have been here for more than three minutes. Three minutes is all *they* needed. Three minutes is all *I'll* need.

• Four •

So I went riding on the rail, took the old Chevy down to 101, up across the overpass and started hanging in the cloverleaf. It was a new thing then, hanging in the cloverleaf. You drove down the downramp, short stretch on the freeway, up the upramp, all in nice, tight curves. Then across the overpass and the same thing again on the other side, and back, and over, down and up, and over again.

After three or four cycles you began to feel that you were hanging in. You found your perfect speed and the idea was never to speed up or slow down. No brakes, no pumping! A dreamy feeling developed. Somebody might pick up on your hanging in and join, and soon there might be four or five cars of different vintage cloverleafing.

It was a merry-go-round, not a race. In fact, you were supposed to keep your position like a wooden horse on the wheel, and everybody turned to the same station so you all had the same music, same rhythm. It might go on for ten minutes, half an hour, even an hour. It was a centrifugal game, good especially for the girls who sat against the door behind the driver to "get pressed." Getting pressed was *their* thing. I drove alone, and I drove couples who got pressed together. Sometimes I drove Titiane Mbuto, the beautiful creole girl.

I liked to hang in alone though. I began to feel that I was in a spiral going down and down, through different layers of freeway, deeper and deeper, always in the vicinity of a different Port Creole, a deeper Port Creole, like the many layers of the ancient city of Troy. It was a spiral in time, and the Chevy was my time machine.

All those machines are dead now, the Chevy is dead, the internal combustion engine is dead, all crunched, stoned to death by the poverty masses. The veils of smog hung deep even then, and the stench was punctual and spreading, but there might still be a sparkling winter's day when the chrome flashed and shone and the deep sea-green of the original paint job beckoned. I kept the Blue-Flame Flathead Six engine spotless as I rode down and down and still farther down.

No thought then of killing Sadoos. No Sadoos in fact. It was Hare-Krishnas, and Clear-Light Premies, and Cosmic Beamies. Only the creoles, the sons and daughters of the original shipload of Africans and French sailor-soldiers, resisted the religious trend, remained fiercely independent, like Titiane. She was the perfect clover-leafer. She even told me when my speed was right, and she told me that she had a perfect way of telling.

"I go by how my heart feels. It tugs and pulls and tries to move over to the left. There's the right pull that feels like candy love, and that's the right speed. Make it pull a little more!"

And after a while she would say: "Now you keep that pull, you keep me happy, Monsieur!"

She was proud of her creole ancestry, and the French men in her lineage, and she loved to speak the flat, lazy, voluptuous patois of Creole County. She was a creole princess, and I was her chauffeur. And she had given her heart to the aging Elvis Presley. In fact, she wore Elvis Presley panties even though she admitted that his role in *King Creole* had nothing to do with what it was to be creole.

"He did a good job though," she told me, "all that chocolate powder with the blue eyes and the dyed hair. It could be like that if there was no creole, if that just came up, then it could have been like that."

It was pathetic for a girl like Titiane to be in love with Elvis Presley.

I knew I shouldn't, but I still asked her: "What's he got I haven't?"

She kissed my driver's neck from behind.

"I don't know but I'd like to!"

"What's a coupla lousy gold records or twenty!"

"It's not the records, but what's on them, sweetie!"

"If I had a gold record, would you?"

"Would I what?"

"Wouldn't you would me would?"

A guy was trying to cut in on me just as I was bearing down out of the curve onto the freeway. He was pushing a fine 48 Olds, deep blue, and he must have seen that I was hanging in. I just kept my speed. He was just a little too slow. He made it ahead of me, still on the freeway, and started his turn but then I had him by the bumper and for maybe three, four, five seconds I actually pushed him. I could feel the weight of the old Olds on my bumpers. I didn't change my speed. If he'd slowed down or tried to brake I would have carried him out of the curve and let him slide off into the ice-plants, I might have made him tumble even. Then he burst free and wooshed off across the overpass and down again.

"He's gonna try to get you," giggled Titiane.

He'd shocked me out of our dreamy conversation and the fun was over. He was obviously a new guy, and he was looking for trouble. It happened sometimes. Some latecomer would come along and try to make a race out of it. The Olds looked great and he was probably turkey, but he just didn't know the rules of the game. He was catching up fast. When I was across the overpass and started on my downward turn he was already hitting the cement on the other side of the freeway, but I kept my speed.

"What you gonna do, meats?"

I turned off the radio.

"I'm gonna listen to him," I said, showing her my profile with as vicious a grin as I could.

There was the hum and woosh of the ordinary cars, all the poverty slaves locked into their unchangeable rhythm and sound. To us then it was just as if those cars and those people were not on the road. We didn't see them, they made only background noise, and they never never got in our way. It was like rain falling through snow. They were the warp of traffic and we were the woof. They drove in straight lines, we wove in and out. They were okay, but here this freak was hot on my tail.

Above the warp hum I could hear the woof roar of his engine, like a waterfall catching up with us.

We made the cloverleaf one more time, then, second time around he was coming down as I was going up on the same side and I knew that this was the stretch in which to do it to him, so I slowed down a little. Halfway across the overpass he came shooting up behind us.

I went down, leaning nicely into the turn and he was right on top of me. I just gave it all I had and in an instant I was traveling at his speed and accelerating and that is how we hit the freeway, one behind the other.

It was so simple he never understood it until he was already deep into the turn, halfway up to the overpass. I just didn't make that turn, just kept right on the freeway. It was known as uncoupling; I uncoupled him. It was all over. If he wanted to come after me now he'd have to go across the overpass, down onto the freeway, up again, back across the overpass and down again. By that time we'd be parked at Howard Johnson's. Not that anybody ever went to Howard Johnson's, we only parked there. We'd park at Howard Johnson's and dash across the street to the Taco Top.

And even the Taco Top was a decoy, as was the small parking lot behind it which bordered right on bushes and a steep, rock hillside which contained three caves, all hidden. And *that's* where we liked to go to smoke!

• Five •

Captain Mikhael "Mike" Voronov, Missing Persons, playfully challenged his lieutenant.

"Okay," he said, "let's start with the A's. Scott Adari."

"It's Adair!"

22

"All right, Adair, Scott, missing since April 5th, last year."

"Nothing new!"

"No corpse, no letter, nothing?"

"Nothing."

Voronov took the "O" stamp, adjusted the date on it and gleefully stamped the Adair file "O" for Open.

He put the file carefully to one side, starting a new pile on his desk and began reading off the names on the succeeding files.

"Applebaum, Joseph."

"All we know about Applebaum right now is that he may have been abducted, maybe killed, for unorthodoxy, heretic ideas!"

"No body?"

"Not yet."

Voronov stamped the file "O" and transferred it to the new stack.

"Bone, Barbara."

"We got a good lead on the girl just last night," said Lt. Mahoney. "Some of her jewelry turned up on the Market, and one of my men managed to buy a ring. We're questioning the seller, just a kid. We've threatened him with five years for blackmarketeering, but he has trouble remembering the face of the man he bought it from."

"Well?"

"Looks like she's dead, sir!"

Reluctantly, Captain Voronov stamped it Open.

"Better fed than dead," he grumbled. Mahoney didn't grimace. It was too early, even for jokes from his superior. He picked up the next file.

"Exley? What the hell! Nothing under C, or D? What about Carpenter, is it Carpenter?"

"Carpentras, sir. Don Carpentras, a self-styled writer. Carpentras turned up last week. Says he ran from all the publicity, fans, autograph-seekers."

"Didn't he write that book, that . . ."

"No, sir. Carpentras has never written a book in his life. He's monomaniacal, delusions of grandeur, nobody ever asked him for his autograph. In fact, we got a bad check charge on him, but he says he'll pay with his next royalty check. As far as we're concerned he's a harmless nut!"

With great relish, Captain Voronov lit a cigar. Then crushed it. He compressed his lips grimly.

"No D's either?"

"No D's this month, sir."

Voronov picked up the next file as a light started blinking on his intercom box. He threw the switch.

"Yeah," he said, turning the mutilated cigar in his hairy fingers.

"A kid, Captain. His name is Alfons."

"Send him in!"

Captain Voronov flicked the switch.

"Alright, what about Exley?"

"George Exley. An engineer. Left suicide note near the Three Roses Motel on 101. We found his clothes, too, but no Exley."

One of the secretaries opened the door and let me in. The door closed behind me and I stood, facing the two men.

"Could be a second set," said Voronov.

"Exley had been out of work for over a year, Captain," said Mahoney, "I doubt if he'd leave his only decent outfit by the side of the freeway if he didn't intend ever to use it again."

"Sit down, kid," Captain Voronov said to me. I sat down and looked at them. Mahoney nodded briefly at me, Voronov paid no attention. Voronov was at least ten years older than Mahoney. He was a heavyset man with broad shoulders and he looked enormous behind his desk. But when he got up later he was shorter than I. He looked like one of those crablike remote control tanks they used to have in the Fifties and Sixties to control riot crowds.

"We found a shoe with blood in it on the other side of the freeway and traces of blood leading into the hills," Mahoney went on.

"No foot in it?"

"No, sir."

"Maybe somebody dragged the body off the freeway and up into the hills, though it doesn't make sense, does it?"

24

Mahoney knew better than to agree with his commanding officer.

"I don't think it was murder, sir. Too elaborate, too clumsy!"

"Alright," said Voronov, "Open!" and slammed the stamp down on the file.

"I wish there was a body, though!" he added thoughtfully, turning his attention to me.

"You're the Populi boy, right?"

"I live on Mr. Populi's spread," I said.

He started going through the stack of files on his desk, lifted the greater part of it to the side, shook his head.

"Kline, Kovacs, Kwock," he read off. "Lohengreen, I didn't know Lohengreen was still open. Well, I guess it is. McDougall, damn that McDougall, why couldn't he have stayed in line. North Bay!"

He ripped out a file and swung it through the air. Then, with deceptive calm, he began fanning himself with it.

"Pray tell," he teased his Lieutenant, "what is a file marked North Bay doing in here?"

Mahoney reached for the file, but Voronov leaned back in his swivel chair with a dainty gesture of refusal, playing the part of a prim geisha.

"No you don't," he savored his moment of triumph.

"I believe that is the North Bay summary file, sir," said Tim. "It has comparative missing persons statistics on the entire North Bay. It should be at the very bottom of the stack."

"Well, Lieutenant Mahoney, how are we doing? Comparatively, that is!"

"We're in third place. Just barely. That means in the actual number of Open File cases. Prorated by population we're way ahead of everybody in the whole Bay Area, sir!"

Voronov slammed down the file on his desk. The jet of air that shot out from under the cardboard threw back the cover of the file next in line. It turned out to be Populi.

"Aha, Populi! Bianca, Innocencia, is that right?"

"Yes," said Lieutenant Mahoney, glancing at me for approval.

"Yes," I said, "Bianca."

"Well, Lieutenant, I haven't read your report. Just give me an idea."

"The only clue we have so far, Captain, is Pierre Brasseur, the ex-fighter."

"Creole, ain't he?"

"Yes, sir, creole. I went to see him yesterday. He tells me that Bianca Populi would come to see him whenever she came to Port Creole, but that he hasn't seen her for weeks and that he found out about her disappearance when he tried to call her Monday. He sounds as if he's telling the truth."

"Can you help us in any way?" Captain Voronov asked me.

"I had a dream last night," I said.

Voronov got up and moved his bulk over to me. Halfway around his desk he stopped and, turning, stared helplessly at Lieutenant Mahoney. Mahoney also got up, walked over to the desk and idly picked up the North Bay summary file, put it back, turned and stood by his superior's side. This maneuver gave Voronov a chance to recover.

"Sure," he swallowed, "anything that might help. We have to follow even the remotest lead. Go ahead, tell us your dream."

"I'm certain it means she's alive," I said.

"Goddamn it, kid!" Captain Voronov's consternation released itself in a thunderous shout. "Don't tell us what the dream *means*, tell us the dream, just the dream. *We* draw the conclusions. That's what we're here for. That's what we get paid for!"

"In this dream I saw Bianca on top of the big hill above the spread, right by the big eucalyptus tree. It was weird. She started shivering, as if she was cold. Then she faded, so you could see through her. She turned to shivering glass. Then it was just a see-through column of mist that started spinning, flattening out as it spun, about the size of a car wheel. It shimmered in the moonlight and it started going up. It took off, higher and higher. Then it was gone, but the dream wasn't over. I suddenly had a calendar in my hand, a tear-off calendar, and there was a wind that turned the days; it turned fourteen days. I counted along as they turned, and then I looked up and that shimmering wheel was coming back down in the moonlight. Then the whole scene happened again in reverse. The wheel turned into a spinning column of mist which turned to shivering glass with a human outline, and then a faded kind of Bianca, and then it was Bianca again, smiling. Then the dream was over. I woke up. I got up and had breakfast. I came down to Creole first thing."

"And what makes you think anybody could survive turning into a car wheel?" asked Captain Voronov.

"It was just a dream," I told him, "but it's given me a lot of hope. I think . . ."

Voronov waved me to shut up with one hand. He got back behind his desk and sat down. He started fondling his chin, re-examining his cigar, which gave him an idea. He threw the switch on his intercom box and said: "Send in Bundubu!"

A golden-skinned creole officer came in and saluted. Voronov pointed to the cigar on his desk.

"Put that thing in a safety envelope!" he ordered. "Send it over to the lab. Don't tell them where it comes from. I want them to examine it and tell me what they come up with and I want them to treat it like an emergency, top priority!"

Officer Bundubu used the fingernails of his right thumb and index finger to pick up the cigar. He carried it out like a dead rat.

"Alright," said Voronov when the door had closed behind Bundubu, "I'll tell you what I think of your dream, Alfons. I think it's a fine dream. I think it's a poetic dream. In fact, I like your dream. But, but . . ."

He leaned forward confidentially. His face was serious. He seemed to know exactly what he was going to say. But then everything sagged. His ears, his mouth, his shoulders.

"It's not scientific," he finished lamely. "'Like the cigar. *That's* scientific. See, now in a couple of hours somebody's gonna burst red-faced through that door and hand me the results of the lab test. They'll say that they're sorry, but the fingerprints on that cigar match mine. Or else they'll try to cover it up, you know?"

I honestly did not understand what he was talking about.

"It's a great dream. It's everybody's dream: mine, yours, Mahoney's. But it ain't scientific. I appreciate your coming up here to help us, and I want you to know that I'm gonna think about that dream. Not only that, I know it'll give me *pleasure* to think about it. Let's let some time pass on this, shall we?"

I got up and walked to the door.

"Anything you come up with, Al," Captain Voronov called after me, "don't be insulted. I'm a little gruff sometimes. Give us a buzz."

I just walked out, took the express elevator from the 36th floor of the enormous Civic Center and jetted down. I wasn't hurt. I had gone there to tell them about the dream. I had a notion that where Bianca was they could never get to her. Nobody would tell them where she was either. She would come back when the fourteen days were up, I knew it. I felt as if I had been given a secret which meant power. I knew more than anybody in the whole world about Bianca Populi.

In the Captain's room, Voronov was staring at Mahoney.

"It's so awful," he said. "It's so goddamn awful, Tim! Why does it have to be like this?"

Voronov began picking up the files again. He tried vainly for a minute to pick up the broken continuity. He let them slip from his hand. His face was a tragic mask of insupportable sorrow now.

"Goddammit, Tim," he sighed heavily, "I wanna go back to Mother Russia!"

• Six •

I took my sweetheart riding around the county. We went through the cloverleaf a couple of times to see in what direction we would be expelled, and it was north.

Creole County occupies about a quarter of the pie

of San Francisco bay lands. Its eastern boundary runs just slightly northeast from the shore, in the north its outline is curved and adjoins Sonoma and Cool counties, and in the west it slips into the Pacific Ocean which itself even then had lost its horizon and qualified even on the clearest days for no more than a very large lake. To the south the Creole County headlands form the northern foundation of the Golden Gate, its bridge, the throughway to San Francisco.

From above, especially in the spring, the county is heartshaped, but a heart tilted to the right at perhaps a forty-five degree angle. Port Creole lies where in a real heart the pulmonary artery would be discernible. We started out from there and were soon in the Sunday morning woosh and wheel, bound for nowhere and everywhere at once within the county lines.

Titiane was in a happy picnic mood, the radio was on and she had expertly selected the creole station which now at the time of the great Bicentennial was full of carnival music, traditional shouts and rhythms, whistles, fifes, rattles, rolls and the cheerfully plaintive voices of young creoles aspiring to stardom. Titiane loved her native music. She loved to dance. She could barely sit still, squirming and tapping her feet.

She wore a light, shortskirted dress and had her feet up on the immaculate chrome of the glove compartment. I didn't mind. It was sturdy old chrome. It had already lasted almost a quarter century. It was permitted now to start flaking, to crack and peel, though it didn't. Her skirt rode up on her thighs and once in a while I glanced to the right, taking my eyes off the road, admiring her slim, tawny stems whose muscles stood out in shadowplay, in long shallow valleys and low, smooth ridges.

She wanted me to move down into Port Creole from Pops' spread, and to live with her.

"I know you could sing, Al," she teased me, still clapping her hands with the song. "You could become a great star."

"Can't sing if you don't have a tune!"

"Any tune, it doesn't matter. Just listen to yourself, you'll hear creole music, I know you will. You're French, right?"

"Partially."

"French blood, a little is enough. You'll sing one day, I know you will!"

The Chevy was in a traveling mood. We drove as far north as we could and then swung off 101, turning west to cut across the coastal hills and mountains, some of which border right on Populi lands. All we had to do was get out and start walking south and we'd be home. I couldn't help stopping the car at one of the summits. We jumped out and ran up a hill. It was misty and cool, but Titiane didn't care. I had calculated my gesture, it would be all-embracing, sweeping the crests of hills in the far distance, but all there was was fog, creeping slowly upward. Still, I announced:

"Some day, my girl, all of this will be mine!"

She flew into my arms and we stood for a moment, looking out over the enchanted landscape.

Back in the Chevy it was pleasantly warm. We sat, warming up. Titiane reached into the bag and came up with a thermos of coffee. It was delicious. Then we drove on.

I started humming along with the music, while she played the dashboard chrome with her heels. She was wearing black-and-pink panties. Most of the time she was watching the trees go by, but once in a while she turned to me and smiled, nodding with the rhythm.

Soon we broke through into the sun and she made me stop, took off her shoes and started running ahead along the road, beckoning me to follow her. She ran at about eight miles per hour, steady, for about a mile, then she got back in and asked me to run. What could I do? She slipped behind the wheel and I got out and started running. It felt better than I had thought it would.

After a while I let her catch up with me and jumped on the front bumper and she drove me another mile or so through the wind. Then I got back in, and she let me drive again.

We wheeled on through the hills and came out near the coast, not far from a place called Oriental. It had once been a Chinese labor camp, but now only a laundry and a restaurant remained of the original population. We had shrimp chow mein for lunch and finally got to the ocean about one P.M.

I don't think people go to the ocean anymore. Even

30

then the beginnings of the stench which now makes it hard to approach any large body of water was developing. There were lumps of black glistening coal-like substance everywhere on the beach. We called them Nuggets of the New Age. They were coagulated oil slicks that drifted about the oceans of the world and were washed ashore by the slowing surf. Titiane picked one up and aimed it playfully at me. She threw, I dodged, we started running side by side, simulating the ancient game of lovers on the beach, just as the ocean itself was simulating the great life force it had once been.

A group of people huddled nearby, I did not count them. As the wind turned suddenly, we could hear them chanting. They were nodding at the ocean and the clouds, their long hair hiding their faces. We ran on past them under the steep shore, on until we were far away, and then we took off our clothes and ran even farther.

I let Titiane lead, and then she let me. We held hands when we ran together. Then we walked. Then we fell into the warm sand, looking up at the simulated sky and real seagulls fighting for survival above us.

Then it would never have occurred to me to kill one of these birds. Now I live off them. I go down to the lake once a week and trap two or three. They are still large, strong birds and their meat is tough. But I pound it tender and chew it well. Rabbits and deer, and even lizards have long abandoned hill and valley in these parts. Mushrooms still grow, and once in a while I catch a harmless garter snake. I have stopped thinking of seagulls as graceful.

Titiane followed them with the tip of one long index finger, painting their flight patterns into the sky. Her lips were a perfect blue, her teeth whiter than soul or sand, her tongue was red as fire. A wide streak of sand ran along the side of her body when she got up. Together we walked out to the tip of a spit, and there we spent the afternoon in the dunes, talking and chewing reeds. We squinted into the sun. We found a pool of water the tide left behind. It was ice cold and deeper than a mountain lake. Titiane dived in, but I didn't dare, and then I rolled her in the sand to warm her up.

When we got back, the band of praying people had left and the beach was deserted. The Chevy was waiting for us. We got in and drove down the coast, sparkling with energy.

We drove through the community of McNamara Beach, named after a former patriot, and stopped for a while to watch the sun set, but I could not think of it as the sun setting. There was no longer enough visual evidence even then to support the phenomenon that once caused the illusion that the sun was setting on earth. It was our earth turning one more time in its envelope of filthy air, far far away from the sun that still shone in purity, as it had before the invention of the internal combustion engine, even before the discovery of fire. We watched the earth turn its shoulder on the sun. We huddled before the night. We made the Chevy purr back across the hills, turning east again, south of majestic Mount Tamalpais, crossing 101, and driving into the lights of Belveron, the city that had constructed the largest Mechanical Museum in the western hemisphere. Titiane loved only one game there: Earth vs. Saucers, a patented electronic environment which simulated an attack of Flying Saucers.

She loved to be the attacker, while I took the part of the defender. We adjusted our seats in the little, tightly curtained enclosure. We fed two dollar bills to the machine and pressed the button, and were in space, I in my rocket-fighter, she in her saucer. I was scanning her in my radar screen, as she dodged and weaved before me. On the control screen she pitted her mobility against my numerical superiority: there were three rocket-fighters but only one saucer.

The saucer fired invisible laser beams, while the rockets dispatched miniature rockets. It took her only a minute to demolish one of my fighters. I saw it go trundling down in flames to my right. In a way it made it easier for me, for I could now manipulate one fighter with each hand and there was no longer any need for switching. It took a perfect center hit to bring down the saucer, and I was right on top of her, pressing the rocket release buttons.

She darted up and away at incredible speed, zooming off to the far limit of the illusory three-dimensional space in which we played our game. I frantically turned my scanners, but she was gone. Not a trace of her. It was impossible! We were separated by a cardboard screen and I could hear her rattling the handles and punching the buttons, so I knew she was still in the game. But try as I might I could not locate her. She was moving at incredible speed in an unknown direction, probably at the farthest boundary of the space created by this electronically co-ordinated system of mirrors and lights.

Just when I was about to give up, I caught her streaking down on me from behind, managed evasive action, and let go of my last burst of rocket ammunition. It missed. I was still flying, but I was helpless. It had now become truly a game, and she took full advantage of it, staying behind one or the other of my fighters as I turned and twisted wildly. She let me have it suddenly and de-liciously, and my left-hand rocket went down in that long, exaggerated spiral of fire, programmed to look the same no matter where or when or how a rocket-fighter was shot down. Then she came after the last of my air-force.

I gave her a good show. She was forced to fire twice before she hit me and I burst into flames. She kept her saucer idling casually just above the crash and flash and roar where the rocket hit the ground.

When we came out of the booth our faces were red and our eyes shiny and we avoided looking at each other until we were back in the safe, dark enclosure of the Chevy. Then we started necking.

• Seven •

Certainly they are coming to get me for the silly act of expediting three pious souls to the happy hunting grounds. They are making a big production out of it. Three sheriff's cars park down by the gate, a fourth crawls up to the Populi ruins. I hear the baying of dogs, shouted instruc-tions. These sounds come floating up to me in peaceful bubbles to collide softly with my ear. All this nervous commotion while I try to drink up the sunshine.

I have about an hour, I figure. They advance cautiously, even though Tim knows I have no rifle, no explosive weapons. Maybe he suspects traps; camouflaged tiger pits with sharp stakes at the bottom to impale the law enforcement officers! None of that! The Sadoo corpses were my only protection, and they were taken away. I alone will have to face the cops.

There is nothing much to face. I know Tim. He will use force only if absolutely necessary. He won't shoot. He may not approve of what I did, but he would never shoot a friend. They are trying to enforce a law which no longer exists. Seventy-three murders in a county with a population of two-hundred thousand. In one month! Murder is what the people want. It's what they're *doing!*

I assumed until now that the police had degenerated into a self-protective club, a uniformed club of privileged citizens. Obviously this is not so. They are actually coming out of their fortified headquarters to pluck a man out of the wilderness. That is what they are doing. They are already three days behind, almost four. They are trying to catch up with the past, proceeding on memory. The corpses of the Sadoos have long been incinerated, packed, stored in the library of infamous deeds. They have been assigned their numbers, their place in history. A minimal role they played!

On the platform atop this hill I, on the other hand, must play out a more dramatic part. There is no question that they are serious, that they will inform me of my rights and that, if only for the record, I must state my position. There are a number of alternatives. I can climb up to the fort and make a stand from there. I can go north and never come back. I can try to talk them out of it. Or I can choose the hideaway. Even with dogs their chances of finding me there would be slim.

In the end I do none of these. Tim comes up onto the summit meadow and I am still sitting here, sunning myself. What a waste of time!

"Alright, Al, let's go!" is the first thing he says.

I get up and face the three of them.

"I thought you were going to come alone, Tim!"

"Regulations!"

"Well, read me my rights, then."

One of Tim's men starts reading my rights. I have the right to remain silent. Anything I say may be used against me. I can waive my rights and discuss the case with the law enforcement officers. I am instructed to surrender peacefully.

"Just for the record, Tim. What about my right to fight?"

"A man can always fight for his freedom, Al, you know that."

We stand there in the sun, staring at each other. If the saucer came now, right now, I know I could hold them off. They would be immobilized. They have come to arrest me, not to kill me. The musical dish shimmering in rainbow colors would plop out of nowhere, appear in time and space just as it did twenty years ago and suck me up, beam me aboard. I realize that I still don't know how they do it, how they did it with Bianca. Bianca will be aboard, and maybe my daughter. She is coming right now, I can feel it. Now is the time, right *now!*

"Well?" says Tim.

"You're a coward, Tim," I stall, pulling my knife out of its sheath. "You know damn well you couldn't take me in by yourself."

Tim says nothing, staring at the ground. After a while he turns to his men and talks to them almost in a whisper.

He starts taking off his jacket. Then his tie. Now his shirt. He looks good, grey hair on his chest.

"Okay Alfons Anton," he challenges me

I throw the knife away and he unbuckles his gun.

"You can come peacefully or fight," he tells me. "One way or the other you're coming in!"

He takes a few steps in my direction, his two men watching. He begins circling to the left. I don't make a move. It isn't necessary. I know I can beat Captain Mahoney. He must be a little surprised that I don't move or change or even turn my head as he comes around behind me. I spread my arms and the next moment he's clamped his arms under them behind my neck and is trying to bring me down with a full-nelson hold. It won't work. He isn't strong enough.

He tries to press his knuckles against the back of my

neck, but I've tilted my head back and the muscles are bunched close together, too thick and strong for his bones to penetrate. He is working heavy. It takes a lot of strength. Then, in a pause, I go limp and slip out of the hold.

"You can never do it, Tim!"

He comes at me again.

"It's too late to do it now, Tim!" I tell him. "When I was a kid I admired you. I was a good kid. Now I'm too big. I can afford to be bad."

He keeps coming and I hold on to him as soon as he's within reach. I've clamped my arms around his and he can't move. He's trying to throw me off by jerking out his hips this way and that, but I'm in front of him, and I just hold on.

"Come on, fight," he snorts. "What is this kid stuff!"

"You like pain?"

He angrily buries his chin on my chest and tries to press down on my collar bone, so I release him. He is sweating profusely. He comes in again, swings and hits me on the shoulder.

"First time I hit you, Tim, all the fight will go out of you!"

He tries to hit me again, but this time I block his punch, catch his wrist and pull him in again, holding on to both his wrists. He tries to kick me away, knee me in the groin, but my knees are up just as fast, deflecting his. Now and then there is a bony clacking sound, and it hurts like hell.

I let go suddenly, catching one of his legs and he goes sprawling in the grass, but is up in a flash. I can see that he is angry now.

"You're just a kid, Tim," I tell him. "After all these years, you're just a kid. You think I'm crazy. You think I'm a kid. You think I'm nuts. But I'm having a good time. What are you having?"

I can half-see, half-sense the two cops approaching. They are sneaking up from behind, and they mean business. So I turn and face them, taking a chance on Tim.

"Gentlemen, gentlemen!" I caution them.

They stop and Tim comes around.

"Come on, Al," he says.

"Sure."

"You're gonna come along quietly?"

"Sure, what else can I do? Aren't you going to shoot me if I don't? Or club me, or hurt me?"

"We may have to, Al!"

"I want to stay up here," I make my speech. "I like this place more than any other I know. Besides, it's vital to me. This is my pickup point. This is where she told me to wait, and this is where I must wait. They may come for me while I'm gone, and then I miss my chance. On the other hand, my body is more important. If I go with you now I may come back here in time for the rendezvous. You said yourself it was possible. Even if they come while I'm gone, they may come again. It's a calculated risk. I go trapping sometimes. I go for water. I try not to stay away too long and it's the same thing now. You guys can take me in and I'll try to get back as fast as I can. It's a chance I have to take. So that's why I'm coming in with you now!"

So we start walking down the hill. I walk slowly in order not to embarrass them. It was not as good a show as I expected. What is there in self defense? Not much!

Tim is trying to keep up with me. He wants to say something, but apparently he can't think of anything.

We trudge through the eucalyptus forest and down across the big meadow, then the path along the weed fields of the old Populi spread.

Tim hasn't bothered to put manacles on me, a noble gesture. I ride in the back of his car through the familiar landscape. We bump through the gate, onto the county maintained road and along the public camp grounds with its broken-down campers and dirty children's laundry spread out on branches and bushes. I wonder why they keep washing laundry and with what. There is no soap, there is only little water. Some of the filthy kids are screaming and jumping up and down, waving at us as we pass.

We get out on the highway and pick up speed. Tim is still trying to talk.

"I bet you're wondering why all this has to happen," I tell him, just for conversation. "That's because you still think you live in the best of all possible worlds. It's still alright with you, ain't it, Tim? You still eat your steaks and your salads, and you get your oxygen allotment, more than three or four times the quota, right, and only the purest stuff. So what have you got to worry about? You get government oxygen, and it won't run out. You wear your mask, and you got your uniform. You actually enjoy this. You figure it wasn't you who did it. If you'd sat still all your life, it would still be just as it is. So it's not your fault. *They* did it, right?"

Tim just can't get it out, even though I wish he could. I'm sure it will be sympathetic. He knows, he must know that he shouldn't have taken me off that hill.

"You're right, too," I tell him. "It wasn't you. Nor anybody else either. It wasn't me. Nor him, what's your name, sonny?"

The driver doesn't immediately react.

"You, driving this car, what's your name!"

"Shut up, Anton!" says the driver.

"Smarten up, kid," I tell him, "you got lotsa time to do on this planet, lotsa time. You may need me sooner than you think. Now what's your name!"

"Mwaba," he says.

"Creole?"

"It's against the law to distinguish ancestral origin by genetic or ethnic derivation, sir," he informs me, almost polite.

"Okay, kid, it's against the law to kill saints, too, though for the limb of me I don't see why!"

We drive along, each enveloped in his own thoughts. I feel fresh and free. The Azydians must know of this; they must be monitoring these developments. They are working within the cosmic plan, no doubt, and they know their role better than I know mine. It *had* to come to this! They will let me be carried to the periphery of life down here, and *then* they'll pick me up.

"I used to think people were worried about what would happen, Tim. I used to think they cared. No way. They were having a good time. Look at this kid Mwaba here. You havin' a good time, Officer Mwaba?"

"Yes, sir," he says smartly, almost winking into the rearview mirror.

"See," I tell Tim, "Officer Mwaba is having a good time. So are you. So am I. So, all is fine. Always has been. You can pick it up from a book, can't you? You can just read it off the paper, or through earphones, right? A little of this and a little of that, and *that's* what it's all about. No need to plan for the future, is there? You got religion, Mwaba?"

"Yes, sir, sure do!" says Mwaba now enthusiastically.

"You like to chant?"

"Any time of the day, sir. I was chanting just before you started talking to me. I was doing it silently. You don't have to chant out loud."

We were driving through Old Town. The stench was unbearable and Tim turned on the vaporizer which made it worse.

"Turn that thing off," I told him. "I don't like you to make a monkey of my nose!"

He turned it off. Mwaba handled the little car expertly so that you could almost imagine sitting in a big six-cylinder gasoline engine automobile. We turned right, and right again, and were on the approach to the Civic Center. The parking lots were crowded with tents of the Latter Day Crusade, but there was no wind, so that their banners hung limp in the air.

I hadn't expected anyone to know about my arrest, but I was wrong. Held back by policemen, two thick lines of Sadoos watched me get out of the car and walk into the building. They stood silently, their arms and hands raised in yogic positions, their eyes rolled upward toward the center of their foreheads. It was impossible not to perceive that they wanted revenge.

• Eight •

Pops Populi drank wine to get over it. He could not accept that his daughter had finally left him. He sat in the dusty vastness of the barn with a half-gallon bottle and a glass while the wine sought its own level.

"Take the Irish. Take a guy like Mahoney," he was

saying. "He probably doesn't drink. That's the price he had to pay for coming to America. Every European who comes here has to leave something behind. That goes for their kids, too. The father still remembers what he lost, but for the kid it's worse. The kid just feels the spot, but doesn't know what's missing. Pour!"

I poured more wine. The floral sheen of California wine lay thick on his face, his eyes were damp and brimming with moisture. His lips were cherry-red like those of a child and the veins stood out on his hand as he raised the glass.

He was talking to cover up. His pride was hurt, and much deeper than his pride, a real ache reached for the surface. He did not miss his wife, never had. But he did miss Bianca. My role was to listen. Even Emma the cook listened while she prepared lunch. Soon the workers would come in from the fields and a little later they would show up, washed and combed, humbly, to take their places at the patron's table. He didn't need them or his fields. They worked short hours and were paid twice the minimum wage. Among the Mexican laborers of California these dozen occupied a special place. Stories were told about the Populi spread, the bonuses, the gifts, the paid vacations, the medical insurance. Pops paid them to provide a little work, a little company, a little atmosphere. It was the best thing he could do short of living in Mexico.

"Ireland, such a blessed country," said Pops, "Mahoney lost the green, that's what it is! That's why he's in Missing Persons! Green is hope, green is spring, and he lost it. Good thing he's a bachelor. It's no good for a baby to be born without green. They walk around like ghosts, blown this way and that by the wind, like Mahoney himself. How's he gonna find my baby without the green?"

It was more the wine speaking now than Pops.

"I had a dream," I offered. "She'll be back!"

"Sure, sure, but she isn't back *now*. She can't be back *now*, it would be too perfect. She can't be back while I'm going down. I know, I know, she'll be back when I level off. It's always like that. They want you to taste all of it, and me, I like to leave a little at the bottom of the glass. So pour!"

40

He had indeed left a little at the bottom of the glass and I freshened it up with more from the voluptuous looking bottle that represented the sensual consensus of half a dozen design researchers and their recommendations. It was a perfectly democratic body, shaped like the girl next door, everybody's ideal concept of how a half-gallon bottle should look and feel. You poured just to pick it up.

"If you want something bad," he advised me with a florid grimace, "be prepared to wait until you don't want it so bad anymore, then you may get it, and when you do, your thank-you will come out just right, not-a too big and not-a too little!"

He put on his best Italian accent and vintner's wink. There was a little wine on his chin just under his lower lip. Emma came in to start setting the table. She was a large old girl from Switzerland and she loved Japanese food. She especially loved raw fish and a couple of times a week I would take her over to San Francisco, to Chinatown, to pick out the best fish there was. There was still fish, thank heaven, because when there was no more fish, Emma had resolutely informed Pops on a number of occasions, there would be no more Emma either. The fish was going. So was Emma. Periodically no fish could be sold because of the sewage problem, or the oil problem. The bay was dying, the fish were sick, the ocean often vomited them up to shore. They stank when you cut them open. Emma's nostrils were billowing. She inhaled deep, apprehensive breaths. She shook her head. No, no! No good, this fish!

"I wish I could pray like I did when I was a little boy! This would be a good time to pray. But you can't pray to nothing. I can't pray to the Holy Virgin. It's too easy and it doesn't help. And I can't pray to her son; he's too tough. Such a stern face, such commanding eyes. Will you pray in my place, Al?"

There was nothing to pray for. Bianca would be back. I knew it, but everybody else seemed still to have problems with it.

"I'll play instead of pray!"

"Play what?"

"The radio," I grinned.

"Yeah, you, go ahead you," Pops mumbled not

unfriendly, "play your radio. Creolize the music, creolize the world. Maybe it's better that she's gone away from here: shake the boobie, wiggle the butt. If she could find herself a decent man, a real man. Even Mahoney, even him. I don't like the Irish in America, or the Italians. The only thing worse is the Irish in Ireland or the Italians in Italy. If I send Bianca to Italy it's like throwing a fly in a honeypot. For a girl like her to walk down the streets of Palermo, or even Napoli it would take her half an hour for a block. I tell you what Italy is: it's-a sticky!"

He drank more and spit some of it out to the side, a scarlet spray in the muted light. This was characteristic of him when he got drunk. It signaled a new phase.

"Oh yeah," he said, "they lock her up every day. You can't see her in the afternoon. You can't see her in the morning. They keep them in prison. They keep the whole damn family in prison. They don't even have parades, let them see the sunshine, the air there is, whatever. Everybody deserves an exercise period, even Jesus. So dark and dank in there, such solemn music! How I hate the Italians, how I hate the Pope. The Pope is like a crow in India!"

When Pops got drunk his mind jumped. He did not care to put his listeners in the picture. He could go on for hours, only now Bianca wasn't listening, and when she wasn't there he talked differently. I had never heard him insult the Pope. He did it like a man of the world, without much emphasis, but his images were deadly.

"You've seen it in the movies," he said, slipping and sliding through his sentences as if they were built on ice, "the corpses floating down the river, the Ganga, you know, and there's always a crow sitting on a corpse, pecking at the throat, pulling up strings, eyes, jewelry too. They can't wear it, so they drop it in the water. That's where the Pope is different. There's an Italian for you, from century to century through eternity. They have stolen *his* mantle, cast lots. The Pope won. He wins every time. He sits on the corpse of Italy as it floats down the Ganga. He pecks out the eyes of Italy, the throat. He doesn't want an Italian boy to come in and praise the Lord. He doesn't want Italy to *sing!*"

Luckily Emma came in with an enormous bowl

heaped full of steaming potatoes, her only concession to Switzerland. It was potatoes, rice, thinly sliced veal, chutney and soy sauce, and steamed spinach. Cheap beer for everybody who wanted it, mainly the Mexicans. Lots of ice-cold water. Even delicate little cakes that, according to Emma, were good for the digestion, the liver. She had found the recipe in a German translation of a Japanese cook book.

"I smell potatoes," Pops exclaimed, rising with some difficulty. He walked slowly back to the table and sat down at its head. I followed him to take my place at his side. A moment later the workers came in. There were the two senior men: Carlos and Julio. They had been with Pops for a decade or more. They came at first to earn the money to build a house back home. They saved faithfully and sent back what they saved, but it didn't work out. They missed their wives, their children. They had a choice of returning or bringing up their families, and Pops let them bring up their families. In a few years they formed the nucleus of the workers. Young men came up, relatives. Friends. No one worked less than a couple of years. Pops nodded at them and they sat down. The others followed suit. In a moment the eating began. Long ago Pops had given up trying to maintain silence at the table.

The food calmed him down. He ate quietly in the din and chatter of his protégés. Then he laid down his fork and waved me closer. He said:

"I don't care about the Pope, you understand that. Whenever an Italian gets mad he curses the Pope. You said you had a dream about Bianca?"

"Yes, it was very clear in the dream that she'll be back soon!"

"Soon?" he said. "And in your dream, soon was when?"

"Two weeks," I told him. "End of next week, I'm sure!"

He picked up his fork and laid it down again.

"She could at least have called," he said, drunk and tired, "we have a telephone and it's still working!"

• Nine •

I've been in here for three days now. As soon as I got in I missed my cards. Tim assured me that he would send someone to pick them up, but I have not yet received them. He told me they'd send a man up into the tree to put a lock and seal on the fort, but that nothing would be taken out.

The first day was whittled away by formalities. Fingerprinting. Taking down data: name, date of birth, height, weight, color of hair and eyes. It turned out that I am thirty-nine years old, six feet in height, weigh two hundred and ten pounds, and that my eyes are the color of my hair, both brown. My name is still Alfons Anton, and they still call me Al.

My jailers could not quite hide their surprise at my tan. Apparently murderers (for that is how I have been categorized) rarely have a tan. What they really wanted to see, though, was my anus. A man poked his finger into it and crooked it inside as if beckoning something or somebody in there to come out. Then he turned it slowly. They do this routinely in search of what they call contraband. It was not an unpleasant sensation, despite the predictable reflex contraction of the sphincter. It's a form of initiation, an old con whispered to me.

"They just feeling you out," he explained.

Yesterday was spent learning the routine. For now I am merely an accused, a suspect. I have liberties, may move as others do, line up for food in the chow hall. But I have my own cell. It's astonishing how quickly memory takes over. Already I dream of my hill, the grass, the buttercups and crocus and the silvery lichen moss on the trees in the moonlight. I can feel the swaying of the enormous tree that holds me in the palm of its three-

44

forked trunk. Still, I'm here, not there. What I miss more than anything else is the motion of the tree. I'm not used to sleeping on level ground. I'm the sailor, beached.

"Watch out," says the old con, "they know who you are in here!"

"Who *am* I?" I whispered back.

"You kill holy men! They call you a mudra!"

I'm not afraid of anyone in here, but I sense that it is good to keep my distance. I know, too, that they will want to make contact with me. The mob can never stand to be ignored. Mudra, mudra, what a strong, attractive word! Is that why I am here, to learn what it is to be a mudra?

They have given me a public defender, even though I need no defense. He is a young, eager man, with greasy black hair and a hideous beard. He does not seem interested in defending me, either. He spends his time explaining the law to me.

"When you kill a man, Anton, you put yourself outside society!"

"Them, too!" I told him.

"Them?"

"Those whom I killed."

"Then you do admit that you killed the three Sadoos?"

I told him that it depends on your philosophy and since I have none, it does not apply to me. Killing is a word that comprises only the body and as much or as little as is known about the metaphysical. If they cling to the idea that murder is the killing of a body they themselves will be doing the Sadoos injustice. The holy men believed, as all of them do, that the body is merely one of three vessels, all of which must be broken to allow the soul to escape and merge in the ocean of divine bliss. The young man is dumbfounded.

"I can't tell the jury that. They'll tear you to pieces!"

"Only my body, kid, only my body!"

I can never explain to him that what I am giving him is a bit of *their* philosophy. *I* believe in the body. Wholeheartedly. I *am* my body. They are trying to sentence *me*. I make no separations. They are them, they are mean, and they are after *me!* They want all of me, even though they may say that it is only my body they want. The spirit is not free, I happen to know. I am *not* on the hill. I *dream* of being on the hill. My body is me and *I* have trouble slowing down, having been a part of a eucalyptus tree for five years. Having been outside for two decades. Having got used to watching the hawks.

"Do you want to plead Insanity?"

"Nobody would believe me. There are too many people who hate Sadoos. Think of all the Cosmicians, and the Jesusians. The Dervishes, the Pastorians. All the splinter groups! They think I did the work of God. Some will say I *am* God. Vengeance is mine!"

"Well, Anton, you show no remorse whatever. How are we going to get you out of here!"

He needs to plan my defense. He wants to plead Guilty in order not to upset the judge. He feels in a case where it is so obvious that the accused is Guilty, it would anger them to receive a plea of Not Guilty. A long drawn-out trial. What will be my defense, if it isn't Insanity? And if I am not convicted, which is likely, the sentence will be so much more severe for my having wasted their time while outside the murders go on, the rapes, the kidnapings. While others wait in line for *their* sentence.

In the afternoon, yesterday, he came back. They let him in my cell; he does not sit down.

"It doesn't look good at all, Anton. Nobody likes the idea. You should plead Guilty. They will let you off."

"Am I guilty?"

"Well, what the hell, did you or did you not kill those men?"

"I slipped a knife between their ribs, yes. Did *that* kill them? Or that they were there! That they stayed when I told them to go? That they wanted to feel that knife? That they were tired? That they climbed the hill to the execution! What am I guilty of?"

"It's a criminal offense to kill a man, in this county, in this state, in this union. Anywhere in the world!"

"Do they arrest a man called Conditions? A man called Poverty? Doom? Starvation? Despair? Are *they* under arrest? What about Fate, is *he* in jail?"

He told me that we have a week for plea. Why does he run around like that, with shiny, baggy pants, hiking boots tied with fibrous old string? He wears a length of rope for a belt, proudly, and his belly hangs over it straining the grimy, spotted shirt. He even wears a tie, this worthy, which makes him look old-fashioned. Even so, compared to the correctional officers, he is what would have been called a badlookin' dude when I was a kid.

The correctional officers are civilians, most of them volunteers. They work for three meals a day, for soup, bread and crackers, noontime sandwich, all the coffee they can drink. Every once in a while an onion, an apple, a few carrots. Now and then they take home a quart of milk for the family. A man gets an extra visit and in return they get a cube of margarine, a quarter pound of coffee, a pair of shoes for the oldest daughter. The Sheriff has posted a notice in the Visitor's Room for everyone to see:

Keep Smiling
Outside We May Be Falling Apart
But In Here We Hold Together!

This is true to the point where it has been adopted as a mode of salutation. "Together" has replaced the Thank You, the Hi, the Good Morning or Later.

My cell is ten feet long, five feet wide and at least fifteen feet in height. The bed is a metal rack, regulation size with a thin plastic mattress, no sheets, one scratchy blanket. There is a toilet, a sink, a metal mirror that has been furiously dented by the fists of former occupants. The result is that my face changes everytime I look into it. The nose crooks to one side, the mouth droops pathetically or is torn apart in an explosive grinning grimace. One ear may be nothing but a flaring stub of flesh, while the other looks like a defective dish for catching solar energy. And my neck is broken up into layers that could be the reflection of a mirage of a human neck in the lazy ripples of a muddy desert water hole.

The floor is bare and pockmarked and around the center of the bed the occupants' heels have steadily battered it, scraped and polished it into a shallow concavity, an indentation that bespeaks the victory of persistent nervousness over cement. I, too, might be nervous. I'm prepared for it, but I'm not nervous. It just doesn't happen.

My best strategy will probably be to go along with what I can sense or recognize as their wishes. I should

plead Insanity. I should plead Insanity and No Contest. It's
a plea I have always admired. Latin is lost in the world,
but in the stubborn courts of California, even now as the
world prepares for the apocalypse, the true Second Coming, as the clouds gather and every night the multitudes
search the skies for the Divine Light that has been promised them, even now a man who wishes may still plead
Nolo-Contendere.

Night falls swiftly over the Creole County Civic
Center which contains the Creole County Confinement
Facility. The light of torches and the drone of mantric
chanting takes over the walls and airwaves. Outside, the
Latter Day Crusaders have turned their faces upward in
ecstatic expectation of their saviour. They are roaming the
streets of Port Creole jabbering of the true peace, the
cosmic soul called the Christ who will liberate those who
believe in him and cast out the wicked. They say that he
will come like a thief in the night, and that no one can
foretell the hour of his coming, and that therefore it is
good to expect him at all hours, but especially at night.

I do not expect him, not now, not for me. Before the
judgment day I will be snatched away, carried off to
other zones of time, join Bianca, embrace my daughter.
It must be so.

My cot is hard, I close my eyes. And still I feel the
swaying of the tree.

• Ten •

I wake up in the middle of the night, much later, maybe
early morning.

The torchlight still flickers on the walls, the chanting
can still be heard, but there is a strange, hollow feeling in
the cell. It is so still!

I want to rise, but don't. It's stuffy in here, humid,
and no oxygen has come from the grated injectors for a

long time, I can feel it, even though I've been told that oxygen is given three times a day and three times at night for fifteen minutes.

Then I see my trembling. I see it before I feel it. At the footend of my bed the blanket over my feet is trembling. My feet are trembling, all of me! There is a distant sound, too, a whisper of wind gently pressing on a distant forest.

Then a sighing, almost a moan, and then the first wave of the quake passes under me, lifting up the cell, the bed, me. I turn instinctively, lying on my belly now, holding on. I scream. I'm like a surfer, but my head is turned away from the surf. I jump up, get tangled in my blanket, ram my head into the wall. Barely back on the bed, screaming, the second wave passes smoothly under me. This time the metal under me is buckled upward and no longer gives a hold. I bounce up, screaming.

I clutch the bars, hold on for dear life. I can feel the third wave coming, and it's a big one. It's not smooth or relatively shallow. It must be two waves, crisscrossing, breaking each other, ripping up the landscape. It's traveling fast, still far away, and it makes a tearing, thundering noise.

Outside the chanting has turned to wailing. And there will be gnashing of teeth, I think. It is the sound of gnashing teeth, gigantic jaws gnashing and splintering teeth, enormous nails screeching on sky-high blackboards, a glass city strafed with rockets. The Creole County Civic Center cannot ride this one out. It tries to break it, but fails.

It cleaves open. The walls break and crumble. On my tier men are flung through the spaces between bars. I hold on to a single bar which slowly twists in my hands. The ceiling breaks. Heavy chunks of cement fall but miss me. All of this tilts to the side and the door to my cell slides open. The third wave has passed and still I am alive.

I take one step forward, and another. I'm out in the hall. Around me to either side many doors are open, broken, twisted out of place and shape. Inmates' bodies lie crushed in attitudes of death. Some stir but cannot move. I alone stand.

I look up. A portion of the domed roof has slipped away. Stars drown in stench and fumes and incantations.

A crater with jagged edges breaks through all levels down to the ground floor. Only the chanting continues, but it has lost its earthy quality. It's too beautiful, too remote. Have I alone survived?

Finally the last wave: a gentle, little one. One I can enjoy. Three earthquake lessons and already I'm an expert surfer, sizing it up as it comes.

With a little hop, skip, jig and a turn to freedom I dance my way through this one. I didn't know it was this easy! That is all there is to it? When the kingdom has been leveled? Has the resurrection occurred, am I the only just one?

A shiny figure approaches. Jesus! I fall to my knees, I bury my face in my hands, try to kiss the hem of his robe which is filthy from dragging over the grimy floor. Strong hands help me gently to my feet, ever so gently. An arm steadies me. A feeling of boundless peace overtakes me. Yes, it must be Jesus, in the form of a correctional officer. The quake woke him, too. He has thrown a sheet over his nude body and hurried to lead me back into my cell.

With a simple touch he smoothes the metal of my cot. I lie down. His hand touches my lips. I cast off on the ocean of blissful fatigue. In the morning I find the Creole County Confinement Facility miraculously repaired and functioning. I sit up and rub my eyes. There is dried semen in my palms.

I get up slowly and shuffle to the bars and stand there, clutching them, firmly, unwaveringly supported by the silent earth, embarrassed by the useless bombast of my nocturnal emission. I've missed the breakfast call and all I can do is stumble back and lie down to sleep some more.

• Eleven •

The guidelines for my defense are held in place by the consideration that I must return to the hill as quickly as I can. Therefore I have now decided to plead Not Guilty by Reason of Insanity. Bill Blut is pleased. Tim Mahoney is pleased. The jury will be pleased.

Blut is a young attorney, and he sincerely wants to help me. To him I represent a dinosauric phenomenon, a puzzling but interesting paradox. He vastly underestimates me, naturally. He thinks I know nothing of the law and spends long hours enlightening me on the subject, pretending that he, on the other hand, knows exactly what I am talking about.

He has managed to obtain permission to see me in the visiting room, a grimy enclosure with a wooden table and two chairs. The once-golden paint has flaked like my playing cards which Tim has still not returned to me. I can't be sure that the old photograph on the wall shows the current president of the United States of America. The duration of a term is now seven years instead of four and a man may stay in office as long as he succeeds in getting re-elected. I believe Immanuel Chin is still in. His crafty smile, the cunning slit of his eyes, the determined perhaps somewhat brutal line of his jaw, all these survive even in a photo where light and shadow have begun to merge.

Of course there are peepholes, and Blut keeps his hands on the table at all times. But every once in a while, when he thinks I am going too far, he kicks me in the shins and I respond with a hearty oath or epithet in the middle of a sentence. He must know I'm not insane, but if he does, he is putting up a good front.

"A lot of people may feel sympathy for you, Al, but

51

that wouldn't prevent them from sending you to the sound chamber!"

"I understand!"

"They don't have to look at you when they do it, you know. It's not a personal confrontation. Also, they want to get it over with quickly. They want to go home. They're scared. They have responsibilities. It's hard enough these days to get a jury together. So I won't upset them by objecting to certain jurors, right?"

"Okay with me."

"The best thing would be of course if we skipped the jury. Juries are vindictive these days. They're hungry. Their kids are starving or sick. They look at the box and see how the world is collapsing, and then they get a letter forcing them to jury duty. The pay's lousy. They get a pound of butter, two pounds of frozen hamburger, three cans of beans and all the coffee they can drink. It's their first contact with the outside world in months. And the first person they see is *you*. Can you imagine what you would do in their place?"

He glances around shiftily. He picks something out of his greasy beard, examines it with exaggerated care, then catapults it to a corner of the room. I have never seen his teeth. Where there must be a mouth there is a black hole, a burrow, hidden by oily undergrowth. His ears are totally covered, but he seems to hear well enough.

"You mean just a judge?"

"Sure, it can't hurt. The judges don't eat too bad. They're on government oxygen. They have bodyguards. It doesn't matter to a judge if you live or die!"

"Is that good or bad?"

"That's good, Al," he grins, opening the black cave. I can almost see flies taking the opportunity to escape.

"Well how can I convince them that I'm insane?"

"It won't be hard. You tell the psychic examiners all you've told me. Don't hold back a thing! That's all you have to do, Al. That'll get you through for sure!"

"But what I told you makes perfect sense. They can't possibly find me insane!"

"Don't worry about it. Trust me. We're trying to do this the easy way. You've been up there on the hill too long, that's all. These guys don't care if you think it's

52

your mama's titty you've been camping on. You just go ahead and tell them why you killed those men, and how you did it, and they'll pronounce you insane!"

He takes a long time to scribble something on a piece of paper and pushes it over to me. It says:

"Don't be stupid, Al! They know you're perfectly alright. I know you are. So does the judge. Only the jury doesn't know. This play is for the jury only. Now if we cut out the jury, we cut out the element of doubt. Judge'll find you crazy. You'll do two years, probably less. They just want to run you through quick so you get out of the public eye. There's a lynch mob of Sadoos outside and they're growing every day. They're coming in from all over the nation, chanting. We don't want them here. Now let's get this over with! And tear up this paper!"

Bill Blut may be working for the Public Defender's Office, but the more I listen to him, the more sense he is beginning to make. I listen to the chanting, audible even in here. There must be a thousand Sadoos and Latter Day Crusaders out there and only now does it occur to me that they've come here because of me.

I tear up his note and hand the fistful of pieces back to him. He stuffs them in his pocket, getting up.

"Okay, sir," I tell him, "let's waive the jury."

"Now you're talkin', Al!"

I have to shake hands with him and am still reluctant to do it, even though his hands are the exception to the rule of his appearance. They are clean, pale, soft, manicured. It is as if he considers them ambassadors of his touch. Even now they are dry and transfer to my own a faint scent of talcum powder, the rare and expensive commodity.

I'm beginning to see his plan, which is to slip this thing through with a minimum of fuss, disperse the Sadoos and Crusaders, ship me up to the Aberrational Facility just north of Oriental, and then let me quickly back up on the hill where I want to be. When he's gone, I'm taken back to my cell, and then it's lunchtime and I have a chance to discuss this with the old con who talks while munching on the piece of bread thinly covered with liquid butter and enriched with various proteins, vitamins and minerals to provide the daily subsistence minimum, or so it is said.

"Listen to me," he tells me earnestly, "this is the oldest game in the world. Get wise to it. They're heading you for the sound chamber. You'll be a beautiful corpse within a month."

He gets up, walks over to the garbage pail and spits a disdainful mouth of soggy mush into it. Then he comes back and sits down.

"You're out of touch, Anton," he continues. "They're feeding you the old line. Learn your rights. Stall. Drag it out. Insist on jury trial. Don't plead Insanity, plead a simple Not Guilty. You didn't do it, did you?"

I look at him wide-eyed. It has not occurred to me that there might be a person who believes in my innocence. The implications are clear: if there is one, there may be more. I raise my left shoulder and my left eyebrow. I sigh.

"Don't try to rationalize," says the old con. "I've been in this all my life. I keep up to date. I've been in Psychometrics for thirty years. Don't you know anything about your subconscious, man?"

What can I say. He's in for stealing food. He tells me they will give him a year, hoping he'll get killed inside. If he's still alive in six months, they'll let him go. It'll be six months of subsistence food and oxygen for him, not bad, and he, too, sounds as if he knows what he's talking about.

"Your subconscious cannot discriminate between past and present and future," he lectures, sloshing coffee. "Also it don't know the difference between reality and fiction. In other words you can make up any story and your subconscious will believe it. The problem with most people is they believe their memory, even though any kid in the street knows how unreliable memory is. It can be deceived; it fools itself often. You do something; I'll give you an example. Say you step on an ant, you kill it, but you don't notice it, right? So now let's say there's a revolution and the ants take over, and one of these ants comes out and says he was right there when his buddy got it, and it was *you*. He points his antenna at *you!* But you don't remember. Now that's half the battle in your favor. If you're stupid and polite, you'll say: Well, maybe I killed that ant, maybe I didn't, I don't remember. In that case the eyewitness will get you. But why not give yourself the benefit of the doubt and say: No, I *didn't* do it?"

It's a charming story, but I cannot immediately see how it relates to my case. The old con is quick to point it out.

"With people it's just as simple. Supposing you had killed those three Sadoos. Well, you know that that's illegal. So why believe in it? Why insist on believing in something that might get you the sound chamber? It doesn't make sense, does it? If you actually had killed them, you should have stopped believing in it *immediately*. You should have sat down right then and there and made up a better reality. You should have told your subconscious: I got up that morning and went for a walk and there was this corpse, and then another, and another. I was horrified! But what could I do? I *had* to pretend I didn't notice, wait until someone else discovered them, right?"

This is all crazy. How can I possibly get away with such a story?

The old con persists, however. He squints his eyelids and shakes his head, while an idea is occurring to him.

"Listen, kid, nobody saw you do it, did they?"

"No. Nobody!"

He smacks a fist in his hand.

"Then it's all circumstantial!"

"But my knife!"

"To hell with your knife, son. Everybody carries a knife. There's five thousand knives like that in Port Creole and fifty thousand in the county. Who says they were Sadoos anyway? Maybe whoever killed them wanted whoever found them to *believe* they were Sadoos. They may have been Sakhis, for example."

"Sakhis?"

"Yah, where've you been, boy? A Suicide Sect. They'll commit suicide at the drop of a hat and they've been known to knock the damn hat off if it doesn't drop on its own. Hell, that's what they live *for*, to off themselves! So here's three Sakhis ready to go, and they do, and somebody picks them up and dresses them up like Sadoos and strings them up to frame you!"

"That's silly!"

He slurps more coffee.

"Not in nineteenninetynine it ain't," he gargles.

"I must admit that I haven't paid much attention to what is going on in the world."

"You're telling *me!*"

A guard slouches over our table, pointing to the clock. We get up and line up to shuffle out like ducks in a row. The old con waddles just ahead of me. We turn the corner where he branches off and he says:

"Think about it, kid!"

"Shuddup, Pearl!" yells a guard.

I have not heard him called by that name before. Let's hope that he hasn't cast himself before a swine!

• Twelve •

In the small exercise yard of the Creole County jail, a man vomited. The old con shook his head.

"Have you ever puked green?"

"No," I said, "what does that mean?"

He did a quick little feint and sidestep. "It means that there's hope," he informed me.

A rusty old hoop without a net is fastened to a wall at a height inaccessible even to a professional basketball player, presumably because they wanted to prevent suicides.

"This is the toughest court in California," said the old con, passing the ball to me.

I threw it, but it bounced off the wall above the basket and right back into my hands.

"Impossible rebounds!" said Pearl.

We were playing man to man. He is ten, fifteen years my senior, but I found it impossible to get around him. All I could do was back into him, feint to the right and then roll to my left around his shoulder for a clear shot or even a lay-up. Even so he gave me just the shortest, hardest little shove at the crucial moment and, combined with the height of the basket, he made me miss and he was leading, sixteen to ten. So I called time out.

I asked him: "How'd you get your name? You don't look like Janis Joplin?"

"Thank God," he said, "but she gave it to me."

I am too young to know much about Janis Joplin, but even so I became fond of her voice, especially "Bobby McGee," back then when Titiane was in love with Elvis. I think I saw her once. She lived in Creole County someplace, with a hundred whiskey bottles and a dozen dogs to carry them to her, in a dark, old mansion, with plumes and brittle rhinestudded silk, pretending.

"I knew Janis long before she was Pearl, even before North Beach," he told me. "She gave me her name just a few weeks before she died. She was tired and she said she didn't want to take anything along on this trip. She even wrote it on a napkin and had the bartender sign as a witness."

We went back under the basket, I missed my first shot and he sunk his, and immediately after that he hit another one. I didn't know what to do with him. He was too good at long range. Most of the time he didn't even bother to dribble or try to get in. He just stepped back, got a little room for himself somehow, and launched. And he hit about six out of ten, which was good enough.

We were both sweating, I from running, he from age, I guess. I scored, and so did he, which put him up twenty-two to twelve, and he called the game.

"Wait a minute. We're playing full time, aren't we?" Pearl is puzzled.

"Full time?"

"Yeah, sixty minutes."

"You gotta be kidding, kid. We play to twenty-two on this court. What do you think this is, ping-pong?"

I let it go at that because it was just a move to save face anyway. Pearl beat me good and proper, and this was his home court. He was a senior All Star alright, an All American selection from the Creole County Confinement Facility, a man who had done time at Mulatto Point even, in the first state prison in the United States to employ high velocity soundwaves pinpointed at the vital areas: brain, heart, stomach and reproductive system, to cause instantaneous death. There was no need for the stethoscope or amplified audio monitoring of the fading signs of life. In fact, when a man was sounded there was little left to monitor. The first searing shock of penetration killed him. But good.

The man who had vomited was just carrying out a pail with the slop he had mopped up. We had ten more minutes, so we squatted in a corner of the cemented court. It started to rain. Pearl rubbed his bald head vigorously with both hands, grinning.

"Ah, Nature's own. Rain is the best part of jail!"

He was obviously in a poetic mood. My face was red, my chest sweaty from playing. I felt energetic and intelligent, and confident that I could win.

"I'm going to present a strong defense, Pearl."

"Defense is no good, kid. You have to attack."

"But how can I attack them? They're the system. They do what they want."

"Yeah." Pearl smiled ruefully. "Just that they don't know what they want!"

It was just a light drizzle, measured precisely into the oblong yard. It drifted down on us gently, snow in spring.

He consoled me, saying:

"You're not a bad basketball player, but you got to start caring about getting points. If you don't hit the basket you don't score and if you don't score you lose. I know it's slow, but that's how they play it."

"I like to play on a team, make plays." I said.

"Yeah. But to make a good play you've got to threaten, and only one way to threaten in the game of basketball, that's with a basket."

He was talking as if he thought of himself as a better basketball player. The game was still in progress and I had to try to stop him.

"You can threaten with the ball, too!"

"Sure," he grinned, wet and happy, "but to do that you got to be able to hold the ball in one hand!"

It was true. I can't hold a basketball in one hand, at least not comfortably. We got up and walked over to the door.

"If you're so good, why are you in here?" I asked him bluntly.

"This is where the action is," he beamed, "I've always wanted to get a mudra on my court."

I wasn't satisfied with his answer. This old con called Pearl began to unfold before me like an onion, and like the onion he made it difficult for me to see the next layer. He was exhausting and intriguing, even mysterious. I was not sure that I could trust him.

"Don't worry about a thing, kid. Remember what I told you about Psychometrics. If you had a machine that could read minds and make books out of them, you'd be amazed at the story of my life. Only thing is it wouldn't be the story of my life, but the story of my life I *wanted* you to read, see?"

We fell in line and marched silently to where he turned off for his cell and I walked on for mine.

• Thirteen •

"I'm glad you're pleading Insanity," said Captain Mahoney.

My playing cards were lying on the table between us.

"Thanks for the cards."

"Forget it. I went up myself."

He was no longer angry with me for resisting arrest. I could imagine him making the trip all alone, wrapped in thought of the past, pausing at the Populi ruins, remembering his grand play for Bianca, a valiant effort that brought out the best in a dying society. He had all dressed up, had brought flowers, rented a limousine, behaved mysteriously, blushed, kicked up dust and felt surreptitiously for the little velvet gift box in his pocket. I wondered what had happened to the diamond ring in it, and now was a good time to ask him.

"Whatever happened to the diamond ring for Bianca, Tim?"

It was a shocking advance. His head flew up, his

eyes stared. I had opened the forbidden door. Predictably, blackness poured forth.

"None of your business!"

He stared at me as the murderous intensity in his eyes gave way to a dreamy quality mixed with moisture, though not quite tears, the sad film of remembrance.

"Come on, Al," he said hoarsely. "That ring is lost." He did not take his eyes off me.

"Lost forever," he said.

"Well, you know the old saying . . ."

"And what about you," he asked, getting up. "What are *you* hanging on to? You're crazy to think she still loves you, even if you believe in visitors from outer space. Give up on her, Alfons!"

He was walking up and down slowly, a big bulge in the right pocket of his uniform. He stopped, pivoted, planted his fists in his sides. He looked more like a military man than I had ever imagined him. As the world got sloppier, Timothy Lance Mahoney had got smarter. He looked sharp as a fiddle.

"Bianca didn't love Pierre. She didn't love me. Didn't love you either. Face it, Al. She didn't even love Pops!"

"She had my baby."

He said nothing, sitting down again. He pulled an apple out of his pocket and put it down in front of me.

"To remind you of the hill," he said.

I didn't understand, but took the apple. It was a juicy yellow-green apple, no different from the apples they used to sell in stores. Today you might have to go all the way to a special place in San Francisco to buy it.

"It was the only one on the tree," said Mahoney.

I still didn't get it, had no idea what tree he was talking about and it must have shown on my face.

"The old apple tree," he sounded surprised.

"The old apple tree? You took this apple off the old tree?"

He nodded.

"That's amazing. In all these years I've never seen one single apple, not even a blossom on that tree!"

I stopped myself just in time. This wasn't apple season. There wouldn't be any apples anywhere in Creole

County until at least four months from now. I weighed the apple in my hand. It was fully grown, perfect.

"No apple grows on that tree, Tim!"

"That's what I thought, too," he said.

"This isn't apple season."

"Yes, I know."

I rolled it against my chin. It was smooth and firm. I tossed it in the air and caught it.

"Why is it so important to you that I think this apple came from the tree on the hill which I know will never again bear fruit?"

"I'm telling you the truth, Al," he said. "I examined the branch carefully. This apple wasn't put there as a lark, it *grew!*"

"I've been in here a week now," I told him. "I would have noticed it. It wasn't on that tree when you took me in. No apple in the world grows in a week!"

"What do you want me to say," he pleaded.

"Tell me the truth about this apple!"

"That *is* the truth," he said. "And I've already decided what to do about it. Nothing. Why the hell shouldn't an apple grow overnight, huh? Why not a *real* miracle for a change, huh?"

He was extremely agitated, gesturing across the table.

"There are close to three thousand registered holy men in this county, and nine out of ten claim that they've made the blind see and the dead walk. At least *one* blind, or *one* dead. I've never come across a man though who claimed to have been raised from the dead, not one, Al. It's all bullshit. Bull-Shit! This apple doesn't claim anything. It was there. I picked it. What do *we* know. Here it is, eat it! Stop asking stupid questions!"

I set the apple down and slid the cards out of their faded box. I began to shuffle them automatically. Tim was calming down. His outburst had not been about the apple, but about Bianca.

"Tell me, Tim," I shuffled luxuriously, "do you think it's possible for a man to believe he's going to be picked up by a flying saucer and not be crazy?"

He was in no mood to answer my question, so I asked him another one.

"That a man can wait twenty years for his lover and

61

never doubt she will come for him in a flying saucer? And still not be mad?"

I didn't really care; I just wanted to talk. He was the captain. He could stay for as long as he liked.

"That his life was not a dream and his memory a dream within that dream? That great things are in store for him? That he will be a hero, a great explorer and adventurer? And *not* be nuts?"

Tim had placed the apple on the palm of his hand and was contemplating it.

"Maybe that's the most important apple in the world," I said, "but not to me. You can have it if you want it. It's the less difficult of two miracles anyway."

He looked up, his eyes again far off.

"Onion would have been harder," I went on. "You could never say no onion would ever grow in a certain place. All the onion needs is a little soil, a little water, a little sunshine, a little . . ."

He began to laugh and went on laughing.

"Now you're nuts," he laughed.

"A little love?"

He tossed me the apple and I caught it neatly. His green Irish eyes sparkled and the red in his grey hair glowed.

"You goddamn faker," he roared, "wouldn't it be just like her to fall for a sonofabitch like you, wouldn't that just make sense?"

I tossed the apple back to him.

"All the same, Anton, she isn't coming back and there are no flying saucers in Creole County, not yet anyway. They turn up in the areas with a lot of inbreeding, up in French Canada, down around New Orleans, not here. People live here come from healthy stock, yessir!"

His laughter was turning into a grimace. He slipped from comedy into farce into tragic mockery. In his gestures I could see the chanting masses of Sadoos and Latter Day Crusaders outside, the pale, suffering faces, the emaciated bodies. The thinly stocked shelves in the supermarkets, the heavily armed guards who looked like bandits in ancient movies.

"Those poor Africans!" he finished.

"To say nothing of the Irish and the French!"

"What happened?" he asked tragically.

I seized the apple firmly like the great treasure it was and I put it inside my shirt.

"It came, Tim, and it went!"

The grin was coming back on his face now, fortunately. He would leave in a happy mood.

"It came, yeah. And it went," he said. "And it ain't never comin' this way again!"

• Fourteen •

The great Jubilee, the Port Creole Bicentennial, was in full swing. Giant replicas of the good ship *Liberté* had been erected, every inch of these scaffolds packed with fireworks. They were placed to the north, the south, the east, and the west in acknowledgment of the mingling of pagan ancestry with the Roman Catholic sailors and soldiers who seized the ship and steered it to haven back in 1777.

The Mayor of Port Creole, Hon. George Limantour, in conjunction with the City Council, the Judiciary, the Police, the Sheriff and with the benediction of Father Patrick Matanai-McInnis, a proud creole chaplain, had declared a state of benevolent anarchy in the city and county. Sexual promiscuity was not merely condoned, but encouraged. The state and federal laws against nudity and indecent exposure in public were suspended for the duration of the week, and the laws against sale and use of Cannabis Sativa would not be enforced for the same length of time. A well-known psychiatrist from San Francisco, Dr. Jimmy Johnson, appeared on television to describe the event as "an intelligent and sensible way to cleanse the public of dormant frustrations and fears, a fine example of mass therapy."

The Creole County Civic Center, except for the jail, had been thrown open to the public, and even the jail was affected. A general amnesty was granted to all convicts serving time for minor infractions of the law. Many others were made eligible for immediate parole, and charges were dismissed against more, and the result of this was that the county jail was essentially empty, an extraordinary condition. It had been made clear, however, that serious crimes that occurred during the celebration would be punished with great severity.

I and Titiane were dancing at the Club Creole just across the street from the Mechanical Museum in Belveron. Titiane was a great dancer and whenever she hit the floor the other dancers tended to stand back to clap their hands and watch her. At such moments I discreetly disengaged myself and fell in with the admiring crowd. I could never have kept up with her.

Titiane sweated freely. Her face was wet and shiny, her torso far back, her golden thighs trembling in the play of sinews and muscles. Her arms had become serpents that fascinated the spectators, her hands at once beckoning and warning. She was now a dangerous animal, now a goddess of mercy and forgiveness, and now a warrior princess in the ecstasy of combat. She was also a little girl, a poor lost teenager out there on the dance floor, fighting for fame and fortune, affirming her basic right in the pursuit of life, liberty and happiness, a child of the crumbling ghetto and proud descendant of the careless passengers and crew of the three-master *Liberté*.

The Club Creole was frequented by a mixed clientele, most of them readily identifiable by the dusky gold of their skins. The band was all creole, their lead singer an enormous young man with the physique of a jungle prince. He was singing his heart out for Titiane and she responded by turning toward the band, offering undulations of shoulders and pelvis to him as instant reward for his song.

I watched her, them, for a while then stepped out into the moonlit night. Thin veils of smog embraced the stars, assuming the task of funereal helpers for the earth and its companions. I walked down the main street, dodging singing and dancing celebrants. I left the laughter behind, making my way down to the silvery bay, along the beach under the bushy shore, out to the Belveron Lighthouse and beyond the point to a favorite place where I squatted to gaze at the city on the other side of the great bay.

It suddenly pained me to think of Bianca. Could she have gone to San Francisco? Shabby though the city had become, there were still fascinations. Depravity pursed overpainted lips in a flushed face, the workshop of sheer sex was always open over there. It was so simple for a woman. All she had to do was cross the Golden Gate and lay back to watch the procession of a thousand faces crossing her body.

I realized that I had not thought much about Bianca. She was the wild one, the huntress, the child of the hills and the wilderness. She had been at home with her father in his territory, but she had never given me the impression of permanency, stepping lightly wherever she went. I had never seen her sitting back on the couch, and sitting at the table a chair seemed no more than a prop, something to be touched, not used. She needed no support, not from a chair, not from a couch, not from the earth itself. Maybe that's why she liked swimming.

She had taken me often to a secluded part of the stow lake, a place where even the ranger's binoculars and sonar apparatus could not find her, an idyllic little bay made up of county waters for the Creole Municipal Water District, and Populi lands. Theoretically, she had explained to me, this part of the lake was supported by land belonging to her father and so she was not strictly speaking in violation of the no swimming–no wading ordinance. There, without shame, she had stepped out of her clothes, paying no attention to me, and walked slowly and steadily into the smooth, cool water.

Bianca was so much a part of the water that I forgot she was in it, swimming. She did not splash, seemed barely to cleave it, left no wake. Once in a while she disappeared, had gone under without bubble, eddy or froth, and when I stood on a rock scanning the clear water it took long moments to see her, fitted neatly between two boulders, reclining there as if on leave from the atmosphere. She was as graceful under water as above and on land. She climbed trees, too; seemed to walk up at the same deliberate pace. Never had I seen her confronted with an obstacle.

So she made love to Pierre Brasseur! Maybe because he was a cripple, a hero of the professional boxing arena who lost his left hand in a freak accident. A man who would have been middleweight champion of the whole world, certainly. Perhaps his hand was taken from him to save his life. He was a fragile looking man. Black hair, pale face, slender arms and legs. I saw him fight only once and it seemed to me that he evaded his bull-like opponent only by terrible intensity, by having pitched his body to the tautness of the finest violin string. He seemed to operate like a blind man, *feeling* the displacement of air that preceded every move of his opponent. He had obliged fortune to stay with him for the duration of the bout and he struck out only once, with his left, and blew the other man unconscious. When I saw that performance, which was hailed as great even by the hardened writers of New York, I feared for him, I feared for what would happen when he fell from grace, when some night he could not command fortune.

The moon had built a road across the bay from the city to me. I heard singing and tooting and blaring horns in the distance. They reminded me of time. I got up and walked slowly back to the point, under the revolving lighthouse beacon, back to Belveron. When I got into the Club Creole the band had stopped playing, the instruments were idle, but couples were still dancing to music from the music box. I looked around for Titiane, but saw her nowhere.

Then I went out back, past the Men's Room and stepped between two buildings, one of them on stilts against the high tide of last century, a tide that no longer reached this far. I heard giggling and clinking of bottles among the pilings, and the sand crunched. I stuck my head under the floor and when my eyes adjusted to the darkness I saw Titiane, and the outline of the singer, and three or four others. They were smoking and drinking.

"Hey, mawn," said the singer, "come on in, step down, have a smoke!"

Titiane's teeth flashed and her eyes shone. I stepped in under the floor which turned out to be a false front, a facade, and once under it I could stand up inside. A fresh cigarette was lit and passed to me. I inhaled deeply. It was what I had thought it would be. I did not usually smoke this stuff, though it was mild to inhale. I did not usually like to be so stimulated. It made me wild, gave me wild ideas. But it was cozy down here, and for one week it was not against the law.

"Hey, mawn, that is good, is it not?"

"Fine," I said and passed the cigarette back to him.

"No, you keep it, mawn, we have much of this. You smoke, you feel good now!"

"You feelin' good, too, huh Joe?" I asked pointedly.

Titiane pulled his arm around her neck and kissed him. The giant singer flashed a smile at me.

"Pretty good, mawn, pretty good!"

A paper cup with wine was passed to me. I took a sip. Someone started singing the old creole song, the nostalgic blend of France and Somali, the historic tune that had been composed when they saw land and knew they were safe.

> *Aaaah, ah ah, aaaah ah ah*
> *Ooooh, oh oh, ooooh oh oh*
> *Bon bon bon, ah si bon*
> *Non non non, bientôt bon*
> *Aaaah, ah ah, aaaah, ah ah*
> *Ooooh oh oh, ooooh oh oh*
> *Bon bon bon, ah si bon*
> *Bon bon bon, ah si bon!*

Suddenly I wanted to be in the Chevy, wanted to roll. I took two steps, banged my head against the facade, ducked and crawled out amid singing and laughter.

That was the crazy night when Bianca returned. I wheeled the Chevy along the Creole roads, through Port Creole, north, then west into the hills in the moontinted night. The Populi spread lay in darkness. The workers were in town to celebrate, Pops already in bed and Emma, too. I cut the engine and walked up the rest of the way in order not to disturb them.

I had intended to sneak in quietly but found myself walking past the barn, up on the path that led through the fields. Then I began climbing, walked through the silent eucalyptus grove, and turned slightly east again to approach the meadows and grade to the top of the hill. Halfway up I sat down and surveyed the nocturnal panorama.

There were lights everywhere, occasional explosions, flares, small fireworks, all of it far in the distance so that it did not interfere with the breathing of the wilderness.

Southwest to my right lay Mount Tamalpais securely humped, hiding the city. To the east the lights of Port Creole and beyond the shiny outline of the Creole Civic Center. Southeast, on the shores of the bay, pale light illuminated the site of the Mulatto Point Penitentiary under construction. All the northern directions were behind my back, hidden by the bulk of the hill. After a while I got up and climbed farther.

Far in the distance I could sense Belveron containing Titiane and the singer, the flashy brute. He had a job to do that night. Well, they were having fun. She was *my* sweetheart, she was *a* sweetheart, and wasn't that how it went for all the sweethearts?

I got to the top and sat down, out of breath and out of balance. Maybe I should not have accepted that cigarette! From time to time, as I lay back to look at the sky, all became dark. The night itself disappeared without replacement. I saw through the darkly painted backdrop, the stage scenery, the walls of the theater and then my eyes, though open, stopped seeing. My mind had blown away. When called upon to link stars with stars, moon with moon, grass with grass, trees with trees, even me with me, my mind was not there to do the job. Everything was still as it had been, but now no longer identifiable. I saw it all, but I no longer knew any of it!

I lay like a baby with all-seeing eyes. I saw so much that all had lost its label. Stars no stars, moon no moon, even curtain and scenery no longer that! Nothing applied! What they had taught me in seventeen years blew away and into this new baby realm of unclassified reality descended a musical dish in shimmering rainbow colors sustained by a tone, a note.

I could not sit up. I lay unable to move, without will, mindless, but I saw that what there was was not a dream, nor a saucer, though that is how I naively described it later. I saw what a baby sees when it looks into the eye of God.

With my fresh eyes I saw it descend on a path like a ladder leaning against a house. My eyes closed but I kept seeing: Bianca next to me, stretching out her hand to help me up.

My mind came winging back, flew into me, jarred

me. I sat up with a groan. It was truly Bianca's hand that touched mine. She had returned, she was here!

I turned my head, looking up. It was a flying saucer, an unidentified flying object, the upper portion of a musical top. The smoggy night sky pursed its dark and mooney lips and kissed it away. But Bianca was still here with me, kneeling by my side, holding my face in her hands.

"Damn!" I said. "Where on earth have you been?"

"To Azydia, Alfons, nowhere on earth. And soon I'm going back!"

• Fifteen •

Following my plea of Not Guilty, the customary bail is set, plus a tidy sum for so-called non-bailable crimes which include murder of persons in public office, murder of religious ministers, murder of doctors or others engaged in maintaining the public health. When it's all added up at the bottom of the sheet it comes to $5,000,000.–. An extra hypothetical charge is levied for Committing Murder on Private Property—$10,000.–; for Outraging Public Tolerance Outside County Limits—$125,000.–; and finally an uncomfortably high $65,000.– for Failure to Report a Major Crime. Soon upon being returned to my cell I am surprised to learn that the entire sum of $5,200,000.– has been posted by a man named Scott Adair, on my behalf.

I pack up my meager belongings, primarily my playing cards and the mysterious, drying apple and am led to the front desk for checking out. As a courtesy to a man who has managed to raise the highest bail ever set in Creole County, I'm allowed to say goodbye to Pearl. We sit in the Attorney's Room. He looks exceptionally cheerful, smiling broadly at the prospect of my departure.

"You know something, Al, the minute you came in here I knew you wouldn't stay long!"

"How come?"

69

"You never lost the peachy look, the novice look. I call it losing the fuzz. You still have it on you now. Hell, friend, they'll never get you. You got some rich friends out there."

"I'll see what I can do for you!"

"Right. But don't strain yourself. I don't mind it in here!"

Frankly, I had just begun to enjoy his company. My game was shaping up. Pearl was teaching me that my true talent was defensive. He had told me that I didn't need to score high because I could keep my opponent from scoring high. The occasional basket, plop plop, would do! I owed him something. I pushed the cards across the table.

"Here, keep you busy!"

"No, thanks, Al, I don't touch 'em anymore. They've caused me too much pain."

I took back the cards and brought out the apple. I had polished it. I had held it in my hand and contemplated it. I had pondered the question of its origin. If it had indeed grown on that brittle tree, another one was bound to grow, which would reduce the value of this one by fifty percent, and another one by two-thirds, and so on. That's why apples are so inexpensive.

"Take the apple!" I said. "It may be the most expensive apple in the world."

"Gee, thanks, Al. I can use the extra nutrients."

I hadn't really thought of him eating it, and I realized that moment that I'd been treating an apple like a monument. But a monument to what? It was right that it should be eaten, and doubly right that Pearl should eat it.

"You go ahead, Pearl, enjoy!"

"Guess those boys are eager to get you out of here," he said, inclining his head in the direction of the door.

"Yes, probably."

We got up and shook hands. One of the filthy jailers shuffled in to watch him as I walked out.

"Together!" I said.

"Yeah, Al, together!" he sang out the refrain.

Timothy Mahoney was waiting for me in the hall and we went for a cup of coffee in the dilapidated cafeteria. The ceiling there is black with thick layers of grime from coffee machines and ancient calcified hamburger fumes.

They don't make hamburgers anymore, only coffee. And cold sandwiches.

We sat down at a rickety metal table that hadn't been wiped in days. Every time either of us touched it it acted like a rocking horse. Tim finally placed both arms on top and held it down.

"Well, Mr. Anton!" he grinned.

"Well, Captain Tim," I said.

"You got friends. Boy do you ever!"

"I don't know a soul with that kind of money," I told him truthfully.

"It was posted in cash, you know!"

He whistled appreciatively through a tiny gap between his front teeth.

"And who's this Scott Adair, Tim?"

"I thought you'd like to know. Remember when Bianca disappeared, when you came to see us and told Voronov about your dream?"

"Sure."

"Well we had a man by the name of Adair on our files then. He'd been missing for a year, no trace of him. You know the files are kept open for a mandatory ten year period. And then for another ten years. We call it Limbo. After twenty years we close it, stamp it C & U."

"What does that stand for?"

"Closed but unsolved."

"I see."

"Right. So about three years ago that's what we did with Adair's file. I think the man who posted your bail is the same Scott Adair who disappeared without a trace, oh about twenty-three years ago, back in Seventy-Six!"

"You talked to him?"

"No, not yet. That's what I want you to do, would you? Officially there is no issue involving Scott Adair, but just out of curiosity I'd like to know."

"Well," I said, "I guess I *have* to talk to the man who coughed up five million to set me free, don't I?"

"You sure do," grinned Mahoney, "and don't forget: it isn't five million. It's Five Million Two Hundred Thousand!"

I tried to slurp the awful coffee which had been poured lukewarm but burned like fire in my mouth. I shivered and shook my head involuntarily.

71

"You know what the New Chronicle out of San Francisco calls you?"

I shook my head again, this time purposefully.

"The Beast of Mount Tamalpais."

"Poor old Tamalpais," I said.

"You're national news, Al."

"And what do they call me in the East?"

"A lot of names, I've kept most of the articles on you. The Creole County Cutter is one. The Devil's Butcher. A Severe Provocation. Things like that."

"Very imaginative!"

I just couldn't drink the coffee. When we got up, the table rocked and much coffee was spilled, but neither Captain Mahoney nor I paid any attention to it. The elevators were not working so we walked down and I noticed that most of the bannisters were missing. Tim explained that they'd been stolen in two raids last winter and presumably used for firewood.

We walked out a back door and got into his private car, his pride and joy, a gasless mobile. It was a little tight for room, but maneuvered smoothly. There was no vibration, no sound, almost as if we were floating.

"Nice ain't it," he said as if he had read my thoughts. "No more than a hundred or so of these in the county. It's kind of semi-official which means I didn't quite pay for it all by myself. Watch!"

He pressed a button and a cool breath of ozone touched my forehead.

"Best oxygen you can get," he said proudly. "Instant Converter which runs itself and needs no servicing for the lifetime of the car. They call them mobiles, but I call them cars."

Just now I realized how much I was starved for a breath of fresh air. I leaned back and inhaled deeply, feeling the pure stuff spread from my lungs through my body. Supply and demand! More demand than supply. Oxygen was a typical example. Pearl had already eaten the apple, had added a little to the depleted store of life juices in his body. But he didn't have enough oxygen. I began to feel expansive. Things were going great. I was on my way back to the hill, great! Mildly, mildly, that is how the world turns, Tim.

"Wildly, wildly," I mumbled.

"What?"

"I mean mildly, mildly, that is how the world turns!"

"Yeah," said Captain Mahoney, "have a look at *that!*"

We had circled the Creole County Civic Center and were traveling along the northern edge of the enormous, rundown parking lot which now no longer served it's diminishing purpose but had been taken over by the Latter Day Crusaders and great numbers of Sadoos.

A truckload of oxygen in great bulk containers, painted green, had arrived and the holy men, devotees and other faithful were lining up, reaching their pathetically dented and worn flasks up for refilling. Emaciated arms stretched, gnarled and bony hands clutched the air. It was a heartrending scene.

Tim swung the mobile away from it, through the lifeless northern district of Port Creole and onto the familiar roads toward the Populi lands.

"Few weeks make a big difference," I announced idly, amiably and comfortably.

"Things always turn out different, don't they," said Tim.

"All those Missing Person files, Captain. How many have you got? A thousand? Two, three? And after two decades one man comes back with a pocketful of money. It's encouraging isn't it?"

"The 'Open' files of the Creole County Missing Persons Bureau at last count contained thirty-one thousand five-hundred-and-twelve names," he said.

"No shit!"

"And that doesn't include Captain Mikhael Voronov!"

"I thought he was living in Russia; I thought he had defected?"

"Not officially, Al, not officially. As far as we are concerned there are rumors. These are considered presumably unfounded. Over the past twenty years we have petitioned the Government of the U.S.S.R. no less than fifteen times for disclosure of the details in the Voronov case. We haven't even been dignified with a denial. As far as the Russkies are concerned, Captain Voronov does not exist."

"But there were witnesses who saw him gunned down

at the East German border. They testified that he was dragged away by East German border police, right?"

"Right. For all we know he's dead and buried in some dismal spot in Russian Europe. He may even be alive. One way or the other, we can't prove a thing."

Tim took the neat little mobile into the hills and there was no change in the smooth, soundless ride, no added strain to the tiny engine. We proceeded at an even pace, entering Populi territory. We drifted almost lazily through the broken-down gate and up toward the ruins. Tim broke a long silence.

"Mother Russia!" he exclaimed softly and bitterly. Voronov had been his great good friend. Mahoney was a man of loyalty. Even though the Voronov case in its day had attracted a great deal of criticism he had risked his job by defending his Captain publicly. He had gone on record to say that Captain Voronov's integrity as a bona-fide American was unimpeachable; that he must have had a good and valid reason for going to Russia; that he was in all respects a professional: incorruptible and competent, and that without him it would not be easy to maintain order in Creole County. It turned out that he was right. Voronov's departure had been disastrous. In two years crime doubled, which was interpreted by Voronov's critics as another aspect of his traitorous behavior. Voronov was hanged in effigy and the Creole County Police had to issue a disclaimer. For two weeks Tim's job hung in precarious balance. Then the storm had blown over.

We came to a halt by the ruins. I got out, but Tim stayed in the car. He stuck out his hand and I seized it.

"If there's anything I can do, let me know," he said.

I watched him turn the cute little car in a tight semi-circle. As he passed me he waved and called out:

"Good luck, mudra!"

I rolled my eyes and gave him a flattered "tsk-tsk" as he went by. Then I turn and start on the long, familiar walk up the hill where Scott Adair has been waiting for me since early that morning.

• Sixteen •

As I climb the hill, the veils of darkness drawn by the artificial light in the county jail begin to part, my eyes are
unpeeled and through the fumes and smog I nevertheless
enter a virginal realm: the California wilderness. I was
submerged, and now I surface. Slowly, as I move upward,
Creole County unfolds around me, wave upon wave of
gentle hills marches into the muck and gloom that con-
ceals the horizon. I stop to cough and spit, but now even
ten feet difference in altitude has a cleansing effect. I cannot understand why the world has not fled to its highest
peaks.

Scott Adair awaits me by the big tree. Through an
extraordinarily smooth face and trim, supple figure I perceive a man of about my own age, a friendly, energetic
person whose handshake is as good as an embrace. Still, I
sense something dangerous, savage, in him. Something that
is not social. Something distant, cold, forbidding; maybe
cruelty, maybe indifference.

"Mr. Adair?"

"Yes, Mr. Anton!"

It's as if he were the host and I the visitor and I see
abruptly that this is a homecoming for me, that the tree is
still here, that up there among the speartip leaves are still
the shadows of my fortified domicile. Somewhere—where,
yes, over there, its lower half hidden by the bulk of the
hill, is the dried up old apple tree, ready to fall, no longer
food enough for worms. The tree from which Tim Mahoney plucked a startling apple.

Scott Adair wears an old but freshly laundered Citizen Volunteer uniform, something that went out a year
after the Great Earthquake. It gives him a quaint, old-
fashioned appearance. It makes him brisk and efficient

75

looking, someone on his way to a clean-up. He also wears glasses whose upper portion is tinted against the sun. His fingers are unringed and I notice brand-new mocassins on his feet, double-soled, authentic, I can't help counting the silver buttons: six, and more hidden by the trousers. Yes, it may not be conventional elegance, but it *is* elegance.

Still, without decorum or caution, he sits down on the ground, crosses his legs, takes out a pipe, stuffs it from a canvas pouch, lights it, starts puffing, and I, still entranced by the surroundings, do as he does. Three hawks are in view, involved in simple spiral arabesques. The northern flank of Mount Tamalpais lies broad and steady not too far in the distance. Sunlight flashes muted on the stow lake. I follow an impulse, jump up, run to the rope-release and trigger it. The rope uncoils on its way down, its heavily knotted end performs a frantic dance in which I stop it and start climbing.

Scott Adair is puffing and watching as I go aloft, past the first thick branches, my feet touching the wooden blocks that make up the "ladder". Now the turn, and there is the fork, above me, crowning a clean, insurmountable stretch of trunk. I break the county seal and enter through the hatch.

"Mr. Adair, please, will you come up!"

He starts climbing, pipe clenched in his teeth. He makes the climb without losing his breath, scrambles in, I close the hatch. He's a sharp dresser and an agile man. He's an elegant, agile multimillionaire.

"Great view, isn't it, Mr. Adair?"

He stands admiringly, looking out toward the Civic Center.

"You must be happy to be home," he says.

I've fallen on my bed, my gaze goes upward into the leaves, the play of sun on green, the dappled trunk. Yes, I'm happy to be home. I've come home just in time, I realize. I am exhausted. It seemed like play, like fun, but it was not.

He sits down in the armchair and talks to me in profile.

"I want to explain to you that bail was posted not *by* me but *through* me and I want your assurance that you won't reveal your sponsors if I tell you who they are."

"Go ahead, sir, you have my word."

"You have been bailed out by the Sadoo Satsang Society of America. The money is theirs and you are responsible to them."

"But no . . . that can't . . . I mean . . . !"

He smiles carefully.

"Yes, Mr. Anton, that's how it is, but I can understand your surprise. It was anticipated."

Even so, I don't want to sit up. All the tension of the past two weeks is draining out of me. I hear the hoarse baby-cry of seagulls outside. A slight wind has come up, orchestrating the air and choreographing the leaves.

"The Society has chosen me to represent them to you," says Mr. Adair. "It has entrusted me with the message to you that their sole interest in you is your freedom and that they will finance in full your defense, if you so wish."

It's good news, but I can feel the swaying of my tree, which is better news. I close my eyes tentatively. It is necessary to concentrate on what to say to this man. Enveloped in my self-created twilight, inhaling the mentholated eucalyptus air, I sink deeper into the realm of no muscle, no tension. It's so soft, so deep here!

"Well," says Mr. Adair, "so much for the official part. You're probably curious who I am, why I was chosen. Let me give you a little bit of my background."

"I know," I mumble, "you're a missing person."

"Yes, that's true. I was listed as missing, I'm sure."

"You were gone . . . a long long time . . ."

The palm of the wind is pressing gently and steadily upon the tree. It presses and gives, presses, gives. It rubberizes the trunk. It's rocking me to sleep. Adair's voice breaks on the rubber rocks of my fatigue. Fragmented words rush over me, come together again to form water. Here and there, there are pools of it, pools of words left behind by the retreating surf of his voice which is carried also by the wind, answered by the seagulls, affirmed by a foghorn booming up from the bay. My ears are wide open. They have lost their capacity for categorization. They receive the story of Scott Adair's recent years, but they attach no meaning to it, no specifics. They seize and hold on to the basic drone of his voice, that is the scroll with the message, and the message is simple: WAIT!

• Seventeen •

When I woke I had slept all night and it was day again. Adair was nowhere in sight. I had not moved from the spot where I had fallen, my limbs were still heavy and I stirred gradually, regaining my mobility.

I got up and stretched and shook off the last traces of sleep. Dried fish and seagull meat was still stocked in the food box, but there was no time to soak it. I was too hungry. So I let myself down to the ground.

It was one of those nasty, sulfurous days when a windless night allows the stench and fumes to stand unstirred behind the sheltering coastal ridge. There was no sunlight. A cheese bell had been set over the platter of the bay area and all who lived here were caught under it, struggling for air, with stinging nostrils and eyes.

It was what was called a Maximum Day, a day on which hundreds of the elderly and infirm would die, were dying now as I decided nevertheless to make my way down to the stow lake to inspect my snares and to see if anything that had been caught while I was in jail was salvagable.

In the lake few fishes survived, and those that did were clever, seasoned veterans who recognized baited hook and net. It is easier to catch a seagull than a fish, even though to catch a seagull is a feat that takes a great deal of patience and experience.

Over the years I have developed a fairly reliable technique, one that will provide between one or two seagulls a week, sometimes three, sometimes none. I spent days by the lake, gazing out across the water toward the center where the birds like to gather, swaying and dipping on the short waves. I tried to figure out how to do it, how to get to them.

Seagulls are fairly intelligent. They have keen instincts blunted only by their insatiable appetites. But even in search of food they are wary, sensitive, and they shy away from suspicious movement or objects. I bought a stuffed seagull in Port Creole and strapped it on top of my head. A snorkel tube was fitted inside the dummy so that I could hang just below the surface, breathing and watching. Visibility was just good enough to see feet and legs of the most curious birds as they kept a respectful distance.

I devised a snare on a long stick from which another, shorter one stuck up at a ninety-degree angle. Where the two bars joined, the contraption was heavily weighted, being kept in place by muscular strength only. Fine, strong, nylon twine ran along the stick and then up to form the loop. It took me months to become proficient at maneuvering this thing cautiously into position. What helped me was that after a few weeks the seagulls became fascinated with their own facsimile. Not only did they come within snaring distance, but they stayed there, moving little, their paddle feet often hanging limply down.

The trick was for the loop to be just wide enough to fit over such a limp foot, and narrow enough to allow pulling it tight with minimal movement. Once the bird was snared the thing was to pull it under quickly without fuss in order not to disturb the others. Many escaped my first attempts, but always they returned to the decoy, giving me opportunity for practice.

I allowed the bird to drown at the end of my catcher. This took again patience and strong arms, plus the weight of the weighted stick. It was equally important to keep the decoy serenely in place, and then to turn and watertread slowly away, back to shore. After a few months of this I was in fine condition. As for the birds they were either unaware of the sacrificial toll I took of their number, or else they didn't care, never slacking in their attention and curiosity.

Seagull meat tastes terrible. It is tough and stringy even when fresh, and no amount of beating will help. But it is extremely high in protein and phosphorous properties derived from fish food. Even today I hate the thought of a seagull meal. And it's worse when dry and re-activated by soaking in water. It is, however, my closest source of essential protein and, combined with ice-plant and tree moss, has proved itself.

After those first, clumsy months of catching seagulls I began to understand their behavior patterns, the movement of their feet, and developed a self-activating snare which I have never been able to perfect. It's success ratio is no more than one-fifth, meaning that four of five birds escape and sometimes it takes weeks for one to be caught in this way. My fish-cages are only slightly more functional. So even now, except in the coldest months of winter, I paddle out and wait for the birds.

I found nothing in the three snares, and a single medium sized fish in one of the fish-cages. I started a small fire, fried the fish and ate it. It tasted bitter. Maybe the time has come to stop eating fish from this lake. For a while I could not decide whether or not to go out for snaring seagulls but then I found myself walking on by the narrow strip of sandy beach, toward a creek which provides perfect mineral mud for a mudbath, and a pool of water for meditation in warm suspension.

Few people know of this place and I have taken care to scare off those who do. A troupe of American gypsies once camped nearby, on Populi lands, clearly trespassing. They had brought along a good half dozen mutts and mongrels which were starved and savage. Nevertheless I succeeded in killing two in one night: a pathetic little poodle-type with matted braids of hair, and a large, emaciated shepherd bastard who put up a good fight and managed to get me in the shoulder. I slit them open and detached their entrails at the top so that they slid out and hung down, warm, dripping blood. I hung them ostentatiously on either side of my mudbath, and the next morning these superstitious wanderers broke camp, presumably passing the word about my atrocities. I have not been bothered much since, but maybe it would be wise soon to repaint the signs which delineate Populi property and which state simply:

STRANGER BEWARE!
BEYOND THIS POINT YOU'RE
ON YOUR OWN!

I took off my basketball boots, trousers and shirt and slipped into the mud. Stirred, it gave off the pungent scent of rotten eggs, but in the turning, in moments, as the fumes penetrated and as I penetrated this olfactory facade, I was enveloped in the sweetest of beneficent fumes and could feel its soothing, healing action in every pore of my body. Moving languorously in the warm, soupy mass of stinking muck I felt free at last. With this freedom came the thought of Pearl, my basketball teacher in county jail. What was there I could do for him? As this question had risen, so it subsided, and I sank deeper into the mud.

A long time went by in comfort. To my mouth and nostrils I was perfectly protected, perfectly safe, but still I had to breathe and even though the technique of breathing fast and shallow had seen me easily through many days such as this one, it was not quite sufficient for today. I spat and coughed, upsetting the rhythm of my breath. I sat up, slipped, fell back into the mud and went under, momentarily panicked. I came up, struggling for air, shot straight out of the swampy, shallow creek bed and managed to steady myself against its bank. It was getting really bad!

In the yellowish twilight I walked slowly downstream to the deep, rocky concavity which I call the tub and let myself into the warm water. My breathing had steadied and my body, its weight reduced, began to turn like a compass needle, adjusting itself to the magnetic currents of the earth: head south, feet north, as Bianca had taught me. In moments I regained my composure, my mind was calmed, I closed my eyes.

Bianca had returned at night, and departed at night. Some of the citizens in the area who had seen the saucer arrive had mistaken it for Bicentennial fireworks atop the hill, and Pops had received telephone calls with drunken voices congratulating him on the magnificent display. Because of these calls he was still awake when we came down that night of the full moon.

She had seemed to me like a fairy-tale apparition, luminescent, light, still vibrant from her passage through non-physical dimensions and naturally I then fell in love with her. I put my arm around her waist and pulled her close and told her of her beauty. And she told me again that she would not be here long. But I said:

81

"I don't care if you go back to the moon as long as you take me with you!"

"Can you give me a baby?"

It was not the question I had expected. It was a prosaic inquiry which made a tool out of me, a means to an end. But that didn't matter either.

"Right now?"

She laughed and spread her arms, bending backward from the waist, bathed in moonlight.

"We can start now," she said.

"Ah, come on Bianca!"

"What?"

"You want a baby from *me*?"

"I need a baby," she said, "I hadn't thought about it. I guess a poet is as good as any other man for babies!"

"Where is this poet, who is he?"

"You, silly, it's you!"

I had not written a line of poetry then and still have not. But apparently she did mean me.

"I love you," I said to Bianca Populi.

"Then you're the one," she told me.

"Let's go down and show ourselves to Pops, Bianca. The night has just begun. Was there really a saucer, or was it . . . was it . . . ?"

"There was," she said.

"Or was it my imagination?"

She stood before me, took my hand and placed it on one breast, then my other hand on the other breast.

"As you feel this, so it was what you call a saucer," she said.

What I felt was really Bianca. Now she embraced me.

"As you feel us now, that same feeling, so it was a saucer from Azydia!" she said.

"It's not a name like some of the other names I've read in connection with flying saucers," I murmured.

"What is the difference?"

"Not so . . . harsh," I told her.

"They want a baby," she informed me. "It will be my gift to them in return for what they showed me and taught me. Do you want to help me with it?"

"Sure, kid!" I said.

I know now that I was hurt, driven back into myself.

I'd seen too many movies, read the papers, the comics, been to the dances, driven the old Chevy, necked with Titiane. What she wanted did not happen in America except among the freaks, the filthy victims of poverty, the shoot-ups and burnouts who didn't care. It was a crazy demand, asylum-love, extra-terrestrial nonsense, and I could see that she meant it. Such a question was asked only among those who had occupied territory, the foreigners, the immigrants. Never among the natives.

"It's an honor for a young man to be chosen," she said.

"Did *they* choose me?"

"No, *I* did. They don't want to choose because this is my world, not theirs."

"What good will a baby do them on some other world—why a baby?"

"Well," she said abruptly, stepping away from me and turning once more her face to the moon. "You don't have to!"

"Ah, come on, Bianca. Don't talk any more. Let's go down and wake up your father. He misses you. I've missed you. I don't care where you've been, and he doesn't, I know. Just as long as you're back!"

Then she stepped out of her clothes: the spanish shirt, the velvet suit of green, the delicately high-heeled sandals. And she stripped off her white shorts. And she stood there in the moonlight, her arms crossed behind her head, smiling.

"You are a beautiful young man," she said, "but you know nothing. You are protective of your semen. You are shy. I should ask a man. A man would know! You have masturbated, you've flushed it down toilets, spread it among the leaves, rubbed it in your hand. You have tasted it and you know that it tastes salty, don't you? You have spent it abundantly, you have given your girlfriend . . ."

"No," I protested, "never. None of what you say. I . . ."

"You lie," she went on. "Now you lie to me and you say you love me. Not *my* love, Alfons Anton, but *your* love. Your little love. I want to adore you. I want to teach you. Even so you will never learn what I know. Not unless they invite you to where I was. Not unless you come to Azydia!"

"Yes," I said fiercely, "I want to go there. With you!"

"Everyone I tell will want to go," she replied, "you are no exception."

"Well, what? Not enough room, not enough tickets?"

She was getting too damned otherworldly for me. Here we were on top of a hill in filthy Creole County. She'd been gone for two weeks without a word, except my dream, and now she was pulling this superior, well, shit on me!

"Tell you what, sweetheart, what do you know about *my* planet? What do *I* know about my planet? Not much. Nothing. I'm free, see? Even here, right here, here in Creole County, right here I'm free, can you imagine? Here among the creoles and the creeps, here I'm free. I got myself a fine Chevy that flies and a radio that sings me where to fly with it, a cherry girl and a mint condition, and here you stand, glowing from some place called Azydia, privileging me! For what? You think I'm just a little boy, just a teenager. It's *you* who don't understand! This is my perfect body. Perfect now, for this whole year, and next year, and many more, and you'll be thinking back to it and wondering how you could not have seen it. I occupy no space, my mind goes away. Azydia my . . . Azydia my . . . !"

"Oh no, Alfons, please," she pleaded.

"Azydia my heart," I finished. "Azydia my semen, my spleen, my fulcrum!"

"I love you too," she stammered, swaying in the moonlight.

"My father fought at Verdun," I sang out. "He fought on *his* planet. The bloody planet, the planet of rape and murder, gore and pus. He told me about it. They built monuments to the blood that ran ankle-deep in the trenches and in the gullies and in the fields. Thousands of men died fighting for five acres of soil and still today nothing grows there, not even grass, and what looks like grass is still nothing when the night falls around Verdun. No one can rest there. Those who live in Verdun flee it and those who don't live there pass through in a day. That is where France broke Germany. That is where France stood and broke Germany. This is the planet of

84

the machine-gun, not the deathray-gun or the laser-gun, or even the anti-gravity principle. This is the planet of death, and this is my home. I want to go away with you. I want to go away with you. I want to go away with you."

She was caressing my face and kissing me. She kissed my eyes, my nose, my ears, my mouth, my neck. I stood still until she had done all that.

"I understand," I told her then, "no baby belongs on this planet. A baby is invincible, a baby is life, and this is the planet of death. I did not understand at first what you were telling me. Tell me now, again, what is Azydia the planet of?"

She took my hands and kissed them.

"Azydia is the planet of us," she whispered, "Azydia is *our* planet!"

Then we made our way down the hill, through the eucalyptus forest, along the fields which are now weedy wilderness. Primitivo Populi was awake, drinking coffee for a change. He held her, weeping, confessing his love, telling her about the past, about her childhood, even about her mother who had met a timely end, but mainly about himself and his love for her. At last they broke away from each other, but still held hands. We all sat down at the table, and Emma came sleepily down the stairs from the loft to do her weeping, and to make soup and sandwiches.

"Now," said Pops, "we, too, can celebrate. Bianca will sleep and I will watch her while she sleeps. I swear that I will never sleep again while you are sleeping! A father who cannot guard his daughter in sleep is nothing. You will sleep and stay, Yanca."

"Yes," she said dutifully, "I will sleep and stay!"

"You will promise never to leave again without telling me!"

"I do, Papa!"

"That's enough for now. Open the doors, let the night air in, and the moonlight!"

Emma groggily managed to open the large doors.

"The moon brought her back," I joked.

"So I'll watch for the full moon in the future," announced Primitivo Populi, "that is the dangerous time! Incidentally, where in the devil's name have you been?"

"Nowhere in the name of the devil," said Bianca, "I've been to Azydia!"

Said Pops: "Never heard of the dumbfounded place!" just as the telephone rang. He picked it up himself.

"Yeah," he had said. "Right. That's right. My daughter has come home, I don't have time. Yeah, maybe. She made a firework on top of the hill, that's right. We're celebrating her homecoming!"

I opened my eyes from these reveries. Above me was the silhouette of a young man looking down on me as I floated in the still, warm waters of my natural tub.

"Hey," he said, "you Anton?"

He didn't wait for an answer, but ran down the steep shore, took a leap in two stages, touching a large rock in creek and bouncing off it to the other side. Then he came walking up on the lower bank.

"I gotta talk to you!"

I lifted my head slightly.

"Shut up," I told him. "Stop wasting your breath!"

He ran back, flew back across the creek in the same way he had before, ran up the steep side and bent down to pick up a portable oxygen cylinder. He let it down to me by its straps, the plastimask dangling.

"Take a hit, old man," he said, "you look as if you need it!"

• Eighteen •

Because I had to, I accepted the oxygen, drank in the force of life propped up against the bank in the water.

"Take as much as you want," urged the visitor.

Once more I fitted the mask and inhaled the precious gas. Then, re-energized, I waded to the other bank and sat down in the sulfurous twilight.

"What a day!"

The young man once again crossed the creek and came up to me. He picked up the oxygen bottle, checked gauge and flowmeter.

"Plenty more where this came from!" he said, the look of concern on his face changing to one of irony.

"Gets worse as you get older, don't it?"

I nodded, still trying to preserve precious breath even though my condition had greatly improved. He patted the cylinder and cunningly squinted his eyes, peering out into the gloom of the forest.

"Somebody paid five million to get you out," he said. "I need paper!"

"Paper?"

"Yeah, money, you know."

"That isn't my money," I explained. "I don't have any money. Well, maybe a little. How much do you want?"

"I don't want," he said, "I *need!*"

"It's the same," I tried to instruct him, but he shrugged me off impatiently.

"You got property. You own this place, most of those lands around here. I have information that can be paper for you. All you got to do is promise a fee!"

"Look, kid . . ."

"Don't call me kid," he said vehemently.

"Well, what's your name, kid?"

"Don't call me kid," he said, handling the oxygen flask menacingly.

"Tell me your name and I'll stop calling you kid, kid!"

"If you keep on calling me kid, I won't tell you my name!"

"Beat it, kid," I said to him. "You and I got nothing in common."

Instead of beating it, he sat down and started picking up pine needles. He assembled them in the palm of one hand and made neat bundles of them. Then he tossed them in the air over the creek, watching them float slowly in the circular current of the tub. I, too, watched.

"You got a lot of problems, Anton," he said after a while. "You got obligations. You got to show up for the trial. If they convict you, they'll do you in. If they do you in, all of this goes to waste. The state takes over, you know. You're all alone, except for that rich friend of yours. But you know nobody puts out that kind of paper for nothing in return. You owe him something. There's something he wants, and it's worth five million New Bucks to him. The only thing I haven't figured out yet is what is worth five million. It can't be your life. You don't look that good to me!"

It was no use denying it: I liked the kid. He stopped with his game, leaned back and took a casual sip from the bottle. "My dad used to call it the sin of pride what you're doing," he said. "You wanna go it alone, and the only way a man can go it alone is if he's got some big card up his sleeve. Only this card has to be so big that there's no card like that. You *think* you got an out, don't you!"

I didn't answer, and he went on, eagerly now.

"There's no out like that," he assured me. "Whatever it is you think you've got, it ain't real, it ain't gonna work. You killed three men, three holy men, and you act as if it doesn't matter. That's too casual, man, and I don't care what it is you think you got, even if you're one of those Second Coming nuts.

"Well," he added urgently, "are you?"

"In my case it's more like the third coming." I tried to be truthful. It didn't pacify him.

"Sure, I can tell. You're an end-of-the-world nut alright! You're not wearing a robe, but I bet you sit up there prayin' when the sun goes down. You pray for forgiveness for your sins, don't you? And you want a ticket when the Lord comes, don't you? When the earth opens up again, this time for real, you don't wanna be swallowed up in it, do you?"

"What do you mean, 'for real'?"

"Ah, I see," he tried to batter me with sarcasm, "you're one of those guys who believe in the Great San Francisco Earthquake. You went along with that, uhuh! I get the picture. San Francisco was destroyed, right? More than a hundred thousand people died, right? Three of five bridges came down, but the Golden Gate held, isn't that true? In a miracle of national fervor everything was rebuilt in a year, better than it was before! Oh yeah! My foot!"

"You're the one who's nuts," I said. "The earthquake is a fact. There were two great quakes this century, the last one twelve years ago."

"See what I mean? You believe it, I knew it. Well, it doesn't matter to me. A lot of older boys think the same way."

"Are you calling me Old Boy?"

"You call me kid, I call you Old Boy. That's fair, isn't it?"

"Okay, kid," I said resolutely, "I've had it!"

I got up, dressed, and walked away. The kid got up and followed me.

I followed the shoreline around the lake to the spot where I hide my buckets. I brought out two, filled them, hung them on the wooden carrier which somebody had brought all the way from China, hoisted it on my back and slowly began making my way up the hill. It was an awful day, maybe the worst ever. I had made the mistake of filling both buckets when I should have carried them half empty. Now it was too late. The kid was right behind me. "Sin of pride," I kept thinking. I was just deciding how to keep up a facade while setting down my load to rest, when the kid himself unwittingly, or maybe not unwittingly, overcame my dilemma by offering to carry the water up the hill.

I set down my load. Casually. I turned to him.

"It may not look like it," I informed him, "but this is a heavy load!"

He got his shoulders under the carrier and slowly strained upward to a standing position. The veins on his neck stood out, but he kept a good face. Without further comment he began to climb. He walked just as slowly as I had, and I could feel that he was up against the same problem I was, in reverse. In his case it was youth. After a very respectable distance, he set down the load without a sign of embarrassment. He got out from under the harness, unstrapped his oxygen cylinder and handed it to me. It would be better if I carried it. It kept getting in his way, banging against his thigh. He took five minutes of rest to explain to me about the oxygen cylinder. It was a clever, legitimate maneuver and by the time he was climbing again with the water, I was ready to make some offer of peace at the first opportunity.

He stopped a dozen more times on the way to the top, but he made it, set down the buckets, heaved a great sigh and reached for the oxygen. In a few minutes he was as good as new.

"What you need all this water for, Old Boy?"

I calmly went about my routine, dividing the water into three portions: for drinking, for washing, and for soaking dried fish and seagull meat. I started a fire and boiled the drinking water. Then I remembered Pearl, the apple, the tree. I walked a little way down the slope and put my hands on the old, gnarled trunk. It was utterly worthless and dry. A large, main branch had broken off and broken again where it had hit the ground. Its wood was turning to powder.

I inspected the branches within reach. They were all in the same condition.

"Hey," called the kid, "what you doin' there, Old Boy!"

I calmly continued my inspection. If the kid wanted to be here, so be it. Something had happened to me while in jail, I no longer minded company.

I was just about to give up when I found the spot. It was a twig, off a secondary branch, bone dry as all the others, but at its end was a spot unexpectedly green, fresh wood now browning in places, a recent break. I broke off the entire branch with small effort. I carried it up to the plateau and carefully detached the twig. Then I hacked the branch into half a dozen pieces with my knife. Everywhere dry, old wood, in places turning to grainy powder, in other places moldy, dead as death can be. No juice had flowed through here recently.

I now picked up the twig and looked at it very carefully. The kid was watching me silently.

Except for the very tip, the twig was in the same condition as the branch and the tree itself: it was dried up and dead. It had been dead for years! But at the tip there were still the vestiges of life. Where the apple had been plucked the process of decay had been reversed. Certainly there might have been an apple here!

"Is that the knife you used on those Sadoos?"

"The matter is before the courts," I told him, "it should not be discussed by me in public!"

"You did, didn't you?"

It was the nastiest day within memory.

"Shut up!" I said roughly. "Shut up and pass me that bottle!"

• Nineteen •

I sit in the shade, shuffling my cards. No matter what I do, the kid seems to be amused by it.

I cut the cards on the palm of my right hand and shuffle some more. I fan them out a little.

"Pick a card," I tell the kid, "any card!"

He picks the 4 of Hearts.

"Four Hearts. Now what kind of a card is that!"

I put his card aside and shuffle again. He picks another one. This time it's the 5 of Hearts.

"Five Hearts. Oh no!"

His next pick is the Ace of Hearts. At last we seem to be getting somewhere.

"Hey, what kind of a game is this, Old Boy?"

"Ace of Hearts stands for requited love," I tell him. "If you don't have a girlfriend, get one. If you do, where is she?"

"Well," he says, "I left her down by the lake."

He isn't kidding, either. His girlfriend is waiting for him down by the lake.

"I figured it would be easier this way," he says.

"Why didn't you tell me earlier?"

"I wanted *you* to bring it up!"

I tell him that this is clever, very clever of him. I tell him to bring her up here and he walks to the edge, cups his hands around his mouth and lets out a sweet, high-pitched hoot like that of a great, dangerous bird in love. An instant later comes the echo. He hoots again, and once again, and each time there is the same, precise response from the valley.

I shuffle the cards some more, picking out little ones and big ones while we wait for her to climb up here.

"How's the war going?" I ask, just to pass the time.

"What war?"

"Ah, come on, you know!"

"No, really, what you talkin' about?"

"Listen, kid, you're a deserter. It's written all over you."

"Oh yeah?"

"Yes, it is. And from the looks of you I'd say you've been in the Southern Brigade."

I've been noticing the way he moves in the wilderness. The choices he makes in the terrain, his approach to the hill, how he prefers to walk off the path rather than on. I can see he's been on the land, in the woods. He carries his oxygen bottle like a military man, almost like a weapon. When he encounters natural obstacles: fallen trees, branches, thickets, a creek, he doesn't hesitate. Nor does he attack them with unnecessary zest. He behaves calmly and confidently in nature. He's at home. I urge him to confide in me:

"Well, come on, how is it going?"

"I could have been in the Northern Brigade!"

Sure he could, but he wasn't. His face is deeply tanned, and it's too early for that in the north. Nor could such skin have survived a long winter in northern parts. He's been accustomed to heat and sun, the southern borderlands where the fighting is treacherous and fiery. President Chin has declared his determination to place the security of the borders above all other considerations. It is difficult to say what this chronic bloodletting is meant to accomplish: keeping Americans in America, or preventing Canadians and Mexicans from entering. The two borders have become a permanent testing ground for the young. And even though they are volunteers, desertion is still a capital offense.

It is a vicious war, complicated by the insistence of American troops to penetrate into Mexican and Canadian territory in order to "catch offenders in the act". This, President Chin has said, is necessary for positive proof of unauthorized attempts to leave the U.S.

In this way this is both an ordinary guerrilla war and a civil war. Few prisoners are taken and the true toll of Americans shot in cold blood just outside U.S. territorial limits is not known, never will be either. Still, the myth continues that it is easier to make a living in this country than in Mexico or in Canada. Often the so-called "leavies" attempt crossing in disguise, using the cover of "freedom of religious choice," and a number of bloodbaths as the result of mistaken identity have come to public attention.

"It got boring," says the kid. "After a while your reflexes get so that you no longer anticipate trouble. You just pick it up as it comes along. Between periods of shooting ignorant, unarmed slobs you hang around in the landscape. Something moves, you shoot it. You shoot a lot of Americans that way. Also, you get used to the idea of moving as little as possible. Then, when you get across, they treat you the same on the other side. To them suddenly *you're* a leavie. Then it gets really ugly. There's a big trade in monkey tags, because the monkey tag is what you carry to determine your nationality. We were issued two sets: American and Mexican, but it didn't help much because in some places there's nothing to mark the borderline, so you don't know what side you're on. I saw a friend get blown up a hundred feet in front of me for showing his American tag in Mexican territory!"

He snorts derisively, spitting into the grass.

"Can they find you?"

"Sure," he says comfortably. "But the computers are two years behind. Nobody has a proper name anymore. It's all aliases and also-known-ases. Then you come home, if you have a home, and you find that everybody's changed his name there, too. Old Bill's turned into old Jim and old Jim's turned into old Frank and old Frank into old Johnny. And you can forget the last names. The older guys, like yourself, they still pretty much stick with their names. This means that a lot of guys that are listed as missing aren't really missing, they've just changed their name. Also, you put on a robe and you become invisible. This friend of mine, a real sharpshooter; when he came down from the Northern Brigade with a reputation for picking the spots off a leopard without the leopard noticing even though I've never heard of leopards in Canada, well, we thought he wouldn't last long down south. But one day, I couldn't believe my eyes, he turns up in a

93

green robe. Made him blend into the landscape, he claimed. Plenty of room for his arsenal of deathdealers under the robe, too, he said. He was just as good with us as he'd been up north. One day he just dropped his arms and ammunition and walked away. Disappeared into a group of Green Monks, as if the night swallowed him up. A guy like that isn't even a dot on the computer screen. Nobody'll ever find him and if they do they won't know whether to shoot him or issue him a rifle and by the time they make up their minds he will either have shot *them* or be gone. Insane!"

Of course, war has never been officially declared. The two brigades are known as border patrols, and neither Canada nor Mexico are interested in protesting these actions in the U.N. It's just something that has developed, not merely in North America.

"Well, kid, what's gonna happen?"

"Nothing."

"Then why are they doing it?"

"For sport. Just for sport, Old Boy!"

His girlfriend comes up with a loose, swinging walk, breathing easily. She wears Italian hiking boots, no socks, and her thin, sinewy legs gleam dark golden all the way up to tattered shorts and a shirt that does not hide the aureoles of her pointy breasts. She has long arms, a long neck and she looks as if she, too, could have carried the water.

She comes over, not a frown or a smile on her face. She takes up position next to the kid, looking down on me.

"We're talking about the war," I tell her. "Join us!"

"Sit down, Dooda!" says the kid.

She sits down without ceremony, never taking her eyes off me.

"You remind me of somebody," she says.

"You do, too," I try to return the compliment.

"You look young for a mudra!"

"Do I?"

"Some people say that no man can kill a saint unless he himself is a saint among saints!"

"I'll try to remember that during the trial," I say.

The kid interrupts ironically: "Oh, incidentally, this is Old Boy. Old Boy, this is Dooda!"

I take them up to the fort. They delight in the rope, the pegs that serve as a ladder for the last part of the way, the hatch, the compact, functional interior of the fortified cabin. For a while they become children again and forget the blood and the killing. The creole beauty and her soldier friend! I can't keep my eyes off her.

If a girl can look like this, now, then what has changed in Creole County? Not much! She outshines all the acrid atmosphere. With her long legs, her effortless climb up the old eucalyptus she outstrides time. Her large teeth are set like enormous, flawless rows of pearls in her face. And, by the devilish technology that haunts the world, she wears nothing at all under her shorts!

"Ah, there, the lake!" she enthuses.

She must have been swimming in it. There is still water in her hair, caught in the strange, virid glints of that curly wilderness. Do I still have my face? Is Primitivo Populi's estate still in charred ruins, his daughter and child still gone? Only the kid's oxygen tank assures me that this is so, though even then these vessels began discreetly to make their appearance.

There weren't many. The use of oxygen was restricted to commercial establishments for welding or for therapeutic purposes in hospitals. Private use of oxygen was allowed only on doctor's prescription and strictly supervised. It was possible to obtain it on the black market, though, and its possession and use no more than a misdemeanor. In fact, the public had not yet realized its value. By the time they did it was too late. The government began to dispense severely limited quantities to private individuals. This was at first oxygen of the highest purity. Today you're lucky if you can get 90% purity, unless, of course, like Tim, you work inside. In his authorized biography "The Illusion of Power" President Chin says that: "Oxygen is the single most important stabilizing factor in the world today. Whoever controls it, controls the people. It is this struggle for the control and abundant dispensation of the precious gas which underlies all contemporary thinking and action. It is, in fact, progress itself. With its per capita output of one-liter-per-minute, the U.S. is by far the leader in oxygen production in the world."

He goes on to derive all sorts of conclusions from

these impressive statistics, pointing out how the I.O.P. (Intensified Oxygen Program) first recognized the need for systematic production and distribution of oxygen, and how this lead gained early in the global race for the life-giving gas has never been lost.

The reality is slightly less impressive. Oxygen distribution to the aged, infirm and disabled has never reached the minimum daily requirement level, nor has there been a proper updating of these levels from month to month to accommodate the increasing pollution levels. The now infamous Q-Factor, the pollution multiplication effect resulting from over-saturation, has never been taken into account. Every day thousands of Americans die of causes linked directly or indirectly to oxygen deficiencies.

"I need somebody to take care of this place, anyway," I tell them. "I'll have to spend a lot of my time down in Port Creole. You kids can stay if you like. You can stay up here. When's the last time you've been in a place like this?"

"Never!" they chorus.

"The kid . . ." I go on, but Dooda interrupts me.

"His name is Freddy," she smiles. "His name is Freddy Rainbow!"

"The kid, also known as Freddy Rainbow alias Teddy Tornado alias Wilbur Windfall also known as Pedro Gonsalez, all these aliases, these anonymous nonentities, these folds in the impenetrable veil thrown over the great national computer for deserters, derelicts and . . ."

"And mudras," yells Dooda.

"And mudras, all these names assembled here and adherent to three human bodies namely me and you two, all of us can share what there is which is dried fish and seagull meat, and the kid knows where the water is, how to get it, what to do with it, and I'll show him how to snare seagulls with a dummy and snorkel, and you all can make it downright cozy for yourselves while I will camp at the bottom making sure you won't be disturbed in the least, is that agreeable?"

Dooda launches a furious attack of kisses which rain down on me on my forehead, my nose, my cheeks, even my neck. "And now, if you'll pardon me, you look as if you can use a rest. I'll leave you alone. All you do, Freddy . . ."

"That's not my name," says the kid moodily, maybe because of juvenile jealousy, maybe because of stubbornness.

"Well, at least I don't have to call you kid anymore, so let down the bottle from time to time, will you. I think the weather is changing. Tomorrow will be a windy day!"

If I listen well, if I care to imagine, I can hear the Sadoos in Port Creole chanting for wind, praying for deliverance from the weight of yellow poison that sits upon us, the beast with as many claws as there are pulmonary passages in Creole County.

In three, four days the moon will be full. Then, certainly, the weather will change. Right now the yellow is being mixed with orange and magenta, as if somewhere a defective strip of indirect neon lighting were being covered with colored paper, turning darker, more uncertain, and permitting the silver of the eucalyptus leaves to assert itself in the shiny evergreen of California oaks, and the duller, deeper hues of manzanita and iceplant.

The light is changing, and what has remained of the miracle of the departure of light? Not much, little, just enough to reflect the changing of the times. In this unbreathable time of heaving chests even light has degenerated and this decay is popularly misinterpreted as light fallow enough to herald the coming of a new divine judgment.

The new, the unknown always offers itself for dramatic misinterpretation. The human imagination is pointed in a certain direction by the force of circumstance and, once pointed, must continue in that direction. It can imagine all except its own insufficiency. It cannot for example, imagine that the speed of events is superior to its own speed.

Bianca and I did not sleep that night.

"But if Azydia is *that* far away, then even the speed of light is insufficient to get you there, right?"

"In time, Alfons!"

"In time!"

"Yes, time is a universal concept. It applies every-

97

where in the cosmos. But it's not the *greatest* concept in the cosmos!"

"Concept, concept, it's a reality, isn't it. When a year has passed, a year has passed, n'est-ce-pas?"

She held my hand and kissed it.

"Yes, the seasons are true, Spring, summer, and fall, and winter, they make a year, a stretch in time. Trees grow and mountains shrink. Time is reversed in stone, but still a year is a year only as long as a tree is a tree. Where there is no tree, no grass, no baby, there can be no year."

"Then there is no time on Azydia."

"No, there is time on Azydia, but there is also no-time. The concept of the absence of time, notime, is superior to the concept of the presence of time, time."

Even though she held my hand and her luminous eyes searched my face, I felt uncertain.

"Why?"

"Because what is present is surrounded by and contained in what is absent, not the other way around. Absence is the womb of presence."

"And the womb is more important than what it produces, right?" I tried to joke. "The mother is more important than the baby, right? You don't kill the mother in order to kill the baby, you kill the baby, you kill the product, you kill presence."

"Please," she said as tears came into her eyes, "don't speak so savagely!"

"Ah, children," said Pops, "calm yourselves, take it easy. You don't know what you're talking about."

"We don't know," I said wildly, "but maybe we'll find out!"

"Alright, alright. Good. Fine!" he said. To have his daughter back was all that mattered to him now.

"Then what is this musical note, this vibration you say they use to conquer time and space?"

"You want to know everything in one lesson?" she asked.

"Well, see, I know my Chevy," I said, trying to build up something from my own simple, basic knowledge. "Now, recently, some of these scientists have broken through with gravity. They have discovered the anti-gravity principle and they say that if there are visitors from outer space, if, mind you, if there are, then they, too, are using this anti-gravity principle. Right here on earth, Bianca, we're beating gravity right now."

She looked at me in a strange, longing way, as if I were very, very far away from her.

"Beating gravity is not enough. Intelligence, reason can beat any obstacle, conquer any force. But it can do no more than that. A cannon can fire a missile that will break a wall. But that is all it can do. It will go no farther. Gravity is only a minor obstacle. Anti-gravity will overcome it. That's marvelous for diversion, for entertainment. Men will be able to float in weightless bubbles with feathers for oars, just as you see in old engravings, their most ancient dreams of personal flight will come true. But they will not touch the stars that way."

"You never used to talk like this," I said half to her and half to Pops, realizing that I sounded defensive.

"I never knew," she said.

"Go to Washington. Tell them about this," I said, "Talk to the experts. They'll understand, won't they?"

"That's not why I came back," she smiled and leaned forward, her lips brushing against my ear. She whispered:

"Our baby!"

"Yes," I said loudly, wildly, suddenly ecstatic with the certainty of her desire, the certainty of its fulfillment, the certainty of all the time ahead of us.

"Time," I shouted, jumping up, pulling Bianca up with me.

"Time oh time, yes time and time! I love time," I sang out.

"I *am* time!" chanted Bianca, twirling around the enormous room. And true to the nature of time, she never stopped.

• Twenty •

Alias Freddy, the kid, woke in Dooda's arms, late in the morning.

He was for a moment disoriented by the residue of sleep which had been deep after seminal exhaustion. Dooda looked loose and sleek, having thrown one long thigh over the cover, exposing a jungled armpit to the soft light agitated by leafy shadows. The tree swayed Freddy gently into the present. He remembered. Dooda stirred.

He sat up in bed and slipped off without further disturbing her. Lying only partially on her back, her strong breasts effortlessly resisted the pull of gravity. Her lips had dried, as in death, but in the darkness to which they formed the entrance, a pink divan glowed distantly: her tongue!

He found a mirror and examined his face, tracing the heavy jaw with one finger, touching the softnesses under his eyes, dried and slightly wrinkled in the sun. He moved his shoulders athletically, flexed his biceps and ran his hands through his hair. He had a morning erection that demanded release and so he slipped into his pants, through the hatch, found the rope and felt his weight swing into position as his bare feet sought and found the wooden pegs on the great trunk.

He let himself down slowly, taking note that it was indeed a windy day, as I had promised him. He was beginning to enjoy himself. He let go of the rope much earlier than he should have, fell too long but showed great, sudden agility by twisting at the waist and still landing on his feet. His weight lay too far back. He fell, like a broadjumper, touched the ground with his palms and came up dancing to regain his balance.

He looked idly around, touched the massive tree and peered up at the base of the fort. Then he walked across the summit plateau and looked down to the lake, up toward Mount Tamalpais, then at distant Port Creole and the Civic Center. If he had stayed a little longer he would have seen me emerging from the eucalyptus forest. Instead he turned, stepping cautiously through the grass to the opposite edge. He selected the dead apple tree to relieve himself against.

It had been a long night and he stood for a long time in the peeing trance, looking out at nothing. Even the tree which stood between him and infinity seemed to disappear. His eyes were unfocused, his mind at rest. When he shuddered back into himself with a final atavistic post-urinal spasm, he saw the bananas. There were six of them, in a bunch. They hung from a thick branch to his left and when he touched them they fell and even his lightning reflexes failed to stop them. He picked them up, first the bunch, then one that had broken off, and he carried this extraordinary find back up to the plateau.

It never occurred to him to examine the branch. The appearance of the bananas was truly shocking. So much so that he continued to act as if it had been a perfectly natural event. When I arrived he had polished off the one that broke off and was about to tackle another one for breakfast. My appearance triggered the first proper response. He dangled the empty banana skin like a pendulum and pointed in mute consternation at the apple tree.

"Bananas! A whole bunch of them! On that old tree!"

I was by his side in two leaps, snatching up the remaining five.

"You found these on the old tree? You ate one of them?"

He nodded, frowning. In his half open mouth I could see his tongue searching for leftovers.

"They're great," he said. "Try 'em!"

"You goddamn fool!" I screamed, cluching the bananas. I rushed over to the tree and found the spot in a moment. It was not unlike the place where the apple had been plucked by Tim Mahoney. I fitted the knotty, brown root of the bunch in its place and it matched, perfectly. Beyond the spot, half an inch either way, the branch was dead. I stomped back up to the kid.

"Goddamn, Freddy," I said, "these bananas are not for eating!"

"Shit, how was I supposed to know!"

"That's an *apple* tree," I stormed, calming. I pointed at the tree.

"That's a special tree of some kind?" he asked innocently.

"Yeah, very special," I said, much calmer now. After all, there were still five left. Just to make sure, I picked up the skin, too. I sat down just as Dooda called from the fort.

"I'm down here, honey," the kid called back.

"I'm coming down!" I examined the bananas carefully. They were in perfect condition, perfectly ripe, and not a spot on them. They gave off a subtle scent which the nose had to search for but which, once caught, made the face turn to it again and again.

I scraped some of the inner skin and tasted it. It was delicious.

"Bananas are for eating," said the kid. He didn't phrase it as a question. It was an imperative. He sounded as if he was ordering me to eat one, too.

"Listen," I said, "it's a miracle, it's magic. For one thing this is a dead tree. *Nothing* is supposed to grow on it. For another, even if it should be an apple, not a bunch of bananas, so this is magic within magic. You don't *eat* magic! This is a sign of some kind, a great distinction. We are chosen to be honored in this way, and you can think of nothing better than to eat up these symbols!"

"Eat one," he said calmly. "Don't worry about it!"

I was about to reply sharply when I looked at his face. It was in a state of total, blissful relaxation and it radiated health and happiness. The skin was smooth and tanned, the lips moist and lightly closed, turned up a little at the corners. His eyes were clear and calm, gazing out at the world with balanced satisfaction. A single tear had sat brimming on the rim of his left eye and now detached itself and rolled down his cheek, perfectly intact, until it reached the vicinity of the nostril, where it lost itself on the skin. He didn't look like yesterday's deserter at all.

"Bananas are good for you," he said. "Good!"

It was the special attention he gave to saying good which compelled me to follow suit. I unzipped one of the bananas and started eating. It was as if the years had been rolled back and I was a boy again with my first banana. But it was better than that. It was my first conscious childhood banana sweetened by nostalgia, by manhood, by my wait for Bianca from Azydia. It was the innocent palate sharpened by the taste of killing which now tasted the magic banana. I swallowed, swallowing good for the first time in my life. This banana was good for me which meant that it *is* good for me. It fed me now and would continue to feed me forever. It would be wholly digested, wholly absorbed. I was permitted to take it in and keep it. I partook of the banana while it strove to join me.

Dooda let herself off the rope and came over to us. The kid told her to sit down and handed her a banana. She peeled it and began eating slowly. Freddy's face glowed. I did not have to ask him what it was that made him so happy. It was the virginal, paradisical splendor of the world that surrounded us. All I saw about me was refreshed and resuscitated. In the far distance, brought closely within reach by the crystal-clear air, trees paid homage to a new, gentle wind. A feeling of great, sweet anticipation came over me. I stood up and spread my arms, bathed in clean, golden sunlight, awaiting the wind, following its approach across the valley. Then at last it touched me as a mother touches her sleeping child. Again, it was the first touch of wind in my life, a never-ending caress, a long, intimate embrace.

A hawk climbed up out of the valley in lazy circles. The sun lay shimmering on his wings. The bird was sustained by light, guided by the same wind that touched me, linked us. I, too, was no longer bound to earth, leaning backward, arms spread. I opened my eyes wide to take in the upside down paradise where a perfect world bordered the cosmic lake in which all creatures found refreshment and rest. There was no need for me to cast off. I stood for a long time and then slowly righted myself.

Freddy and Dooda sat side by side, holding hands, looking out at perfection and at me, one of the perfect creatures. They were the first lovers and the last and looking at them brought tremors of sad ecstasy, the fulfillment of the oldest dream: to behold lovers in the purity of their love and youth. Then I remembered the apple. The apple I had given to Pearl! There was a flash of panic, the skies seemed to be rent, but already the moment had passed, and again there was no blemish on the shiny, sparkling perfection of the world in which I lived.

I sat down with the lovers, received by soft grass that bent beneath my greatly diminished weight without breaking. I sat close to them, facing them. They were brother and sister and I was their brother, too.

"Banana!" I heard a voice, remotely familiar. It was my own voice cleansed of intent, the voice of a child.

"Banana!" they smiled.

We sat in perfect peace, watching the change of light, the long, slow, perfect path of our earth in the wake of the sun. From time to time Dooda rose and brought water in cupped palms which she sprinkled over us, bejeweling faces, shoulders and limbs. I watched her go and come until again she return naked in perfect modesty, placing herself between us.

We sat through midday, through the long afternoon, into evening, saying nothing. Then, as the light faded and the colors shivered toward night, I felt compulsion to speak.

"I killed Titiane Mbuto," I told them. "It was an accident. She rode a bicycle. The car ahead of me turned without warning and spun her out into the street. I was going too fast. The distance was too short. I broke her body. I saw the light fly from her eyes. She died in my arms."

The earth's shadow caught and held us while high above a seagull left a shadowy wake in the golden ether.

At last I had let go of my confession. I could see that perfection is not concerned with guilt or innocence. There are no accidents in perfection, either. Nor had the world been perfect when I ran over Titiane Mbuto. It was perfect now!

I looked at Dooda who sat silent, in blue.

"I wanted you to know," I told her. "You remind me of her!"

Then, far away and close by at the edge of the world, the Creole County Civic Center grew a second cupola, an orange bulge, a melon moon which broke away from it like a drop falling on a mirror in slow motion. The Creole County Civic Center had given birth to the moon. I rose and spread my arms and once again bent backward from the waist to see the darkening world by the shores of the cosmic lake in whose deepest depth somewhere, luminous and invisible, there was Azydia, my destination.

• Twenty-One •

Now the almost full moon comes up, and now it's time again for Bianca's most probable return, except that this time it's more likely than ever. The night sky is perfectly clear, the world has righted itself again. Up in the fort the lovers are forever in each other's arms and I'm the doorkeeper, the unbribable guard who whiles away the hours under the jeweled dome somehow brought up from two centuries ago.

"People have to know themselves before they can know the universe," Bianca had said.

"Yes," I said. "Deep!"

"So, all is fake, nobody knows anything!"

"Except you."

"I didn't know; I was shown. Even now I know only *that*, not what."

"But you know more what than what I know, right?"

"Yes."

"Did you ask to be taken, or did they just pick you up?"

"I'd been waiting for a long time, Alfons."

Right here, where I now sit, we sat, together.

"Show me Azydia!"

"Can't, too far!"

"You show me, and I'll tell you!"

"Don't be so tough, Alfons, I love you."

105

She wanted that baby real bad, but somehow we didn't know how to start. It was a perfect place for it, a perfect night, just like this night. Suddenly then, as now, all reason for wanting to leave has disappeared. This is no longer the rotten, stinking planet everybody knows it to be. It's paradise again. A magic bunch of bananas has transformed it from a cesspool to a lake with water clear as the Mount Tamalpais spring in 1777 or before.

"Tell me what you want to do with your life," she said.

"How do you mean?"

"I mean when you're through with your Chevy and cloverleafing?"

"Ah," I said, "wait between lights!"

Waiting between lights was another favorite diversion of ours. It was a hypnotic game. As the light turned red the trance was induced. We'd sit with idling engines and open eyes, suddenly all alone in busy, whirring America. We were insects who had fallen to the center of the machine and found the spot where all activity ceases. We sat transfixed, feasting on nothing, in the trance of nowhere, with unknown origin or destination. Idling. American gasoline zen.

"No, seriously!"

"I wanna leave."

She hugged me closer and kissed my temple.

"Yeah," I said, "I wanna volunteer. I wanna join the army!"

"No," she whispered, "not you. The army is not for you."

"There's a war going on," I told her, "and I want in on it. Nobody else is, so it's up to me."

"It takes at least two men to fight a war," she said wisely.

"You're wrong, Bianca, it takes only one, and I'm the one. I wanna join. This is a good war. I want to win, so I'm getting in early."

"We're not talking about the same thing."

"No," I said, "we're not. We won't, either. I never talk about the same thing. It's not the war you suspect either, or the war anyone suspects. This is a different war."

"What kind of a war?"

"It's the war *I* make. Everybody else has already made their war, now I wanna make mine. Now I wanna show them what a war should look like. A *real* war. Don't you like uniforms, battle music, bullet-torn banners? Don't you like to see men fall and others step over them?"

"No," she said thoughtfully.

"Neither do I, Bianca. My war is different. There'll be no men falling and nor will they get up again. Only I will win. See, now, I'm just learning, I'm holding back."

"You're waiting, too, then!"

"Yes."

"Will it be long?"

"You tell me!"

"Oh, Alfons."

She kissed me again, and stayed close. Then I kissed her. It wasn't easy with Bianca. She'd brought something back from wherever she had been. Maybe it was all-forgivingness, boundless love. I'd been the one she found on the hill, here, in this spot, and so I was the one she had chosen. It was an accident, even though she said there were no accidents.

We hugged and kissed under a moon very much like this one. We hugged and kissed very much like Alias Freddy and Dooda were hugging and kissing in the fort, except that there was no fort then, just this hill and the plateau. I can't even remember when the apple tree died. That's how long ago this happened.

"They bring you up chickenshit," I told her. "They gang up on you, so after a while you just don't wanna see them any more. They don't fight man to man, they're gangsters!"

"Who, Alfons?"

"The gangsters!"

"There are no gangsters . . ."

". . . on Azydia," I finished for her. She nodded, serious.

"See, you don't understand," I went on, "people on this planet don't want to know about that. They'll pick it up, shrug their shoulders, then they'll shit in your trunk or slash your tire. You're not supposed to take it seriously. Like I take you seriously. I'm not supposed to. You go out there and tell them about Azydia, about time and no-time, they'll believe every word you're saying. They'll lip

107

read. They'll love it. See, that's all *free* information. But they want to pay. They want you to make them pay. So you have to find a way to make them pay, and there's only one way, that's with money. They consider nothing else payment. You can put a man in jail for ten years and when he comes out you give him a pill that'll make him live for two hundred years and he'll think he got a bargain. Or you kick him in the ass. He'll *still* think it's a bargain. You could have *killed* him, right? So as long as you don't kill him, he thinks whatever he gets is *free*, unless, unless you make him pay for it with money. But, remember, you can't ask for too much, because the sonofabitch is cheap, really cheap. All the secrets you bring back on that starship, well, let me see . . ."

I looked deep into the nocturnal lake, beyond the moon, beyond the Dog Star, beyond and still beyond every depth until there was only Bianca's kiss and breath on my cheek.

"You charge ten bucks, no more," I said with finality.

"Ten dollars?"

"Yeah, ten. That's all. I don't mean ten for everything to everybody, I mean ten for whatever you choose to reveal to any one person. You charge ten for the littlest and ten for the biggest and ten for each little bit in between, to everyone. If you want to tell a hundred people that there is a planet called Azydia in our phonetics, you charge them ten for that. If they want to know more, they have to pay ten again. I mean a thousand bucks each time, because there's a hundred of them. And you string it out. Do it so that you will never get to the end. You will soon be rich."

"And what about me paying you for all this information?"

"You owe me a ticket to Azydia."

"But I didn't ask for this. I didn't *need* to know."

"How do *you* know? Just wait. You'll be very grateful to me some day for having told you."

"You're not conceited at all, are you?"

"Upon my word, miss, I ain't jivin' you!"

"Well, then, sir, unbutton my dress!"

I had never encountered a dress with so many buttons. When she was naked she commanded me to nudity, too, and I stood suddenly cold in the cold light of moon, shivering.

"Now your courage will be tested, master," she called.

It was not merely cool, or cold. There came from the depth of space a feeling of such desolation, such overwhelming loneliness, such an impossibly piercing assault upon my essential physical self that I was flung to the ground, cowering like a savage. Bianca, meanwhile, stood perfectly erect, in amused repose.

"It's lonely out there!" she said with a voice as gentle and as penetrating as balm in steel.

She stretched on the tip of her toes and I clung to the ground, shaking violently. I was afraid I would not survive. It could not possibly be this cold in California. It had never been this cold anywhere. This was not cold, not ice, not temperature. This was a condition I had never encountered.

"Help me," I stammered.

"There is no help for him," she said. "I cannot help you."

She gave me no assurance, no help. Inch by inch I pushed myself up. I got to my knees but no farther. It was over there, not more than four, five steps from where I sit. I hope it will never happen again. The ordeal went on for a minute, two, five, ten. I struggled to my feet until I, too, stood. All this time Bianca was watching me calmly. To her the moonlight must have been like mild sunshine, but to me it was terrible. Finally I stood alone. All alone in space. I spread my arms as she spread hers. I leaned back following her lead. Then, two perfect swans, we curved gently into the unfathomable pond.

•Twenty-Two•

Pearl ate the apple. Two days later he walked out of Creole County Jail a free man.

Judge Krishna Bavan Krotentoter, at thirty-one one of the younger judges gracing the bench in the New San Francisco area, retrospectively found errors in the proceedings, enough to declare a non-trial and release Pearl. This might seem ordinary, but it is not. It is the first time within memory that a judge has taken the time and made the effort to review a case after it was closed. But Pearl, who has come up to the Civic Center on the occasion of my first appearance in court in my own case, explains everything to me.

"Thanks for everything, kid," he says, smiling beatifically, "that apple was dynamite!"

"Come on," says Bill Blut as we enter the elevator, "we only have an hour or so. Alfons and I have to go over his opening address to the court!"

"Leave us alone, will ya," growls Pearl, "listen, go have a coffee. I'll bring your boy back in fifteen minutes, deal?"

Blut reluctantly branches off into the cafeteria and we walk through the broken-down gate halfway up to the top, the gate that was smashed in the riots of '84, out onto the bare hill, looking down on the camp of Crusaders and Sadoos who are already jamming the halls and corridors.

"As soon as I ate the apple, I knew I would be released," he grins. "Oh, incidentally, I didn't eat it all."

He pulls a small package of tinfoil from one pocket and cautiously opens it revealing about a quarter of an apple.

"Where'd you get the tinfoil?"

110

"No problem," he smiles, "no problem at all. You can keep it, anyway, what do I care about tinfoil. Eat the apple, eat it now!"

I've just slipped back into the dismal present with its surgical masks, oxygen bottles, billowing smog and stench. The beautiful banana curtain has blown away and revealed a grey, desperate scenery on which a sullen, ominous drama is being acted out. We have wrapped the remaining three bananas in eucalyptus leaves to let a few days pass before eating them. And now: the apple.

"What did it do to you?"

"Show me the truth!" he says, apparently without emotion, but I do detect an undercurrent of defiance, a tone struck by a smart, uneducated, non-academic man who has stumbled upon the philosopher's stone but not yet managed to erase the last traces of his faulty upbringing.

"Yes," I provoke him a little, "and what *is* the truth?"

"Nevermind," he says, "eat the apple!"

So I eat, chewing slowly and carefully, mixing in plenty of saliva.

"As soon as I ate it I could see that Krotentoter was in my hands to do with as I please in connection with my case," he says. "So I did nothing. I let *him* come around to it. It was beautiful. I knew he'd free me. Those two days I spent until they let me out were the most beautiful days of my life."

"What did you do?" I inquire, munching.

"Played basketball."

I had barely swallowed the first mouthful when the apple began to make itself felt. In a matter of seconds the curtain of perfection was once again drawn over the scene. I blinked and stared, trying to see through what was obviously a romantic illusion. I focused on details of the deceptive, three-dimensional painting before me but the result was simply that it became more realistic, more convincing.

"Great, ain't it?" Pearl almost smirked.

I gulped and started chewing on the rest. Only a few minutes had passed and time suddenly demonstrated its porosity. I saw my environment, but I saw it ideally, and I saw it as it existed *in time*. I saw it in fragments

111

scattered through timeless space, brought together by the physical eye to form a tangible, instantaneous reality. I saw that I lived among fragments of disembodied *principles,* each drawn to the other by the *need* of my senses, materialized for the purpose of corroborating the presence of me, myself, us, Pearl and every other person.

"Let's go play a game," Pearl suggested, and I could see that there was plenty of time.

We walked down the southern side of the hill, near the pot-holed, quasi-abandoned freeway and found a weedy, cracked asphalt court with a basket which Pearl had repaired. He squatted by a pile of broken crates and pulled out a brand-new basketball wrapped in tinfoil. It was a treasure of tinfoil.

"Where'd you get all that tinfoil?" I couldn't help marveling.

"There's a lot more where this came from, kid!"

He unwrapped the ball, bounced it a couple of times and then threw it, in a casual, aimless gesture. It missed the basket by a mile, just barely making the backboard and, by apparent accident, it bounced off, bounced once on a crack in the court and from there directly and softly into my hand. I held on to it, noticing the perfection of the ball, then recognizing how silly the game of basketball really is.

"It's a distraction," I said.

"Sure."

"We play it to hide in this world!"

"Yeah," said Pearl, "pass the ball!"

I passed the ball to him, he dribbled, passed it back. I felt its weight, let it ride on the palm of my hand way out there, far far away, then I dropped it and slid under it as it bounced, taking two quick, deliberate steps away from it, as if I was tired of the game, then I spun around and caught it off its second bounce.

"Hey, not bad, you're learning."

He showed me a fast, lateral move. It was just a sidestep, more or less, but it was done with total concentration and an expression of blissful superiority on his face. Pearl was the greatest basketball player alive.

"It's not what you do *with* the ball," he lectured, "it's what you do *around* the ball. The game is fascination. You know that the ball always bounces. All you have to

112

do is keep it bouncing. But a man is more fascinating than a ball. You are the man. *You* fascinate while the ball bounces."

He bounced the ball once, very hard. It jumped fifteen feet in the air. When it hit the ground, Pearl was through two pirouettes and frozen in the stance of a classic discus thrower from which he zipped into what looked like a statue, receiving the ball on the palm of one hand as a butler receives a weightless calling card on his tray.

"What do I tell the judge?"

"Tell him you were playing basketball!"

• Twenty-Three •

The courtroom was crowded to the rafters. The little piece of apple, now in the act of being properly digested, transformed the scene into something timeless, a permanent theater which floated through the ages. The costumes changed, the settings, but the subject matter remained always the same. And so did the contending forces.

I was five minutes late. Bill Blut cast his eyes heavenward, appealing to a higher justice on my behalf when I entered. I had played a brisk game with Pearl, and while he had dominated the early going, I learned fast, aided by the immaculate perception made possible by the apple. Finally, when we were tied at twenty, I could see the tiniest, most distant impurity in his game. It was the last, microscopic vestige of his determination to win and it cast him in the role of the beast. It was as if he disappeared. I paid no more attention to him and sunk two shots in quick succession.

"The defendant will stand before the court," said Judge Krishna Bavan Krotentoter, gravely and pointedly looking at the lock. I made my way through the crowd, to the attorney's bench. I inclined my ear to Blut.

"Take it easy," he whispered, "the judge is in a terrible mood."

I nodded and faced Krotentoter.

"You are five minutes late for this important opening phase of the proceedings against you, Mr. Anton," said Judge Krotentoter. "I think you owe the court an explanation for this tardiness."

"I was playing basketball," I said.

"In the future," said Krotentoter, "you will adhere to the precise times of appearance before this body of justice. If not I will find you in contempt! Do you understand?"

"Yes, I do," I said.

"The court understands that you are appearing as co-counsel in your own defense and that you have decided to avail yourself of the opportunity for an opening statement no longer than sixty minutes in time."

"Yes, your honor."

"You may begin, Mr. Anton."

I could see now that a jury would have been terrible. The way the jury is placed in a contemporary courtroom, sitting in a semi-circle behind the judge, their placement would have taken away my focus and my concentration. The way it was now all I had to do was look straight ahead at the judge.

"Your honor," I said, "I move for dismissal on the grounds that you have neglected to inform me of the charges against me, a grave procedural error indicating extreme prejudice. Also total confusion!"

"The charges against you were read before you arrived, Mr. Anton. This court keeps to the appointed time and you may deem yourself fortunate not to have been held in contempt."

"Oh," I said, "fine then."

It was a play perfectly cast against me. The faces were timeless and in permanent array of suspicion and vindictiveness. Krotentoter himself wore all the masks, layers upon layers, of the merciless judge whose verdict is certain to be cruel and unjust. But, with the help of the beautiful magic apple, I saw and recognized the perfection of this arrangement. It gave me certainty. There would, of course, be a limit in conventional time. But within this limit I was given all the freedom in the world.

What mattered now was to use the time for entertainment, for *fascination* as Pearl had called it.

"If it please the court," I said, lifting my right hand elegantly, "I will now begin, and I will begin with an image that might entertain some of you, the image of basketball, a now somewhat disreputable game. Life is like a basketball game."

I let the sentence go as a man releases a pigeon, in this case a carrier pigeon. It didn't seem to carry very far. There was no reaction.

"Well," I continued, "perhaps not a basketball game, but more like a carrier pigeon in the sense that every bird of life is trained to carry a message. It is up to us to recognize this, to attract the bird, take from it the message, to read it, to ponder it and then to act accordingly."

Again, I paused and, noticing no great change either in Judge Krishna Bavan Krotentoter or in the feel of the spectator-audience behind me, I decided to go ahead directly, without further dramatic interludes.

"The world is in turmoil," I said. "Many are certain of impending doom and a majority of these look forward to some form of confrontation with a higher, spiritual justice. To put it bluntly, they say they will be judged by Jesus or Christ or both of these in one who will come again right about now. These predictions are based on ancient prophesies and new revelations. It is not difficult to see why such ideas have arisen. Every day thousands die of suffocation and pulmonary afflictions to say nothing of heart trouble and various types of strokes, tens of thousands as a matter of fact, and the world seems to be crumbling. The oceans are dead, though here and there some of the natural creatures of earth survive, some fish, some animals on land. Volcanic eruptions, earthquakes, floods, droughts, famines, pestilence, strikes and emotional epidemics are the order of the day. The economic situation is desperate. And we have not been able to lay the blame for these conditions to any one man. Human history itself is responsible. The seeds of our present situation were sown a long, long time ago. All we do now is reap. And as it is with our history as a whole, so it is with each individual life. Some people persist in calling it Karma, even though the principles of Karma, or Cause and Effect were so irrevocably repudiated back in the

115

Seventies. We know today that the knowledge of Cause and Effect would have to include a total knowledge of the universe and all its laws because we are not subject merely to influences on this planet or influences within this solar system but are directly, firmly and intricately linked with all the countless galaxies in the universe. We have no such knowledge. Such knowledge is utterly and totally beyond us at this stage of our development. That is precisely why we are in such a mess today. Even to pretend that we know anything is silly. In fact we know nothing. We have lost our contact with the world and its products. We eat synthetically and what remains of natural foods no longer contains the vital juices and foodstuffs that once made us alert and intelligent. In short, we have failed. We are in need of help. And nobody knows where this help will come from or even if there will be help."

I paused again, this time not for dramatic effect, but simply to catch my breath. I had no idea what I was saying, but I was satisfied enough with my delivery.

"In fact, even though there are millions and millions who acknowledge that we are in need of help, desperate need, there are also millions who say that we have never lived in a more prosperous or more propitious time. These are the immature, the deceivers, the exploiters of humanity. It is easy to see for a poor man what the advantages of being wealthy are, but the opposite is not true at all. The progress from rags to riches is a natural one, but those who have riches do not want to hear about those in rags. Nor does any of this matter. It has gone too far in the world. Fakery triumphs. The unreal is represented as the real. And nothing is known about reality.

"People have sought refuge in religion, in chanting incantations, in pious demeanor, prayer. But their prayers are directed to fake images and to deceitful hearts. The show passes for the content. Those who kneel in anticipation of divine judgment do not know what it is to be forced to their knees. They have never opposed the power which they expect to judge them. They hope for a merciful verdict. They cannot conceive that perhaps they themselves are the judges. Nor is it within them to imagine that God may be conquered!"

I threw out this last line. It slipped out of me without

knowing why, or even that I had said it. I heard it as it was spoken, and this finally, brought a murmur of protest from the audience and I understood in that instant that I had taken the ancient position of the heretic with the flaming tongue. I had pronounced heresy.

Judge Krotentoter moved very slightly, but very noticeably in his seat. His worn old robe, shiny and maybe a little greasy with age cleaved open over an unbuttoned shirt, revealing a tuft of greyish hair, also unclean and matted. Beyond this, Krotentoter maintained his composure.

I began to realize that I was addressing the people themselves, many of whom were Sadoos and Crusaders. I was speaking *at* the judge, but *to* the people. So much I understood, but was this the way to acquittal? It didn't seem so. Still, I decided to work on, to talk more or less therapeutically, to let my mind empty itself with words and to hope that at the last moment, before the sixty minutes were up, a stalagmite of truth, something truly moving, truly fascinating would rise from the bottom of the emptied vessel.

"Well," I say, "let God be forgotten, let bygods be bygone, it's all snot under the bridge!"

Now at last Judge Krotentoter is startled. He raises his hand, the court reporter switches off the automatic recorder plugged into one of those newfangled energy-dispensers.

"The defendant will refrain from further obscene or inflammatory commentary!"

"Yes, your honor, if the court will forgive my haze!"

"Would you repeat that, please," says the reporter, timidly.

"Haze, as in maze!"

"Thank you."

Some communication is taking place, an exchange, obscure and clumsy as it may seem. Not quite half of my time is up and a minor breakthrough has occurred. I have, speaking defensively, broken through their shield, but the extraordinary apple shows me that this is still nevertheless no more than a predictable phase of the eternal proceedings, a principle made visible, painted hopeful, to subside into the quicksand of developing history in which each moment carries with it the seed of perfection that must break and wither to permit the ugly flower of human ignorance to rise to the surface.

"It is my opinion," I continue boldly, "that the law no longer exists. What substance it had was always derived from the lawful stance of the people on this planet. When that stance fell below the level on which it could be externally demonstrated it became incapable of supporting a legal superstructure. That you have not realized, that you still sit in judgment, that you still sentence men to jail and to death, is only further demonstration of this absence of a respectable foundation. There is no law! There is no law because there are no people. Both, individuals and society derive their credibility, their raison d'être from their talent for unity, solidarity, from their willingness of one to cooperate with many in return for which the many promise to protect and support the one. When such basic relationships do not exist, there is no society. I'll give you an example. When I came here today I had to make my way through the crowds milling about this building because of my trial. But they are crowds only in an objective sense. Subjectively speaking, that is, from my individual point of view, there are basically only a handful of people. The others are backdrop. They provide the sounds that perpetuate the illusion of life on this planet. They cough, they wheeze. They murmur, they chant. They press forward, fall back. They make way for me. They are members of the eternal greek chorus, the never-ending mass of bystanders which can never be dented. They absorb sound, receive impressions. They clutter and despoil. They are parasites, usurpers. Their greed is insatiable. They have never learned to suffer, and it is this inability to suffer which withholds from them the dimensions that render humans real. They are imitations, shadows, copies constantly striving toward the original as it is manifested in myself. Their envy is boundless, their cowardice has no limits. In their mass they form an ocean which is yet no more than a drop, less than a drop, in the universe. Humans! You can shove 'em! Take it from me: Not a million of these skeletons, compressed and drained of their marrow, yield the strength to lift a finger to the face of their creator. This is why they're always talking of revolution, of change, of progress. Afraid of words, afraid of the distil-

118

late from dictionaries, afraid to follow the lead of ideas for fear of death. In order for these cowardly carbon copies to be entertained, facsimiles, mirror images, are created. God is a Sadoo, or a Crusader, or a Sakhi. The God whose wisdom consists of a perpetual series of suicides. A jargonic God, the God of Vernacular! Brute shit! Is it any wonder that you go around praying for leaks in your oxygen cylinders?"

The hand on the clock has advanced to the forty-five minute mark. It's time to think of more, and I'm nowhere near drained. Just now I feel the apple suffusing me entirely, and what started off as a lecture on perfection has turned into a shambles. I am one man. I stopped long ago trying to stop the world in its pathetic tracks.

"Of coarse course," I say, ready for the reporter to stop me and to repeat this opening. But he doesn't. And the minute hand moves steadily on. Maybe something new now. Maybe take an outsider's point of view.

"Who does he think *he* is, you will now be asking yourselves. Or worse: I see among you the forgiveness that blooms in the cesspool of suppressed murderous impulses. I am a hundred years ahead of you all, nay, a thousand, an eternity! Never will the coward turn adventurer! Never will the backdrop become the play! It has happened that the curtain parts to reveal an empty stage. Never has an audience been entertained by an empty stage! When the time comes, I will rise and leave you behind. I have other plans. You are trying to take my life and play with it. Your vanity makes it possible for you to imagine that you can keep me from leaving this planet. You are trying to tie me up here, to keep me in bondage. You are like the Mindanao savages fifty years ago when they first saw a helicopter. They could understand everything, they were not surprised. It was not so extraordinary, after all. Birds fly. There was nothing new in flight. But the one thing they could not imagine was that one of their number should be scooped up and taken away. Away means nowhere, you think. Since you cannot imagine anywhere but here, you believe there is only here, and here is all there is! In that respect I am more fortunate than any of you. I had a teacher. I knew Bianca Populi and she was extraordinarily convincing.

But for her I would be like you: a gaping, dumbfounded, slow and vicious but fumbling mob of stumble bums!"

There were ten minutes left and I had run out of steam. What more was there to say? All was smooth now, I had glassed them over, glazed their gluttony. Absolute silence reigned in the shabby courtroom. They were now accustomed to my pauses and they sat there, neither impatient nor waiting, merely passing time that was jampacked full of action. They had lost me a long time ago. I could feel it. The field, including Bill Blut and Judge Krotentoter, was far behind. I was running on the dry chalk flats by the bay, in the wind, under the sun. Noise and stench far behind. An egret, the symbol of purity and extinction, had unfolded its wings in trembling majesty to receive the divine light. We stood, facing each other across the marsh.

"I am the original," I said into the silence. "You are the copies."

Then I began to amuse myself by watching the clock. After three minutes had passed, Judge Krotentoter lightly banged his gavel.

"Mr. Anton," he observed, "you have six minutes left."

"Fuck the left!" I said and sat down next to Billy Blut.

• Twenty-Four •

Bill Blut's father's name had been Willem van Blount. He was a Dutchman from Zuiderkoje and he came to America during the Second Energy Crisis as a master peat-moss brickmaker to advise Americans on peat-moss brickmaking. Peat-moss bricks were used in heating, but also in a new auxiliary attachment to conventional gasoline engines which permitted automobiles to run on peat-moss.

"We changed our name to Blut after the class riots of Seventy-Nine," said Bill, slurping his coffee soup, "I was just a kid then, barely in school."

Some of the coffee found its way through the grimy beard, guided by oily spikes of matted hair, and dripped on his shirt to join other patterns of leftovers aging there.

"He was a proud man but, naturally, he didn't want to die. He was no aristocrat, you know. Van Blount is a common name in Holland, and it doesn't necessarily indicate nobility. Still, they lynched him. Maybe because he was a meticulous dresser. He wore nothing but white shirts. My mother had to wash three a day: one for the morning, one for the afternoon, and one for special occasions. He wore suits. You can imagine! Suits in Seventy-Nine!"

He shook his head sadly. Of course, many of those who stuck to wearing suits that terrible year survived. But they were fortunate enough not to be saddled with a foreign name. Bill Blut's story was not an uncommon one.

"Yeah," he said, "he would have made it, too, if it wasn't for his Dutch accent. I was only eight years old, but I remember it as if it was tomorrow!"

He smiled ruefully as he told his story. Willem van Blount was caught by an angry mob on his way to work. He was pulled out of his peat-moss powered car and forced to surrender his driver's license which provided his executioners with the objectionable name. His general appearance only confirmed their impression that he was not merely aristocratic and wealthy but foreign to boot. When he opened his mouth to defend himself he provided the straw that broke his back.

"He must have known what was gonna happen," said Bill. "He tried to make a speech. That did it. The accent did it. They went ape, they Sweded out, except that they didn't do it in that cold, indifferent Swedish way but with American gusto. It wasn't strictly speaking a lynching. They kicked him to death!"

We sat for a while, staring out at the rainy countryside. It was a long, slow, cleansing rain. It was raining jewels and health. The apple still had not worn off and I was drawn into that distant event in which Mr. Willem van Blount lost his life in an imperfect world. I could not

121

imagine the repetition of such a scene nowadays. Was not my name Anton, was I not of French descent? And had I not killed three native Americans, their bizarre make-up notwithstanding? And was I not still alive, bailed out by an organization whose members had a blood right of revenge upon me?

"If he'd kept his mouth shut," said Bill Blut, "he might have made it."

"Well," I said pensively, "what did you want me to do, leave the one hour empty, relinquish my right to an opening address?"

He didn't answer, but it was obvious that he disapproved. Maybe he thought I could always talk before my execution.

"Is that what you think?" I asked him.

"What? Think what?"

"That I can always talk when they're about to sound me out?"

"I didn't say that," he said.

Again we were drawn in by the rain. His attitude had changed in these few short weeks. He still underestimated me, but he had begun to understand that I was not an ordinary person. The class riots had sent fear deep into the marrow of America, for sure. It is estimated that no less than three million, and probably closer to four million people, most of them men, died. They had only one thing in common: their inability to blend into a crowd. Willem van Blount had been lynched precisely because he could not be part of the lynch mob. Bill Blut broke the rainy trance.

"Didn't you use to box?"

"Oh no," I said, "not me. I took lessons from the champ, from Pierre Brasseur."

"I've boned up a little on you," he said and let it go at that, but I could imagine what he had read. The police files, the reports by Tim Mahoney on the relationship between Pierre and Bianca, and myself of course. It was probably all there in the dusty file with no new entries since Primitivo Populi's death until now.

The cafeteria was closed to all who did not have business in the courts. But outside in the halls and corridors Sadoos and Crusaders and a multitude of the poor, malnutritioned populace pressed against the plate-glass

122

partitions which had withstood the onslaught of time and neglect. We were sitting in plain view, but our backs were turned to them. It was not a pleasant sight.

Pierre Brasseur had showed no surprise at Bianca's return. He had obviously not been concerned with her absence, either. We went to see him together, Bianca and I, and he either never noticed the change in our relationship, or else he never showed that he had noticed it. He was pale and serious, as usual, but he began to take a greater interest in me. One day he invited me to box with him. I didn't know how to respond to this, but he was very insistent, taking great care to assure me that I would not be hurt.

I could not have refused without looking silly, so I accepted. He laced on the gloves himself, using his threefingered, artificial left hand deftly, telling me not to worry.

"Most people have the wrong idea about boxing. That's why most fights are so boring."

He tested the gloves by pushing them against his chest. Then he asked me to hit his right hand, which I did, maybe a dozen times.

"Fine," he said, "good. Now, this is the ring," he indicated an area in a room specially reserved for this purpose. The ring-posts were marked with chalk on the floor. There were seven of them and they formed a circle. He explained that a circle was more appropriate for learning the art of self defense. Then he took up a casual stance in the center of the circle and positioned me at arm's length opposite him while Bianca sat on a folding chair, smiling at both of us.

"These are the rules," he said. "You punch as hard as you can, but you aim for a point close to my skin. You try never to touch me. If you do, you will receive a slight rebuke from me. Don't worry, I won't hurt you. The idea is for you to pretend that I am a few inches thicker, taller, more substantial than I am. Okay?"

I thought I had understood and began to advance, looking for an opening. There were openings everywhere, apparently, and I let go with my punches, keeping in mind what he had told me. It was not as easy as I had thought. In my first lunges I made contact with his shoulder, then his elbow, and every time this happened I felt

123

the tips of his fingers tapping me lightly on some part of my anatomy: the forehead, a temple, my chin, my neck, my heart, my stomach. He used only his right hand for this and most of the time I never saw it come or go.

I tried mainly for his face. He was shorter than I, even though I was still growing, and I could punch down on him, but the rule of not touching him made it difficult. In a little while I was huffing and puffing, but though I punched harder I managed to contact him less often. None of this made sense to me, but it apparently pleased him.

"Very good, excellent," he said when I was completely out of breath and just stood there, my gloves hanging limp.

He helped me take them off and told me to take a shower. When I got through with this I found them sitting in the kitchen, talking.

"Ah," said Bianca, "here comes our hero, the future champion of the world!"

Pierre had told her that I had a great deal of talent. We drank lemonade.

"So," he said, "the thing is: you retire now!"

"I sure am," I said, having misunderstood him.

"You see, what I'm showing you is what I've learned. If you get into the fight business, you'll lose more than just a hand. Today, in professional boxing, the idea is to kill beauty."

"Figures," I said.

"That's why there are so many ugly people in the business," said Pierre. He was a practising Catholic and he had lost his hand in church when it got caught in the heavy door to a confessional. It seemed like a minor bruise and it was treated immediately, but it swelled and swelled, became gangrenous and had finally to be amputated.

"I gave my hand to the Holy Virgin," was how he put it. Bianca seemed to be no less fond of him than ever. She treated us both with great warmth and friendliness. She regarded us affectionately, almost as if we were children. She enjoyed seeing us together, at play.

"It was a detour," Pierre told us, "I found out what not to do. And I want to teach you what I know. It will take a lot of practise, but it doesn't take much time to *tell* you what it is. Are you interested?"

"I sure am," I said.

"Boxing is a simulation. It's a simulated fight to the finish. But it can never be real, because in a real life-or-death battle there are no rule books and no breaks. When you fight for your life you always win. This is a secret I'm passing on to you. So, the thing is to be defensive. Your body protects itself. It has reflexive mechanisms which protect you. They are self-activating, they trigger themselves, and what I want to teach you is to let them do this without interference."

"Does this go for any fight, against any opponent?"

"Yes," he said, "any opponent except yourself, your own body. Your body cannot defend itself against itself. Then a suicidal battles takes place!"

Bianca interrupted.

"You're still talking about one man fighting another man, aren't you?"

"Yes," said Pierre, "that's all I know, man against man!"

All through Bianca's pregnancy, Pierre taught me his art. After many months he himself put on the gloves and changed the rules to permit touching. We traded light blows. He initiated me into an advanced form of pugilism by instructing me to try not to defend myself at all as he attacked.

"I'm going to attack you," he told me, "try to evade me, retreat, keep your hands up but don't think of your fists as defensive. Relax. See what happens."

Nothing happened while he struck out precisely, hitting me lightly in places that would have brought me down had he been in earnest. We did this dozens of times and I couldn't understand what he was trying to do. But by this time I trusted him. I learned how to slip his punches, how to crouch away, how to cover up. My footwork got sharp and anticipative. Then one afternoon during one of these workouts he rushed me without the customary preliminaries and this time it was a real attack launched to blow me into unconsciousness. And then, after all these months of feigning and feinting, my reflexes were triggered. It was an amazing thing, even to myself. My right hand was out and back before I noticed it, and it had hit him precisely in the forehead, and with precisely enough force to stop him. It was a stern, paternal touch which I had administered to the overexuberant child and stopped him, on the spot.

He dropped his gloves and an expression of great happiness bloomed on his face. I had never seen this earnest man show such enthusiasm as then, when he picked up my right hand, still gloved, and raised it in the traditional victory salute.

I was very proud of myself and I wished my father could have been alive for me to show him what I had learned. These were not just words: I felt like a master. Never had being an orphan weighed so heavily on me as in that moment of triumph. Why did they have to drag an ancient veteran of World War I into Vietnam? Only because he spoke French and knew the French mentality which had dominated Indochina for so long! And what made him sentimental enough to take to absinthe in the afternoon on the shaded terraces of Saigon cafes. An old man with two wars behind him, a former member of La Famille, the Free France underground guerilla organization. What made him an expert, anyway! There he died, with all his knowledge of French deception and conceit. He had played his role so well that his cadaver was first mistaken for that of a Vietnamese.

Brasseur had a reason for doing all this. Maybe he felt it was a way to continue to stay close to Bianca who had begun to favor me. I was too young to understand. I did not inquire, I was not jealous. It could not be anybody's but my baby. And Pierre had taught me something invaluable. Bianca was teaching me love, and Pierre was teaching me survival. They went perfectly together. Still, there was something more to it, something more ominous. I could not quite pull this idea to the surface then, but there was a feeling in me that I was being prepared for something. But for what?

Pierre gave a party in honor of my graduation. Bianca, heavy with child, still insisted on dancing into the morning.

"And why *did* you kill them then?" asked Bill Blut

into rain and reverie. His question fitted so perfectly into my daydreams that the truth at last came out.

"In a fit of frivolity," I confessed, "I killed them frivolously!"

• Twenty-Five •

The rain turned to snow, and it was snowing in Creole County reminding me that the war was over.

It rarely snowed in Creole County. A week or two Mount Tamalpais might be white in the depth of winter and from its peak, or from the hill, you could look across the bay and see Mount Diablo, the other sentry, also white. You could make snowballs and snowmen, and you could feel cold from the hands into the bone, if you wanted to. But never had I seen it snow like this in late April.

Not only did it snow, and that itself was startling, but it got cold and the snow stayed. As it came gently down it made Christmas out of spring.

It was strange snow, though, coming from clouds that traveled high enough in the realm of thin, clean air, but as it fell it passed through grime and pollution and by the time it entered your field of vision it was no longer white, it was brownish yellow tending toward black. Tens of millions, billions of snow flakes descended and created a moving filter with their porous little bodies. Hour after hour the snow kept falling and then it began slowly to turn white again, covering the sooty snow on the ground. The air was clean once again. But still the snow kept falling.

The holy men who camped in Port Creole interpreted this as an omen, an important sign from the heavens, an act of purification preceding the Coming of the Christ. They huddled under blankets and robes around fires, chanting, eyes turned heavenward to receive yet

127

more snow on brows, lashes, head and shoulders and on their bare feet.

The kid and Dooda were munching on their bananas when I came home and they urged me to do likewise. But I could not. The changes caused by the slice of apple Pearl had given me were still lasting, the perfect curtain was still down, and the single banana which remained from the dead apple tree was well enough preserved to last another day.

So we just sat in the fort looking out at the phenomenon of snow falling in April in Creole County. The little, tubular oven-stove was going and through the grate pale fire flickered.

"How did it go?" Freddy asked.

"I don't know; you can't tell."

I slipped back there again with Titiane Mbuto as I was watching the beautiful Dooda, and I started humming.

"What *is* that tune you hum all the time?" she wanted to know.

" 'The Ochre Yellow Blues.' " It was easy for me to talk to her about this. "I wrote it for Titiane. I tried to get her back from her singer, but it didn't work. I also wrote a tune called 'Tears of Joy.' That didn't work either. Then, when Elvis died, it was all over. I think she burned everything. After the accident I became very close with her parents. They liked me very much and they wanted to take care of me, but I stayed on the spread with Pops, of course. 'Ochre Yellow Blues' never made it, but 'Tears of Joy' did. It was a hit around here, just a local thing. It never got picked up nationally."

They asked me to sing it for them, so I did. I had not sung it for a long time, not like "Ochre Yellow" which I hum a lot. "Tears of Joy" is heavier, more emotional, and when I first sang it for Titiane tears were streaming down my face. It didn't help at all. She sat bored through the performance, impatient, waiting for me to get through. She didn't want to talk either. It was obvious to her that these were desperate tries by me, not in a league with Elvis' "Let's Have A Party" or "Heartbreak Hotel."

It wasn't necessary for me to pretend that Dooda was Titiane. Dooda was now, Titiane was then, but the song still had its magic: first came the tears and then

128

the unbounded joy, the crazy elation that never quite caught on across the nation. It had not succeeded in getting Titiane back, but it was strange to see Dooda melting and weeping along with me. When I finished, alias Freddy was shaking his head.

"Boy," he said, "a lotta good emotion in there, ain't it!"

Dooda said nothing but shot a quick glance at him. I tried to cover up by saying: "How about 'White Christmas'?"

"Yeah, 'White Christmas,' yippeeh!" yelled the kid and we were off on a vigorous rendition of the immortal melody which turned softer and softer to match the snow, the snowy eucalyptus, snowy Mount Tamalpais. From there we slid naturally into "Jingle Bells," then came "Home on the Range," and finally "Sentimental Journey" which neither of them remembered well enough to make it a success.

There was now true Christmas cheer in the room, and the second banana showed a much earthier effect in both of them which expressed itself in talking, reminiscing, even in planning for the future.

"Everything will be alright," said Freddy. "My dad told me so. He always knew he'd come back to America some day."

I looked at him strangely, pensively. There was something familiar in his face, now that I had got past the surface he presented.

"Rainbow, Rainbow," I mused, "that's not an American name!"

"It's not Rainbow," laughed Dooda, "it's Reignbough."

"Yeah," Freddy joined in, "maybe even Rimbaud. Maybe we're fellow Frenchmen, uh, Alfons?"

"Yeah, maybe," I smiled and started singing "The Marseillaise." Then "Pont d'Avignon," and even the abominable "Alouette."

"Dooda," I said, "what's your real name?"

She leaned over and kissed me on the cheek.

"Theophilia," she said, "ain't that quaint!"

"Freddy and Theophilia also known as Dooda," I said, "let me tell you that good times are ahead."

"Good times are here," said Freddy.

"And more ahead," I went on. "I feel as if I'm seventeen again. I think it's Theophilia."

"I think I'll take a walk in the winter wonderland," said Freddy, getting up. Dooda looked at him, and at me, but she said nothing.

"It is cozy here," she said. "Take care of yourself, soldier!"

"Hey wait a minute, the war is over." I laughed.

"Which war?" Freddy asked.

"My war," I said.

"Your war isn't my war," he smiled.

"This is my home," I said cheerfully. "You are my guest. We live in the same home, we look at the same fire, the same snow. We eat the same fish, the same seagulls, drink the same water."

"And we eat from the same apple tree," added Dooda.

"So it's Christmas, Freddy, and the war is over." I told him again.

He squatted near the hatch, his face smooth and young now.

"In here maybe," he said, "out there, maybe."

He tapped his chest theatrically.

"But not in *here!*"

Dooda handed him the oxygen bottle.

"Take it easy, soldier," she said, "we're all in this together."

Freddy lifted the plastimask obediently.

"Here's to together," he said. "I salute the left, the right, and the middle."

"He learned that in Mexico," Dooda informed me happily.

"Fuck the middle," I said recklessly.

Freddy slipped through the hatch, handling the rope easily, peripherally. He no longer needed to pay any attention to the descent. He was at home here.

The hatch fell into place and Dooda moved away from me a little on the bed. She knelt by the fire and poked it with a stick of green wood. Sparks flew up through the grate and emphasized that it was darkening. Her neck was long and reflected the light in shiny, reddish gold.

"You really miss her, don't you?" she said.

"Who?"

"That girl, Titiane."

"Yes," I said, "but it won't be like that again. I won't make the same mistakes."

"What was your mistake?"

"I was too young. I should have waited. I wasn't meant for Bianca. That was a mistake. I could have got back with Titiane, but not with Bianca pregnant. She not only wanted that baby, she *needed* it. I had no choice, not young as I was anyway. Bianca knew too much. I wanted to know, too. All Titiane knew was Elvis, and at that she'd never met him. Just his pictures, his posters, his paraphernalia. I couldn't win!"

She came back from the oven-stove and sat on the bed, turning her face to me. She pursed her lips and winked, once, heavily.

"There's nothing there," she said. "You have nothing to remember. What you remember is nothing."

"It's all I have."

"No, it isn't." She went through me with youthful ferocity.

"I'm waiting for Bianca to come back. She won't let me down. She'll take me to Azydia."

"I'm waiting, too. I'm waiting to see when you'll start noticing me."

"You love Freddy."

She told me that she had never made love while it was snowing like this. She told me that it was snowing like this just for us. What had happened to my world? Three weeks ago I had been a recluse, a bulwark, a lighthouse against the ocean of wailing and gnashing teeth in the world. A symbol of determination, hope. Three weeks ago I had been proud and alone, four weeks ago. It was as she said: there was nothing to remember, I had remembered nothing. I had shuffled cards and watched the night-skies, waiting for the full moon and Bianca. I had been shut like the door to a mausoleum. Now miracles were occurring. Apples grew on dead trees, bananas. The people whose brothers I killed put up astronomical sums of money to keep me out of jail. Lost or missing persons were turning up. The world was casting off its dismal veils, one by one, and what had looked like a leprous body swathed in stinking bandages, soupy, pussy, fly-ridden and poisonous, emerged with immaculate alabaster skin, the rosy translucency of a paradisical past or ideal future.

My watch was growing long. I had acquired companions in whom I could confide. The earth no longer appeared detestable because those who inhabited it were seeking me out, and the first of these, the three Sadoos, I had killed! A therapeutic act to wake me from a somnambulant routine. They might have been robots benevolently constructed for just this short and fateful encounter, built to rescue me from drowning in time. I began to sink back, yielding to yet another deception. Theophilia whispered to me. I could not understand what she was saying. Maybe she was talking about our future. She was rising in me like the instant sap that brought the apple tree momentarily to life. It was true that I knew nothing, that I deserved nothing on the basis of my ignorance.

"I'm no longer beautiful, Dooda," I murmured. We kissed and allowed ourselves the time that was necessary.

"I want to conquer a new world; I want to strike out as a hero," I whispered.

While waiting, instead, the world had conquered me. It's soldiers were in my home, and she was one of them.

"Ah, come on, honey," I mumbled in a dream, "you don't wanna mess with a battered old warrior. Look at my face, look at that smile! I smile so easy now. You've said nothing that amuses me, but I smile at you, and at Freddy."

Inside of me my skeleton was incommunicado. I saw us sinking together as pathetic bone people. I saw our flesh's real purpose: to activate us, to muffle the rattling sound of bones. It was these skeletons that wanted to intermesh, not the flesh. The flesh was distraction, detour. And the flesh was only lips, all of it lips.

"Lips," I whispered into her lips.

She told me that we were all snow, falling through filthy space. She told me that we start out as snow and become filter, and that those who come after us, much later, would be clean again and cover us. Layers and layers of clean snow.

She told me that, for her too, the war was over. We were babies in each other arms, playmates in a sunken castle atop the great tree of the world. We had got it made. There was no better place to be, no warmer glow, no smoother skin, no goldener hues. I held her pressed against me, in peace. I closed my eyes as I sank into her flesh and she into mine, deeper and deeper. We ourselves were snow, falling.

I heard a sound, I opened my eyes, I looked up at the abominable snowman assassin. Alias Freddy Rainbow, holding my broad, trusty knife in both hands high above his head. The low fire glowed in it—ethereal blood, golden tongues licking a silver blade, the final distillate of a late winter night in Creole County.

Theophilia shielded me. There was no way I could have moved without disturbing her. No way to get away fast enough. My choice was between letting her die in peace and warmth and happiness, or in terror. So I said nothing, did not move.

His snowcapped head gleamed above wintry shoulders bearing epaulettes of snow. He was no longer a simple soldier, but an officer, maybe a general, and he was wearing his parade uniform for the execution. For a long moment he stood and I lay, waiting for the deadly arc to be struck between us, the last connection to be made. His eyes flashed into mine. His eyes dulled as if the light had gone out everywhere at once. His hands sank, still holding the knife as Theophilia woke and turned and smiled up at him.

She sighed and touched her forehead. She sat up, touching her hair, her neck, her shoulders, my chest. She reached out and touched Freddy.

"Hey, soldier, the war is over," she said.

The snow on Freddy was melting, glistening, giving off a little steam. There is no way of keeping up with the stream, the current is too steady and too swift and we had already passed the crisis. Dooda remembered nothing. The knife had been a flashy gesture.

"You can't kill love," I told him.

I reached for the banana, unwrapped and peeled it and divided it in three. Silently we ate, each one piece. This was the last part of the winter, the time of vigilance and hope. Maybe tonight the transition would be made, tomorrow morning would be spring. No one here nor anywhere could catch the moment, the moment of victory.

133

The war is over, I knew. So winter, too, had now to end.
The true, irrevocable spring lies before us, I thought. We
were united, we were strong. We were ready for the
fruits of peace.

• Twenty-Six •

In the third week of my trial, during testimony concerning
the circumstances of Titiane Mbuto's death which Judge
Krotentoter insisted on hearing, The Second Coming of
Christ took place in Washington, D.C.

The long-anticipated event was well-publicized despite the demands made upon the media-monopoly by
the reports of an extraordinary series of natural disasters
and catastrophes around the world. It was as many
scientists had predicted it would be: Christ was no ghostly
ethereal being but a messenger from an advanced stellar
society who had been dispatched to sit in judgment over
the denizens of the earth.

His credentials were overwhelmingly impressive. He
arrived in a starship almost two miles in diameter and
half a mile high. The vehicle could neither be photo-
graphed, nor looked at directly. Special sunglasses appeared miraculously in the hands of those in the area to
protect their eyes from the powerful rays of light which
emanated from the ship. Christ was a being somewhat
human in outline, but almost twenty feet tall, a giant who
wore what looked like a robe-like space suit made of material that shone with a cool, whitish light. His face was
distinctly human, though enormous, with large, blue eyes,
full lips, and long, golden blonde hair covered partially
by a hooded cap. The expression of the face was unchanging and very much like that of Oriental saints except
that the largeness of the features made it terrifying. The
crowd that gathered in the half hour before the Saviour
emerged from the starship was on its knees, their eyes

closed under the sunglasses. From the beginning it was indisputable that the King had arrived.

As one, those who witnessed the event felt their ordinary consciousness blocked out. In its stead they received a new awareness which initially took the form of a history lesson. They were acquainted with the true mystery of the life of Jesus of Nazareth. In a simplified, condensed form they were made aware that Jesus had been the good teacher who came to teach His speciality: Love. All the children of earth had been invited to attend, and He had taken pains to dispatch teacher's aides everywhere to teach this lesson. When the lesson was over, the teacher had departed in a manner demanded by His teachings. He had not left without warning. He had told His pupils to go home and study, to prepare. He had told them that He would return, that there would be a test, that some would pass and others would fail to pass. And that it would be terrible for those who had been lazy.

They knelt before the Lord under the hovering starship that shone more powerfully than the sun. Many of those in the crowd that had now swelled to five thousand lay prone, face down on the ground as a new, higher knowledge poured into them. They were told that the giant planet from which the Lord hailed, like our own sun, circled the central galactic sun, which in turn circled the inter-galactic sun once every 576 million earth years. Christ revealed Himself as the direct representative of the distant King known as God or El or Allah, and by many other names on the planet earth. The five thousand received the knowledge that 2000 years was the length of the beginner's lesson on earth and that those who had learned it would be advanced to the next higher grade, while those who had not would have to do the first grade over again. What precisely this entailed was not immediately communicated to them, but even so the assembled crowd was beside itself with fear and lay or knelt trembling, many among them wailing, howling, gnashing teeth, but too afraid to run from the spectacle.

Only the most hardened reporters and cameramen dared raise their heads when Christ finally emerged from the starship. When the film was hastily developed with trembling hands it showed very much what the newsmen had thought they had seen, except that the shiny robe produced light that outshone the Saviour's face and only his enormous shining bulk remained. It appeared to be floating down from the sea of light that was the starship.

Despite His size, Christ appeared barely to be touching the ground on which He walked. Those closest to Him who dared look reported that His feet were made as of brass and fire and where He had walked the earth was seared.

The King took a shortcut across a freeway where what little electric steam traffic there was, stalled. About Him and in His wake, people sank to their knees or fell to the ground, and even Sadoos and Crusaders and other holymen were no different from policemen, and security men, and all the others except for the littlest children, from two to four years of age, who ran after Him, singing, dancing and laughing. And not a mother dared follow to protect them.

Christ, the King, made straight for the dilapidated White House which had just received a fresh coat of paint. His arrival had been timed perfectly. President Immanuel Chin was on his way to lunch with a delegation from the Model World Government Organization and as he stepped out of the front door Christ arrived on the lawn and stood motionless, looking down on the tiny leader of one of the most powerful nations on earth.

Immanuel Chin, an American of Chinese extraction, at the time of this historic encounter, was sixty-seven years old and stood five feet six inches in height, weighing one hundred and forty-two pounds. He was obviously no match for the Saviour, but he displayed tremendous courage and showed no signs of fear or uncertainty. He knelt briefly with bowed head, then got up quickly and resumed his firm stance.

"Welcome to the United States of America, Your Majesty," he spoke the historic words that echoed around the world.

The Christ stood for a long time, surveying those before Him from His lofty height, His face unchanging in that terrifying expression of never-ending love and forgiveness. Then, slowly, He raised His right hand and President Chin, just as slowly, sank to his knees once more, just like his bodyguards and the members of the Model World Government Organization. Tears poured from his eyes, his knees gave way and he slipped with all his length to the floor, trembling even as those around him. Then at last the Savior's voice was heard. It was even and melodious and it filled the starving souls of men with sweetness and hope, for now, as He spoke, the terror of his appearance was overcome by hope. Maybe, just maybe, so each man or woman felt, maybe I'll be saved.

"Immanuel Chin, rise and follow me!"

The President of the United States did as he was told. The Christ turned and together they started on that long historic walk to the suburbs and beyond to the place that immediately became known as the "Meadow of Judgment", there to discuss the technical details of how the judging was to take place, while everywhere on earth, in every capital of every nation, a similar scene was witnessed, making true the prophesy pronounced by Jesus of Nazareth:

"And I shall be everywhere at once!"

• Twenty-Seven •

The Prince of Peace's arrival on earth, though predicted and expected, still took astounding forms. For one thing, there were none of the automatic, coercive forces which had been anticipated. Judgment was not instantaneous and it now seemed as if there would be a period of grace, a space of time in which certain technicalities and formalities would be taken care of.

The Christ operated out of the enormous, sunlike starship from which, in hundreds of locations on our planet, He ventured forth to attend to the business before Him. Wherever He went the multitudes and the cameras followed Him and His Coming overshadowed all of the other numerous and primarily catastrophic events in the world, for example, that the polar caps were melting at an alarming pace, that Greenland appeared to be in the process of breaking apart, that Iceland was washed by thunderous tidal waves and that portions of Tierre del Fuego were already under water. The magnetic poles had strayed from their positions and scientific speculation could predict that this phenomenon, if it continued, would lead to a "capsizing" of the earth in the very near future. Still, compelling though these events would have been in ordinary times, they paled in comparison to the news of the return of the King of Kings.

Apart from His overwhelming physical characteristics, The Christ also acted as a giant, walking deodorant wick. Wherever He went noxious and nauseating fumes disappeared. They were replaced by clean, sweet air that made the nostrils and lungs smart with its sudden pungent freshness. He seemed to be walking at the center of a circle perhaps half a mile in diameter inside of which all pollution was miraculously eliminated. Once people had got over the shock of His appearance and the fear of forthcoming judgment, they flocked to Him from near and far, and even the most calloused hearts were attracted if only to be relieved of the necessity of oxygen from bottles.

In view of these developments it was not surprising that The Christ chose television as His official means of communication with the populace. His first appearance after the conference with President Chin was a one hour program in which He spoke only three words. These occurred precisely halfway through the program. They were:

"Observe and listen!"

The one hour period served as a lesson in meditation. The enormous figure of The Christ shone forth from its position on the Meadow of Judgment. It was this point, repeated in appropriate places all over the planet, which became the focus of attention for the entire world. Many started out sitting in front of their sets but ended up on their knees, hands raised in prayerful gestures. The unspoken, telepathically received message was clear and confirmed unanimously:

"Peace, Peace on Earth and Goodwill to Men!"

The Saviour was obviously in no hurry with the Judgment.

This notion was confirmed when President Chin himself went on the air to explain the situation to the people of America.

He was a man who had undergone subtle but unmistakable changes. The smooth, confident face with the stern eyes had sagged a little here and there. President Chin looked tired and shaken. His lips were tightly compressed. His gestures were abrupt and seemed occasionally to escape his control. He had obviously been through a nerve-shattering experience.

"My dear brothers and sisters in America and in all the other nations of our beautiful planet," he began uncharacteristically, for his general approach to public communication via television was brisk, unsentimental, businesslike. His voice trembled on the brink of breaking. Here and there along the route of his pained speech he broke into what appeared to be an uncontrolled smile, and a couple of times tears seemed to enter his eyes. But with tremendous effort he managed to hold them back.

"You are all aware of what has occurred. The Saviour is once again among us. But this time He has come not to suffer for us but to judge us. Each one among you must decide for himself or herself what this means. The words of Jesus of Nazareth as they are recorded in the Holy Bible assume new significance for all of us and they will prepare us for the trial ahead.

"I have met The Prince of Peace personally and I can assure you that He is indeed that: a prince of peace. We all stand accused, and we may all defend ourselves before Him, and each one of us will receive not merely the benefit of the right to an attorney, as has been guaranteed in our own human Constitution for more than two centuries, but a right quite inconceivable to us. This is the right to judge ourselves.

"I repeat, The Son of God has personally assured me that each one of our number may judge himself or herself and proclaim himself or herself innocent or guilty.

"The Prince of Peace has told me only this: that there will be sufficient time for all of us to make up our minds, but that He will announce the day and hour of judgment soon. In the meantime He has divinely deigned to grant us an hour of His time every day for a period of meditation and prayer such as you have just observed."

Here President Chin paused to drink from a glass of water. The gesture was made ostentatious by the zoom close-up. The camera meticulously recorded the tiniest wavelet on the surface of water in the glass, making it painfully obvious that Immanuel Chin's right hand shook badly. Then he addressed Americans once again.

"The charge against us, individually and jointly, may surprise you as it surprised me. In all honesty I must say that I am still shocked by it. I had prepared a speech, but I want you to know that what I am saying now is not prepared material. I feel that I must speak to you as a brother and a fellow human being. The charge against us is that we have wasted time. The Prince of Peace has made it clear to me that time is God's most precious gift to men, next to His gift of eternal life. It is the second-most-serious charge that can be brought against a creature of God. The charge of wasting life, I have been told, cannot be brought against humans. It is a higher charge, an offense which humans, because of their ignorance, are incapable of committing. This means simply that the most serious charge that can be leveled against humans has been brought in against us, jointly and individually, and that we will be given a chance either to defend ourselves in open court, or to plead as we wish. If we plead Innocent, this judgment will be accepted. If we plead Guilty, this judgment will be accepted. If we wish to present our case before Him, that too is acceptable and the Master Himself will then decide."

Again the President paused, this time simply in order to rest for a moment. He stared somewhat blankly ahead of himself, into the cameras, at his audience. His eyes unfocused and there was something pathetic about his helplessness. Never had he been seen like this by anyone, so Tim, who had insisted we watch the program in his office, assured me. I, of course, had only a vague idea who Chin was, or what he had said in the past. Even before I went up on the hill, I was no longer interested in politics. From what I had heard and imagined, Immanuel Chin was a slippery customer, a man who had not quite managed to contain the strain of cruelty he had inherited. There had, I now remembered, been some executions. In some way, it was rumored, Chin held individuals responsible for the never-ending series of apparently natural

140

catastrophes that plagued the world and the U.S. in particular. There had been witch hunts. There had been secret assassinations. None of this could be reconciled immediately with the shaky little man on the screen who seemed to be pleading for something, though it was hard to say for what.

"I do not know," he now continued, "how much time the gracious Lord will grant us to ponder the charge and to decide in our hearts how we wish to plead, but I urge you all not to compound the errors of the past. Let us not waste any more time! Let us this moment begin to examine ourselves and our lives, each to himself! My brothers and sisters, perhaps it is not too late; there is hope. I have met the Saviour and He strikes me as a being who is profoundly aware of our weaknesses. Mercy and hope reside in Him forever and in the Father who sent Him, let's not forget that. Let's use every second of our time to examine ourselves. And, perhaps, to prove that we are worthy at least of forgiveness in the eye of that distant Father whom we call God, the Ruler of All the Galaxies."

We sat in silence for a while after President Chin had finished, Tim puffing on his pipe. These were serious times indeed.

"Al," he spoke up at last, "I think this means that your case will be dismissed."

"Could be. If not, I'll introduce a motion to that effect."

"Absolutely," Tim Mahoney said. "No judge on earth can now sit in trial or pronounce sentence, since every judge is himself on trial. The way I see it, ordinary criminal law will be suspended. At least until after Judgment Day."

Again silence settled between us. The impact of the Second Coming was beginning to make itself felt even here in Creole County, remote as we were from Washington, D.C. In a number of locations former drive-in theaters which hadn't been used for years were being remodeled for closed-circuit television. After the initial shock, already there was energetic, bustling activity. If at first it had appeared as if the Coming of the Lord would result in universal depression, the opposite seemed now to be the case. Every day brought new surprises. Nothing happened

141

according to the timetable set by the Latter Day Crusaders, for example. Nor did the Christ conform to the popular concepts formed of Him and His return. People, even the most religious among them, were forced to admit that it was different from the way they thought it would be. Already three days had gone by since His arrival and we were still alive, unharmed. Not only that: the world had been given an incredible opportunity to vindicate itself by judging itself innocent of the charge of wasting time! It was almost too good to believe.

"I have to tell you something," said Tim. "I never believed in the flying saucer thing. I thought you made it up to explain Bianca's disappearance. In fact, Al, I have a confession to make. I've been trying to fool you all these years. I've pretended to be your friend, but secretly I've lived only for the moment when I would catch you off guard and prove that you killed both Bianca and your infant daughter."

"But why, Tim, why?"

He shook his head and seized my hands emotionally.

"It doesn't matter, but I beg you forgive me! I know now that you are telling the truth. There *is* a planet called Azydia. And Bianca *did* promise to return from there and pick you up. I know now you'll go there, Al. I'm with you in this. I don't know why you killed those men, and I don't care. I care only that Bianca is alive and that I'll see her one more time!"

I was slightly embarrassed by this show of inner turmoil. At the same time I was touched. I could imagine what he had gone through in all these years.

"I can't promise you that," I said cautiously. "*I* believe she's alive. *I* believe she'll come to pick me up. But look, things have changed. The Lord walks on the earth again. Am I still free to wait for *her*? I don't know, Tim. I just don't know anymore."

I was truly confused. But this confusion did not dampen my elation. It was almost certain now that the trial would be halted. I, along with all other men, would be held accountable directly by the Ultimate Judge, to Ultimate Justice. Had I wasted time? How would I plead? Was I guilty or innocent of this cosmic charge? How else could I plead my case?

One thing I could see immediately: I needed help, I needed advice. It was necessary immediately to confer with my friends, with Freddy, Theophilia. With Pearl, the fox. With Bill Blut. I had to find Scott Adair. Now we were all on trial, it seemed. We could plead jointly, maybe. As far as I could see I had never wasted time, but maybe that was deceptive. As soon as I realized how rotten this society was, when everybody I loved or liked was dead, or had disappeared, or not now available for friendship, as soon as this had happened I withdrew to my own company. Had I not been aware from the beginning that there was no time in the world? And had I not always had the idea that time was being stolen? From Bianca, from me, from everybody? Many nights I had lain awake under the stars, asking myself who the time-thief was and how this theft could be stopped. Hell, I found myself thinking, I'm an expert on this! And maybe that is what the world now needed, an expert on time!

All the long, exhausting lectures on this subject that Bianca delivered to me, often against my protestations, came back to me. Time. Notime. Azydia. Speed of Thought. All that stuff. I was pleased with the way things were going. The Christ had shown Himself without the slightest inclination toward punitive cruelty. He was patient, kind and could not be opposed because of His size and apparent power. All He had failed to do so far was to inform the world of what the nature of the punishment would be for those found guilty. Maybe it was better not to know! If your hand is going to be chopped off, wouldn't you rather not know about it in advance?

Yes, yes, it was as I had felt: exciting times lay ahead for me. Things were developing. Maybe there was something I could do about this situation. One way or the other, though, I could see that I would have to make a decision. I would have to decide whether to go with Bianca and Azydia, or with the Prince of Peace.

I shook hands with Tim and bounded out of there on springy, youthful legs. Downstairs in the parking lot the Sadoos and Crusaders were busy erecting a large screen for closed-circuit reception. This was the first time I had seen them work. Yes, the Lord was good for all, even for the laziest among us. Good for business, too. Maybe there was something to the old saying that when people are up against it, they fight like hell. For the first time in ten years I felt as if I, too, was part of humanity. I, too, was fighting like hell. But it was fun now, because I had company.

• Twenty-Eight •

Judge Krishna Krotentoter banged the gavel, lightly, symbolically, surveying his court with cool eyes.

"Court's in session," he announced, "step up, Mr. Anton!"

I took my place in the witness chair and the County Prosecutor, a tall, storklike man swathed in bandages continued questioning me. I found out later that he was suffering from one of the many forms of scurvy that were now common but that he wore his bandages more for reasons of vanity and identification than out of necessity. This gave him the appearance of a badly wounded veteran who has escaped a military hospital. He spoke in a metallic, cracked-up voice and his name was Ferguson. His method was sarcasm and he seemed determined to get as much exercise out of his work as he could, stilting back and forth in front of judge and witness on legs that might have been welded at the knees.

"Would you tell us again, Mr. Anton, what prompted you to arrange for Titiane Mbuto's funeral and burial in one of the graves adjoining that of singer Elvis Presley?"

"Your honor," I said, "I realize that this is slightly unusual but I would like at this time to move for suspension of all proceedings against me until the larger matter of the guilt or innocence of humanity as a whole has been settled by the Lord Christ who is now preparing us for Judgment!"

Attendance at my trial had drastically diminished. So much so that there were empty seats in the once sumptuous now shabbily upholstered spectator section.

144

Every day, at noon precisely, The Christ appeared on television and the nation knelt for prayer. Already my case had been superseded. We were swimmers in the stagnating backwaters of startling new events. Still, from those who were there, rose a sigh and murmur of approval. I had popular support.

"Motion denied," said Judge Krotentoter evenly. I thought that I had caught a swift smile as it slipped across his face and was gone.

"The Saviour has made it clear, sir," I said, "that we are all on trial. It makes sense that a man, any man, who might be guilty should at least withhold judgment on the guilt or innocence of another man!"

Now Krotentoter smiled. Faintly but unmistakably.

"Mr. Anton," he said calmly, "your motion is denied. But since you disagree with me, let me digress for a moment. In order to try you I have generously interpreted the most generous provisions of both constitutional law and trial procedure. I have applied judgment to the circumstances of the murders with which you are charged which permits you to be free on bail. I have admitted you as co-counsel in your own defense. I have not objected to what other judges might well have interpreted as an excessively confused opening address. Now you raise the question of the return of our Lord and Master, The Christ, our Saviour, and I will again apply my best and most generous judgment to this new situation. I am denying your motion because I believe that bringing this trial to a swift and fair conclusion is a task I must discharge before I can begin to devote myself to personal soul-searching which, I assure you, I intend to do the moment this trial is over!"

He leaned back and eyed me expectantly.

"Yes, your honor," I said, "with all due respect, I consider these proceedings a waste of time!"

"Once again, Mr. Anton: your motion is denied and your opinions unwelcome. You are approaching the thin line that separates orderly courtroom procedure from chaos. I warn you. If you insist on questioning my authority in this court I shall hold you in contempt. Do you understand?"

"Yes, sir, I do!"

"Mr. Ferguson," said Judge Krotentoter, "continue!"

145

While the County Prosecutor had the recording clerk re-read the question concerning Titiane's funeral, Bill Blut was making prominent little gestures meant to caution me, no doubt. Tim Mahoney was sitting back against the wall, looking glum, and in the same row, over in the corner, was Scott Adair. As I had expected, Pearl was nowhere in sight.

"Well," I said in answer to the question, "Miss Mbuto was a fan of Elvis. She called him The King. She collected the commercial items produced by the Presley industry: cigarette-holders, sweatshirts, gloves. She made entries in her diary, like: Elvis Reigns Supreme. Or: Elvis Lives In My Heart. She told me that his dancing on stage was divinely inspired, a great gift from God. She once tried to rent a room next to his suite in a big hotel, so I thought it would be what she would have wanted, a grave next to his."

"I see. And would you say then that after her idol died, she became despondent, careless, perhaps so much so that she herself was to blame for causing the fatal accident?"

Bill Blut was up with: "Objection, your honor. This is irrelevant and immaterial. Miss Mbuto died accidentally, that was established in court. The County Prosecutor is putting emotional pressure on the defendant. Miss Mbuto's death was a painful event for Mr. Anton. I can see no purpose in exhuming this dark episode!"

Bill Blut was pulling all the stops of what he had learned working for the Public Defender.

"Sustained!" said the judge.

Ferguson tacked before this unfavorable gale.

"Now, concerning the death of one Primitivo Populi, I wonder if you'd mind . . ."

"Objection," called Bill, "again this is irrelevant and immaterial!"

"Your honor," said the storklike creature hotly as a touch of pink crept into his emaciated features, "I am trying to lay a foundation."

"What foundation, Mr. Ferguson?"

"This will come out in the questioning, your honor."

"Alright," said Krotentoter, "the objection is over-ruled."

"I was asking you, Mr. Anton, if you have reason to

believe that Primitivo Populi was murdered, that the fire which destroyed the buildings of his estate was arsenous in nature, that . . ."

"Objection. The answers to these questions call for an opinion on the part of the defendant!"

"Sustained," said Judge Krotentoter. "Mr. Ferguson, may I suggest you rephrase your questions!"

"Yes, your honor, thank you," said the County Prosecutor. "Mr. Anton, do you know of anything that would tend to confirm the notion that arson was used to murder Primitivo Populi?"

"No, I don't," I lied.

Ferguson turned away from me abruptly. Maybe he had information which told him I was perjuring myself. But it was impossible now to cling to this dramatic fleeting moment in the distant past. He shook his head like a surfacing diver. He was not sure of whether or not he had succeeded in whatever it was that had put him on the track that led past these deadly stations in my life. Obviously he was implying that I had something to do with all of these tragic events. And, of course, I did. I was involved. He knew it, I knew it, the judge knew it. Everybody had known it then. People had suspected me. In a way, killing the Sadoos was corroborative evidence, even though it had not yet been established. They were trying to cast me in the role of a mass murderer.

"Mr. Anton," continued the prosecutor, "you have been quoted as saying that Bianca Innocencia Populi, Primitivo Populi's daughter, was taken away by a flying saucer, an Unidentified Flying Object, that she returned from a distant planet called . . ."

For the first time his memory failed him. He looked at me, turned to look at his assistant, a fat, young man with shaven head, one of the so-called Legal Monks and member of an organization that had sworn him to lifelong service to humanity without demand for or expectation of monetary reward. The fat humanitarian raised his motheaten brows. Ferguson scratched the bandage on his left wrist in dismay.

"Azydia," I supplied.

"Yes, from Azydia. That she stayed for a while, gave birth to a daughter—your daughter Fox . . ."

"Vox," I corrected him.

"Vox, yes, how clever. *Vox* Anton! That means the Voice of Anton, your voice, doesn't it, Mr. Anton?"

"Yes, it does."

"And that she then climbed aboard this flying saucer and returned to Azydia with her little daughter Vox, and that she'll come back for you, Mr. Anton, isn't that correct?"

"I believe it is, yes," I said.

Bill Blut was up again, affecting the demeanor of a man whose patience is being put to a test.

"Your honor," he said, "I can't see where this is leading us. Perhaps Mr. Ferguson can tell us. I have the impression that we are really getting to a point which if we go beyond it will be, forgive my conjecture, sir, a waste of time!"

He sat down, apparently immensely pleased for having managed again to bring in the idea for which I had almost been held in contempt of court. The idea for which the world was on trial.

Now at last the County Prosecutor put his cards on the table.

"Your honor," he said, "I have studied Mr. Anton's history thoroughly. As thoroughly perhaps as any man. And it has occurred to me that wherever Mr. Anton has gone in his relatively short lifespan, death has accompanied him. People have died. People close to him, people he liked, or even loved. People whom he owed a debt of gratitude. Finally even his wife, if we may sanctify what is even now at best a questionable relationship. The fact is, if it please the court, that people around Mr. Anton die or disappear. So much so that the law of averages just doesn't fit anymore. I can't help feeling, your honor, that there is some insane method here, that all these tragedies are linked and that the link in every case is Mr. Anton, the defendant himself. And I hope to show that, far from being an isolated act of violence caused by the long, fruitless wait for an imaginary spaceship, the murder of three holy men on the hill above the place where Primitivo Populi died so violently and so inevitably, followed a pattern. A pattern, unfortunately, that none of us could have foreseen. But still, a pattern of murder, cold and premeditated, a bloody fabric in which the defendant has cloaked himself as if it were the immaculate garment of a respectable life!"

Judge Krotentoter glanced at the clock. His hand felt, maybe unconsciously, for the grimy, matted tufts of hair under his open collar and he tugged at them. For a moment it seemed as if he might smack his lips or spit down from his considerable elevation.

"In view of the broadcast from Washington, D.C. in thirty minutes," he said, "this court stands adjourned and will reconvene at 2 P.M. precisely!"

• Twenty-Nine •

2 P.M. precisely never came! Nor did 3 or 4. Next thing anybody including myself knew it was 5 P.M. Three hours had passed without anyone noticing. Three hours had disappeared.

Pearl thought that three hours of amnesia should make America sit up and think, but it didn't. Once the curious fact had been noted, fixed instrumentally and by employment of the zero meridian, Americans went back to their preoccupation with the impending Last Judgment, reassured that everywhere on earth three hours had been lost. But neither Pearl nor I, nor Billy Blut, nor Freddy, nor Scott Adair and not even Tim Mahoney got over it so easily. And certainly not Judge Krotentoter who had once again to postpone the proceedings against me for another day, now with the added uncertainty of whether or not there *would* be another day. What had happened once could happen again! We might be taken out of time altogether. Pearl fondled his chin.

"But time passed," he said, "though it wasn't used. When the pulse beats, time passes, but we don't know if the clocks kept ticking for example!"

"What else?" Bill wanted to know.

"Maybe they jumped," Pearl speculated.

"I remember nothing," added Scott Adair. "I looked at the TV picture, then—nothing."

"I never watch television," said Pearl, "but I don't remember nothin' either. So it's not the TV!"

"But the Saviour in Washington did it, don't you think?" I suggested.

That much was agreed. There was no other explanation. It had to be Jesus the Christ, the Lord from the distant galaxy come to judge the world for wasting time. Somewhere, we all felt, there was an ominous and profound connection between loss of time and what lay ahead for all of us. We felt the day of judgment drawing near. And then, we knew, this time lost would play a role, perhaps an important one. Certainly an important one! Still, that wasn't good enough.

"Bill," I said, "I'd like a legal opinion from you."

He stared at me in consternation. His eyes bulged from the jungle of hair.

"Well," he recovered at last, "it's *about* time. I thought you knew it all."

"Bill, the last judgment is like a trial, right?"

"Yes, sure, I'd say so."

"Well, three hours are missing out of my life. I don't like it."

Bill Blut looked around at the others huddling in the grimy cafeteria as if to say: you're not alone in this, Al.

"So," I went on, "I feel this is a form of punishment. But we haven't been tried yet, have we?"

"No," he admitted, looking abruptly thoughtful.

"You get what I'm driving at?"

He wrinkled his forehead and tried to nod, but didn't quite manage.

"Is it legal to incorporate punishment in the trial itself, or better, is it legal to punish *before* the trial?"

This time he shook his head with determination.

"Absolutely not!"

"Wait a minute," rasped Pearl, "this ain't just any old judge, you know. This is *The* judge."

"Yeah, but still, even He has to stick by the rules He sets up. He told us that we had time to think it over. He said He would tell us the day and the hour. Then, kerplop, three hours go by, disappear, nobody remembers anything. At the very least it isn't fair!"

There was reluctant agreement. For the most part, these were not religious men. Still, they found it hard to resist the powerful compulsion to submit to the Saviour's unchallenged authority. There was a long, long silence. Scott Adair broke it.

"Well, Mr. Anton," he said crisply, "what are you suggesting?"

I was ready for it.

"I'm suggesting, Mr. Adair, that the King of Kings is a thief!"

These were all hard men with the exception perhaps of Bill Blut who was hardening fast by association. All of us had lived and faced death. Some of us had killed. Tim Mahoney had done it in the line of duty, and so had Freddy. Pearl had done it in a bloody rage. Scott Adair had been gone for over two decades, but I could read it in his eyes. He, too, had killed. Yet now they all blanched. I followed up my advantage.

"He's a thief," I said in a low voice, trying to be as persuasive as I could under the circumstances. "He is not a common thief, of course, but a thief. He's come here to steal time. You and you and you, and I, we are the victims. Figure it out!"

I dipped one finger in the lukewarm coffee and used the table for my calculations.

"300 million people in the U.S., 5 billion in the world. 900 million hours in the U.S. alone, 15 billion in the world. That, gentlemen, is . . ."

In fascination they pulled their cups toward their waists to make room. My index finger moved on.

"625 million days," I said, "makes 1 million 736 thousand, give or take a few thousand. That's one million, seven hundred thirty thousand years. Over one and a half million *years,* friends. And that, I may say, is a lotta time!"

They were stunned. I wasted no time.

"There's no way we can get it back," I pressed the attack, "no way. But there *is* something we can do and do it legally."

"What?" asked Bill.

"We can collect," I said. "The Christ owes us money."

Now Scott Adair's finger was on the slippery surface.

151

"The minimum wage is $5.–per hour. That's 75 billion New Dollars for the world!"

"But how . . ." stammered Bill. "This is crazy . . . how are we gonna collect?"

It was a good question. I had brought them this far with my audacious arithmetic, but now I was stumped. So I got up.

"Maybe we can't," I said, "but I'll be damned if we don't try!"

• Thirty •

I didn't even know if old Miss Montstream was still alive when I took Theophilia for a Sunday afternoon stroll through the noxious, deserted streets of downtown Port Creole which now to me seemed clean and sparkling with new vigor.

We were of good cheer and bouncy step and the pale, heavy sunlight that twilit the cracked walls and made grey ghosts of our shadows seemed golden like eggyolk once again. What I saw was and was not, all at the same time. Here is where Bianca and I had joined the festive Bicentennial crowds, where I had seen her drunk on sweet, red wine, where she had spoken Dionysian stanzas, senseless, visionary bursts.

"The world is always waiting, Alfons. Waiting for the little things, waiting for thimbles and thumbs. Rainbows in dewdrops, spoon in the moon . . ."

"Hey," I said, "spoonin' the moon!"

It was a great title for a great new song I would write. It was a natural. As the sun paled behind veils, the moon became instant batter in Bianca Innocencia Populi's nights, and I for the first and only time the naked shepherd with glistening loins by her side, tending the flock of ourselves. Spoonin' the Moon, all the world would croon. What did it matter that I crooked a little finger to lick its sweetness out of the sky. We didn't need spoons. It must have been love if honey is love.

"This place gives me the creeps," said Dooda. She had reason to talk like that. Lizards had come down from the hills and lived like scavengers. They had become meat eaters in the process and though they did not run for cover as we passed, they averted their eyes, having lost their pride and their independence.

"Look at that—there, the fat one!"

The one she pointed to was as big as a rat. She made a move toward it, but had to take two determined steps and raise her arms before it scurried.

A bunch of little kids came running down the street after a boy riding a bicycle with tireless wheels that were no longer circular so that he bumped and wiggled along barely able to keep his balance. They paid no attention to us as they clattered by.

Then I found the entrance and rang the bell which had once been electric but didn't work. I banged the door with my fist. Dooda sat down on the doorstep, stretching her long legs. She was not used to towns. Old Miss Montstream opened.

There was a slimy, whitish film over her blue eyes as if they were frozen and had just begun to thaw. She did not recognize me.

"Miss Montstream," I said, "Al, Alfons!"

It was as if the message had been spoken into a seashell. Her head turned slightly, quickly, like the head of a lizard on the folds of her old neck. She understood.

"Mister Al," she said, "Mr. Anton, my!"

And we walked in.

It was as it had always been: dark and cool, with all the shutters closed and venetian blinds let down parted just enough to simulate dawn and dusk at high noon, while at night she used candles, living in a forest of stumps and wax mounds. She became indistinct in an ancient armchair.

"You want a suit, Mr. Al!" she said and I realized how much older she was now. I had not seen her in years, and if I had she would then have accompanied her words with a cackle or a wheeze. Now she spoke flatly with the last breath of available air. The pressure inside Miss Montstream was dropping. It was now barely enough to

153

round her out, giving her living bulk. But soon, I could see, she would exhale one time too often. She would exhale and collapse. How could she have lived this long!

Dooda stayed by the door, crossing her arms.

"Are you alright?" I asked her solicitously. She did not answer, but got up and used her hands like a wedge to pry the tightly hung suits apart. She pulled one out and brought it over. I could not make out its true color or pattern. But I fingered it politely and voiced approval of its quality.

"You're taller now," she mumbled, "you get younger?"

"181 centimeters," I said.

"This is a forty-two," she said. "Are you 6'1? I never got used to the decipers."

She meant the decimal system.

"Take off those pants!" she ordered. "You still bare? Last time you were here . . ."

She was caught in time, in principle like all of us, but in her own particular detail, peculiarly, a dried, flattening old woman of Port Creole, California, in a room full of suits with one of them in her hands, stuck in the resin of nostalgia.

"Tell your girl to sit down," she said.

Theophilia's eyes had got accustomed to the scarce light and she found a chair.

"Missy Montstream," I said, "I want an outfit!"

"You haven't changed," she said. "These men are dead!" She shuffled the suit back to its rack. "But their time will come, they'll be worn again!"

"I want something bright!" I said.

"Ah you! I got nothing bright!"

She stood by the rack, her long old monkey arms reaching up and holding on to all the empty shoulders. Some time went by. Then she turned.

"Come!" she said, beckoning to Dooda with two fingers. They walked through a door and I followed them. There was no way Missy Montstream could disappoint me.

In this room she began to light candles until a fine, soft light warmly filled it. Dooda stood awkwardly by the rack in her fraying shortpants. She gingerly detached a dress from its sisters and held it up. Miss Montstream pushed past her.

"Here," she said, sliding her hand expertly into the lot. It was something shiny, something light and almost transparent, as if spun by spiders and peacocks. Dooda gave out a sound, a low, startled moan as the fabric touched her skin. It was an assault of beauty that took her by surprise.

"Come on, put it on," said the old woman. "Don't be bashful!"

Dooda slipped off her shirt and in one motion slid the dress over her head. Her breasts dipped once, once again, and under the dress she divested herself of her old, battletorn pants.

"How are you gonna get up the tree in that?" I teased.

"I won't," she said. "I'll take it off and sling it round my neck!"

"Sold," I said to old Miss Montstream.

She came over to me and thrust her face up at me. The film was still there, shining in the candlelight. Her eyes were expressionless. She no longer played the game of love, having become invincible.

"All right, my boy," she said in her deadflat poker voice, "you want an outfit, I give you an outfit!"

There was another rack in this room. It was smaller and the clothes hung loosely on it, with spaces between hangers.

"Bottom up or top down?" she croaked.

"Hell," I said, "top down!"

"Okay," she mumbled, "he wants top down!"

She closed her hands in the ancient prayerful gesture of all the displaced misunderstood mistreated persons that have ever come to America from other parts of the globe to fight their way to the top. It was a gesture both of submission and proud mastery. Then her right flicked out like the head of a striking rattlesnake, flicked out and returned having pierced the sound barrier in that short flight. An almost audible boom still reverberated through the room, stopping even Theophilia's adoring fingers in their caressing slide over the delicate fabric of her dress.

Miss Montstream swung around and thrust the windbreaker at me. It was eggshell white, a forty-two. Its weight was perfect, that of a light cape made of wool, cotton and a dash of acrylic. It was cut modestly in the shoulders, straight to the waist where the seams were re-inforced. It had a heavy, golden Fun-Matic zipper, and it was made by Top-Money, the Palm Beach sportswear manufacturer now long gone and defunct, their looms rusting in carcass halls whose padlocked doors hung vandal-broken in their hinges. I put it on. It was a dream.

"Sold, Missy! Done it again," I beamed.

She came up with a shirt of silken beige. She brought out sturdy, timeless slacks from Desert Brothers, Inc., so loose and bulky at the knee, fold over foot, Pro-Swing by name, also long, long gone, blown down the corridors of fashion. She gave me jockey shorts, two pairs, but I re-fused the socks.

I changed right there, while they discreetly left the room and when I presented myself to them I realized that only the knife was awkward, didn't fit. I took it off and handed it to Dooda.

"You carry it!"

Miss Montstream came up with a perfect belt for her and then the bargaining began.

"What you have given us is worth its weight in gold," I opened. "Just that we got no gold!"

"I hear," she countered cagily, "where our beloved President will pioneer again by putting the dollar on the oxygen base, but now that the Saviour walks the earth as in my day, what will that help?"

I thought I saw the opening.

"We may be wasting time," I hinted.

"Don't gimme that crap, Mister Al!"

She came closer again. The film had melted now, her eyes were clear.

"You gimme pleasure, my boy," she wheezed.

I smiled down on her.

"You've been waitin' a long time," she said, "when are you going to come through for the old broad?"

I smiled some more. It was no use fighting her. All withered before her boundless love and her insidious breath.

She reached out and pulled open a drawer. Again

one hawk's hand dived in and emerged with a pair of sunglasses. They looked like welder's goggles. The glass was thick and on each side they had leather blinders.

"These is the best there is, my boy!"

I took them from her, the bargaining was over, she had again humiliated me. Missy Montstream accompanied us to the door. She stood well back in the room as we walked out. The film was descending over her eyes. But she made one last sound of farewell, a plaintive growl, half moan, like a man trying to imitate a seal. It rose, maybe involuntarily, from her innermost self. I turned back and kissed her on one cheek, which was old, soft and damp.

The moment the door closed behind us we were enveloped in a gust and whirl of feathers, as if somewhere a pillow had been ripped open in a passing car. I still held the sunglasses in my hand. It was a passing car, yes, and it had caught and run down a wood dove. The bird lay still in the middle of the road as the feathers settled. I put on my new glasses. They bathed the world in soft honey gold, including the pathetic heap of feathers in the street, and Dooda running for it.

"It's dead," she called.

"Shuddup!" I yelled back.

I took off the glasses and examined them as she brought back the dove. They were made in Germany, by Zeiss-Ikon, trademarked Everest. Maybe the ill-fated German Everest expedition of 1987 was equipped with glasses such as these. Seventeen men buried in an icefall. Seventeen men and seventeen pairs of glasses protecting against the cold, deadly glare. They probably suffocated as well as being crushed, and the dove's neck was broken. Above its throat delicate feathers still shone and shimmered in green and ruby irridescence. The immaculate neck was flecked with bright blood of pure innocence. The damned stiffness of deserted flesh had not yet occurred. The bird fitted limply into the curve of my palm. Its eyes were closed. Similar to the eyes of old Miss Montstream, a bluish-grey curtain had now been drawn over the cancelled interior show, closed after so short a run!

The sunglasses she had given me as a parting gift

did their work well. If this was the dead dove of peace in my hand, its passing was made bearable by the soft warmth of golden light in which Zeiss-Ikon dipped the world.

• Thirty-One •

Some fool group of academic intellectuals, writers, artists and armed forces officers have put together an assault platoon and physically attacked the King of Kings. They used mortars, flamethrowers, hand grenades, submachine-guns and the devastating laser cannon, all to no avail. It turned out to be a popular bloodbath. Hundreds of the thousands who ring Judgment Meadow in prayerful meditation are dead, hundreds more seriously injured. The Christ Himself stands serene through the assault, never moving, never speaking.

The consequences of such insane action are incalculable! President Chin has sternly dissociated himself from these men and embarked on a fast which he says will last until America is cleansed by the act of divine judgment itself. As on every day, The Christ has returned to his starship.

Observers claim that the laser beam passed not through the luminous Emissary of God, but around Him, and from this it is concluded that the entire figure of the new Jesus is surrounded by a force-field, a magnetic shield of some kind. Naturally! *I* could have told them that. So could Freddy, or Bill. President Chin has ordered all troops at the borders to cease operations. Presumably Mexicans and Canadians are now streaming into this country. Now at last we'll see how this affects us.

At the Creole County–Cool County line young militants are attempting to seal off Creole County. Armed patrols of creole guerillas seized and held the northern lanes of the Golden Gate Bridge and were dislodged in a five-hour gun battle with police, sheriffs and state troopers who had been flown in by helicopter. The county is in turmoil, as is the State of California, the nation, the world.

In view of the attack against the Christ, Judgment Day is now presumed imminent. The men responsible for this action have fled and significant portions of the population consider them heroes in hiding. Maybe they will become the rallying point for resistance to the Divine Messengers open court and judgment. Nevertheless, my trial continues, Judge Krishna Bavan Krotentoter seeming not in the least disturbed by these developments.

The thin headband is firmly placed about my head, and another strip around the chest to pass over my heart. In this way I will have to tell the truth. Ferguson's silly questions are posed triumphantly. He is sure of himself. Now that Krotentoter has approved use of the Veritas device, just recently perfected and still contested in other states of the nation, they will learn at last whether or not I killed the three holy men atop the hill.

For three days Bill Blut fought valiantly against Ferguson's request to use Veritas. Krotentoter during this time has seemed extraordinarily obliging. He has discoursed on points of law, has engaged in persuasive argument both with Bill and myself, and at one point retired to his private chambers to ponder a question and consult books of law.

The most significant objection to employment of this device is that there is a 0.05 percent margin of error. It is to this slim percentage that we have clung like sailors in a hurricane. I have pointed out that this possibility of error may assert itself precisely at the crucial moment and that the danger is that I will be convicted just on five percent of a percent. Finally Judge Krotentoter went along with Ferguson, and the stork gestured to a door which opened to let the Veritas device be wheeled in.

It is still rather large, the size of an average computer, but its function differs greatly from that of computer technology. To put it simply: its inventors claim that they have created a machine capable of contact with what we have called the conscience. They explain in their propaganda brochure that the ambiguous and emotional term "conscience" is simply the traditional way of naming

159

what amounts to *two* forces whose traditional labels in turn are "courage" and "cowardice." "Courage," they explain, is that which makes a human being go to the limits of his or her intelligence there to admit ignorance or defeat. "Cowardice," on the other hand, is that which insists that individual ignorance is perfection. Other contemporary terms for "courage" are "humility," "modesty," "tact." Terms for "cowardice" are "certainty," "expertise," "sophistication." The interplay between these two tendencies creates what is known as a "good" or a "bad" "conscience." These fluctuations in the Veritas device are not merely noted but intensified and fed back into the brain and heart of the subject for corrective action. A Veritas interrogation is an agonizing process of self-evaluation, so exhausting that subjects have died. Bill and I agreed not to object to its use on such grounds. We feel that it would prejudice the judge in his interpretation of my testimony.

The first questions are designed to relax me, to make me feel at ease with the device. I answer them in this spirit, lightly.

"My name is Alfons Anton."

"I am thirty-nine years of age."

"I am single."

"I have a daughter."

"I did not kill Primitivo Populi."

"I did not kill Bianca Populi."

"Yes, I killed Titiane Mbuto. It was an accident. There are no accidents."

They pause for a moment while Bill Blut, Ferguson and Judge Krotentoter whisper out of earshot. Then Ferguson asks me if what I am saying is that since there are no accidents I did not kill Titiane Mbuto accidentally.

"If you know that there are no accidents, then her death was no accident. If you don't know that, then it was."

That's my answer. I'm fully conscious. I can see, hear, smell. I can feel and touch. They've given me extra oxygen, top purity government stuff to keep me alert. It's nice to be able to see things so clearly. For the time being there is a feeling of exhilaration. I smile at Bill, and even at the bandaged Ferguson. I smile at the world. And I keep my palms lightly on the fine, firm cloth of these excellent golfing trousers. I follow Pearl's advice not to fight it, kid!

"I did not kill Primitivo Populi. I do not know who killed Primitivo Populi."

What a marvelous thing the conscience is when its molecular structure is amplified to re-enforce what we call truth. With ninety-nine point nine percent certainty Emma Holzfäller killed Pops. More than likely she was assisted by the Mexican laborers. Her motive? Jealousy! The demented jealousy of a post-menopausal cook. Maybe Pops tried to rape her. He took his daughter's return much too matter-of-factly. While she gushed forth of distant, space-shrouded Azydia, he sat smiling blissfully, the proud father proud of his daughter. But his heart wasn't in it. Emma had nothing to be jealous of, that was the irony of it! The inevitable parting of father and daughter had already taken place. Pops was now truly an old man. What he really wanted was to be alone. To drink his wine, to make peace with his vicious fantasies, to nurture in his heart the wounds inflicted by his daughter. How else could they all have escaped the blaze, except Pops in his bed? Maybe the Veritas device is not such a bad thing after all, since it will not base the truth on circumstantial evidence, such as the thick leather thongs from Emma's sandals with which Pops wrists and ankles were bound to his bed. What good would it have done if I had passed these on to Tim Mahoney instead of throwing them away? Emma was tired of America, tired of poisoned fish. She wanted to go home. So I let her. Carlos and Julio, their friends, their families. When Pops died, when the spread burned down, it was all over. What would have been the use?

"Who killed Pierre Brasseur?" Ferguson wants to know.

"I do not know," I say, even though, here again, I'm almost perfectly sure that Pierre killed himself. It was suicide. Every bone in his body was broken. He fell off the cliffside behind the Taco Top where I took Bianca after Titiane broke up with me. He must have followed us. How could a man as surefooted as the incomparable champ have lost his footing? It was either suicide or fate. It was either Pierre's will or decree from the Father in that distant galaxy which had now dispatched the Son to judge the world.

"I know nothing," I say between questions. The Veritas device reacts strongly to this statement. It is fed back into my brain and my heart again and again, amplified each time.

"Nothing," I groan.

"Nothing," I shout.

I scream the word. I wail: nothing, nothing! I know nothing.

"We don't want to know *everything!*"

Ferguson is trying to use his voice like oil on the seething ocean of my torment. It doesn't work.

"Don't you see," I bellow, "knowledge is a tooth, an iceberg, a dove with a broken neck. It has roots. Holy cow!"

Ferguson: "Holy cow?"

"Yes, the holy cow, the divine udder!"

Ferguson: "What is this 'holy cow'?"

Blut: "Objection, Your Honor! This is patently absurd and irrelevant. I object to this line of questioning on the grounds that it constitutes a grave and dangerous misuse of the Veritas method and equipment!"

Krotentoter: "Overruled, Mr. Blut!"

Ferguson: "What is the 'holy cow'?"

I feel a little calmer now. Just when it seemed that my senses would take leave of me, that my mind might absent itself as it had that night when Bianca came back, once again I see the world as it is. A picture that can be understood.

"This sphere, this planet," I tell them, "we are the divine udder on the cosmic cow. There are five billion titties on this udder, give or take a few. Every day thousands dry up, shrivel, shrink back. Every day thousands grow and the udder fills them up with the holy juice to make new titties."

"Fills them up with *what*, Mr. Anton?"

"Divine milk of love. Cosmic juice!"

Bill Blut objects again. What can be seen of his face is red, whether with anger or embarrassment would be hard to tell. He contends that I have clearly been mentally disturbed by the ordeal of the Veritas procedure and that to continue in this fashion will present a real and present threat to my health and life and may in the extreme constitute cruel and unusual punishment, a priori.

Judge Krotentoter sustains him. Ferguson at last is shocked into popping the big question.

"Mr. Anton, who killed the three Sadoos whose bodies were found hanging from trees on the slopes of the hill where you live?"

"Three stopped-up titties," I reply. "I opened them up, drained them dry. But the udder is still full. Push one titty in, another pops out somewhere else. Hydraulic principle. More pop than shrivel, though! Used to be just little goosebumps on the udder, plants and animals. Then one day: kerplop, the first titty."

"You mean teats, don't you?"

"Teats, titties, teaties, all the same. Milk the cow when the moon I mean the udder is full! Try it yourself! See, feel! Taste the juice, the cosmic milk, so warm and sweet. Forgive me, forgive me for I have milked . . ."

No more questions now. The last thing I see in this segment of time is a shadow. The shadow of a full-face oxygen mask with humidifier attachment. They are placing a cloud over my face. The cloud is thin. First my nose pushes through, then all of my face. Its vast, smiling surface turns to the honey-gold Zeiss-Ikon sun above the cloud. I float before the throne of the natural God, bathed in the forgiveness of His light. I smile and smile. I start singing as tears of joy stream down my face. I smile and smile, smiling. I am face only. From my eyes shoot rays of freedom energy that meet the sun's rays. I am blinded.

When I come to, I'm on the floor in front of Judge Krotentoter's bench. There are some boots around me, some pants. I sit up and brush off my Top-Money windbreaker, my Desert Bros. slacks. I am helped to my feet. They lead me to my seat. The courtroom is almost deserted. Detonations pulse in the distance. Long after Judge Krotentoter has adjourned his court, I sit with Bill and Pearl, recovering my breath.

"How'd I do?" I manage finally to ask.

"You spilled the beans," says Pearl.

"You told them all you know," says Bill.

"Yeah," I beam at them, "it's a great day, ain't it."

•Thirty-Two•

The 51st President of the United States of America, Immanuel Chin, has a vision. This occurs a week after the Christ is attacked at Judgment Meadow, late on the seventh day of the President's fast.

He sees himself clearly in his placement within time and circumstance. The rush of time particles slows to a trickle, the waterfall of passing winks and moments dries. What remains of time is flattened and thinned so that seconds become minutes. It is only moments to midnight, but in Immanuel Chin's life much will occur before the new day.

President Chin has had his fortified main conference room cleared of all furniture except a chaise longue, a small writing desk once owned by Abraham Lincoln, and a plain chair with straight back. Never before in his life has he fasted. Now, in this short and turbulent week, he is catching up. He is calm, but full of energy. His mind is keener than ever.

For seven days he has maintained silence as well. He is prepared to fast to death. He has been reclining on the chaise longue and now rises, approaches the desk, sits down, arranges paper and pen, pauses in deep meditation, then begins to write. This is what he writes.

'I am Immanuel Chin, an American. My country had elected me President and that is the position I now occupy. I have been fasting for seven days. I feel that I am ready to be judged. Every moment that now passes is for me a gift, a precious grant of time.

I see my life, not only behind me, but around me. I see that my life is linked to all other lives,

164

in the past, the present and the future, which are inseparable one from the other. My life is human. I am human. The principle of my life is the principle of all human lives. Therefore I write these words humbly.

The Mystery of the Coming of the Christ is no longer impenetrable to me. Humanity has been judged by the fact of His Coming alone. The Saviour is a great Consul from the Divine Domain. We here on earth have lived in a remote province, and the Master has come to accord us citizen status in the Great Empire of the Lord.

It does not matter whether we find ourselves guilty, or innocent, or whether we let Him decide. The Judgment is His Coming, and His Presence is the Great Gift of His Father, Our Lord!

I am responsible for the death of many thousands of human beings. But I see that I was meant to be responsible for it. Each one of them individually, and all of them together died for me. They are martyrs. They laid down their lives for me. They cut short their precious time which I wasted. And yet I see that I owe them nothing. That I understand this is repayment of this great debt. And that this is possible is Divine. That I am granted time to express this in words is proof of the Great Lord's infinite Wisdom.

I see that my affairs are placed in order. Many times in my career I have faltered and feared. Many times I have been powerless. Now I see that all power has been taken from me so that I may see. The Saviour has shouldered it. It is He who now carries the responsibility for our great nation.

In these past trying weeks many have cried out for vision, that their eyes might penetrate the future. To them I say: the future is as the past, which is as the present. As it was, so it is and will be. To those who cower in fear and ask: what will the Judgment be?, I say: the Judgment has taken place. We have been found

worthy by our distant Father of the Presence of
His Son. We have been blessed!'

Immanuel Chin rises from his chair and walks to one
of the windows. He touches a hidden release and the
heavy steel shutters slide away. The President now opens
the window to the faintly illuminated night sky. To the
left can be seen the reflective glare of the torches at
Judgment Meadow where the masses await the Saviour's
return. The Christ's presence has purified the air. Stars
twinkle peacefully. President Chin takes a deep breath.

For a long moment he stands, his face turned upward. Then, the window still open, he walks back to the
desk. He stands by it, looking down on the paper, holding
the pen lightly.

There is nothing to add but his signature. So he sits
down, angles the pen, and again is lost in thought. How
many documents have I signed? How many sentences?
How many reports by how many Special Commissions?
How many declarations? He begins to write his name.

Immanuel Chin,

He has placed the comma precisely. It has given
him great pleasure to do this. He has placed this comma
proudly. It means that he is not alone, that his name has
a foundation. And so he continues to write:

President of the United States

He pauses again. Yes, tomorrow he will walk out to
the meadow and take his place among the others. No
more fortified limousines for him, no more anti-gravity
traps, no more security cordons. He is a free man once
again, the White House no longer his prison. He does not
see the shadows behind him, but he knows they are there.
He is praying for time now. He sees himself as an arro-
gant man who has wasted his life, who has been granted
absolution and who is still not satisfied. He wants to finish
writing, and so he prays silently for time to finish. His
hand is uncertain and slow, but the pen obeys. He writes:

of Ame

and as his pen's tip curves into the "r" of "America"
they move swiftly into position behind him. There are at
least two men, perhaps three. Though Immanuel Chin's
remaining-time is scarce, still the "r" emerges. Then his
writing hand flies away and the pen, as it falls and slips

off the desk, mutilates the letter. The "r" becomes "n".
And below the "n" only splashes and drops of ink mingling
with blood that spurts from the President's throat as his
head is almost servered by the sharp wire. They work like
cheese-cutters, and the 51st President of the United States
is the cheese.

Yet, as Mr. Chin's eyes bulge, they receive one last
impression of his own signature:

Immanuel Chin, President of the United States of
Amen.

This final Amen explodes in his brain, gushes up and
dissolves in the bloody spray from the fountain of his life.
His mouth gapes and gasps Amen, Amen, Amen! Amen
is the last code in this computer. In the vast halls of Immanuel Chin's dying head a million silver hammers tap
out this last message on reams of coiled, metallic tape:
Amen.

They let him slip to the floor. They step back. One
of them still holds the bloody wire, gingerly, between
thumbs from index fingers of gloved hands. They withdraw
quietly from the historic scene, so that the last President
of the United States of America may be found as he fell.
So that the fateful tableau will stay in order. So that the
scene will be preserved forever in every detail as it has
indelibly been drawn into the living mists of human history.

Though the masses wait at noon the following day,
the luminous figure of the visitor from space does not
return. The starship that has shamed the sun vanishes.
Judgment Meadow lies empty. And everywhere on earth,
in key spots of the 350 nations, the noxious fumes close
in again and smother the pockets of pure air.

I look down from the court floor during noon recess.
The Sadoos and the Crusaders are amassed as usual. But
now there are thousands of others, young and old, in public worship. The giant TV screen flickers but no picture
is sent. Maybe faulty transmission, maybe sabotage.
Technicians frantically check their equipment. Still
nothing. Then, suddenly, a clear picture of Judgment
Meadow. There, too, the enormous, silent crowd still
patient in prayer.

The seconds tick away, the minutes pass. The

clock triumphs and it's time to get back into court. Judge Krotentoter rises solemnly, but there is a newness about him, a warlike confidence. He knows the Visitor has not returned.

• Thirty-Three •

I'm sentenced to death by Sounding on what a hundred years ago would have been a fine day in May.

I still remember the period known as The Weatherbreak, maybe ten years ago. This was just after the Class Riots, and the time of Quick Succession in which no less than nine Presidents followed one another in a period of little more than a year. There may even have been a single day in which the weather changed from "critical" to disastrous. That was the Weatherbreak, and oxygen became the world's most precious product.

Maybe these weeks will be dubbed similarly but in regard to politics rather than the weather. There is a national slump which has nothing to do with my sentence. Nathan Canaan, the Vice President, has disappeared. The Speaker of the House, Carlos Montanaya, is in the hospital, in critical condition. And so America has an Acting President whose dwindling life force is maintained in a heart-lung machine.

I, too, am at the mercy of certain machines. My appeal is automatically processed. It takes only about twenty-four hours for the tapes to run through the appeal computers all the way up to the Supreme Court where the decision is automatically made whether or not my case will be heard. The word that comes back is that my case will not be heard. We can trust the computers. The sentence stands as pronounced by Judge Krishna Bavan Krotentoter.

Bill Blut makes the last move open to us, an appeal for Presidential Clemency. There are more than seven thousand such appeals now pending before the presidency, and Immanuel Chin is dead. No one can say who will be head of state. Therefore I am handcuffed and transported to Mulatto Point Penitentiary, after a tentative date for my execution has been set a month hence, late in June. It seems that the still prevailing law is determined to stop me before the end of this millenium!

We drive away from the Civic Center. Tim Mahoney has managed to be placed in charge of this detail. He sits next to me in the rear of the armor-plated mobile. There is a creole driver, and next to him a slim, dangerous looking cowboy type with long, blond hair who wears the wine-red uniform of Mulatto Point. These state employees still care for outward appearance!

My sentence has been quietly received by the populace. The Sadoos who might have been expected to rejoice in it, have barely reacted. In fact, they are breaking camp. The TV screen has been dismantled, and state militia is digging in around the Civic Center. The Creole Independence Party has petitioned the Supreme Court for issuance of a Federal Restraining Order and the computers have favorably processed this request. But until the Supreme Court convenes on the issue, the fighting goes on. Bill estimates that there are dozens of similar petitions before the court at this time, and that the court cannot reconvene until an authoritative new president confirms it. According to confusing dispatches from the nation's capital, Washington, D.C. has turned into an armed camp.

"Well," I tell Tim, "I may be safest at Mulatto Point!"

"For sure, Al. At least for now."

The wine-red man from Mulatto Point turns his head and grins viciously.

We drift along the still usable bands of 101, through the Mulatto Point cloverleaf, and out toward the bay, past the former site of Fort San Quentin on the narrow finger of land that juts into Creole County from Marin County. The terrain raises; we have a view of the doom-shrouded bay stirred by no wind. We drive through a pass cut into the prevalent basalt rock and come down on the great Mulatto Point expanse, two thousand acres of what may still be the most progressive execution center in the world!

They are very polite with me, very accommodating!

169

I ask for something to eat, they bring me a delicious tomato-and-lettuce sandwich. I want to drink, they procure milk. Now they obligingly switch on the radio and search the airs until I'm satisfied. Times have not changed for condemned men. When a man has been sentenced to death, the public imagination is destroyed. They cannot imagine that I will not be executed. I am that timeless marvel: the walking dead, more precious than any other known species of man! By law and avocation every man in charge of me would feel obliged to lay down his life for my right to die as has been decreed.

It's been some time since I've listened to popular music. In fact, I can't imagine that there still is popular music. The young driver nods his head to the rhythm, moves his lips to shape the words. I can see that he would like to sing along with the tune. But it all sounds false and thin to me.

"How old are you?" I ask him.

"Old enough to know better," says the man from Mulatto Point.

"Twenty-two, sir," says the driver.

He was born when Bianca left.

"Do you know 'Ochre Yellow Blues'?"

He shakes his head, still nodding and silently singing along with the terrible tune.

"K.G.Moon?"

"No, sir."

It's no use. They probably want to forget everything that was done before the Class Riots. Bianca and I came down this road in the old Chevy just after the pass to the bay had been cut, and I was trying to make up a tune called "Spoonin' the Moon." Bianca liked to ride close to me like a young girl, her legs drawn up, her chin on my shoulder. She was like a beautiful dog, maybe an Afghan. Mulatto Point was just a construction area then. The ground had been broken open, landscaping was in progress, bluish light illuminated everything at night. Mulatto Point was generally considered a good sign. Maybe things were getting better after all, people were thinking then. The kids drove out to marvel at it. It became a favorite target for night rides as the enormous complex slowly took shape. Even when there was no moon there was artificial moonlight at Mulatto Point.

"You like music, sir?" asks the driver.

"Yes, certainly. Sure. I like music. You don't know 'Ochre Yellow,' do you?"

"No, sir. D'you know *this* tune?"

I tried to make it out, but couldn't. It had surf sounds on it, and detonations, and the background was like jam made of electronic organ-music.

"No," I say, "what is it?"

"Don't you recognize it?"

I look at Tim, who shrugs his shoulders. I listen some. No results. I want to tell him again that I can't make it out, but just then there is something new, some connection, a pattern of sound. It can't be! I can't believe it.

The driver lifts his chin to watch me in the rearview mirror. Concentrating, I look out the window. In a turn of the road I see Mount Tamalpais and then, for a fleeting moment, I catch a glimpse of my hill and a sigh escapes me. It's, it's . . .

"It can't be!"

"Yes, sir," he grins broadly.

"Bon, bon, bon—ah, si bon!" he hums.

It's the Somali tune, the first song of Creole County, the time-honored melody. They are mangling it. They have cut it up and poured syrup over it, squeezed it and now they are using it like a washing machine used to be used.

"Would you turn it down, kid," I suggest and the uniformed Mulatto Pointer obliges immediately. We come to a stop. Two men in wine-red coveralls attach gravity blocks on either side of the mobile and we move slowly across the moat. On the other side the gravity blocks are taken off, and we glide down a wide, well-tended mall lined with poplars.

Mulatto Point is a marvel of landscape architecture. The idea was to outdo even the futuristic design of the impressive Creole County Civic Center. Parklands surround the area. They are placed just inside the moat that encircles the entire kidney-shaped area. There are bungalow-type buildings, three golf courses, an amusement center, a supermarket and a complex of service buildings. And at the very center the circular Sound Institute, a euphemism for the Sound Chamber itself, the central place of execution where all Mulatto Point inmates are destined to end up unless their sentence is commuted in some fashion.

Mulatto Point is a maximum security institution, and only two men have ever escaped from here. That was back in the days before the anti-gravity trap, when the anti-gravity principle had not yet been perfected and the moat was filled with a special acid solution. Today the moat is empty. It has been rigged as a gravity-free zone and there is no way to cross it for a prisoner. Many have tried. The most ingenious devices have been constructed. Spray-cans and plastic bags full of air have been used in attempts to maneuver in the no-gravity zone. There is no way to do it, and the central anti-gravity device from which the Mulatto Point Penitentiary receives its impulses is located in Sacramento. Only a conspiracy at the highest level of state government could open the moat. Nevertheless, this is straw to which some of the men here are said still to be clinging. And maybe, in view of recent developments, the straw has become a piece of wood. Maybe even a beam. The nation is in chaos, and California is no exception, despite the calm routine that seems to prevail here on the afternoon of my arrival.

Tim gets out first, then I. We shake hands.

"This is a good place under the circumstances," he assures me.

"Take it easy, Tim!"

He gets in where the long-haired cowboy type got out and the creole driver gives me a casual salute as he turns the mobile.

"This way," says the cowboy.

"Yes, sir."

As we walk over to a pink and white complex of shops, he explains the pecking order to me.

"There's only two kinds of men out here, Anton, Mulattos and Pointers. You're a Mulatto and I'm a Pointer, get it?"

"Yes, sir."

"The basic difference is that you Mulattos end up dead, while we Pointers stay alive."

"Yes, I understand."

"Some men think that the color of their skin en-

172

titles them to privileges. They are wrong. No matter what you look like or where you come from, in here you're a Mulatto. Sure you understand?"

"Yes, I do."

"Now we sound on the average about a dozen men here every day, and the average population is around a thousand, so there's a pretty good turnover. Don't worry about it. Our bookkeeping gets a little sloppy, but the record is okay. We've never sounded anybody early."

We've come to a row of shops, places called "Top Drawer," "Le Buffet," "The Icy Pole Ice Cream Parlor," and the "Fresh as a Flower in June One Hour Martinizing" establishment. I can see that meticulous care is taken to make it easy on the condemned men. What am I saying: *the* condemned men! Care is taken to make it easy on *us!* We'll be able to walk the last mile in style.

The Pointer smiles and shakes his locks.

"Can I keep my outfit?" I ask.

"Sure," he says, looking me up and down. He shakes his head again.

"You got it all figured out, mudra, haven't you?"

I smile right back at him. Just a moment ago I've finally understood that I'm as good as dead unless a miracle occurs.

"Whatever you do, kid," Pops told me on a number of occasions, "don't live on the bay flats. No protection down there. After a while the wind gets to you. More people I know drove themselves crazy that way. Stay up in the hills, stick with the hills!"

Now they got me dragged down here on the flats and there's a big no-gravity moat to make sure I can't get out. I can see Mount Tam from where we're standing, but not the hill, not quite.

"You lookin' right up and snazzy and I expect you'll be showing the folks how to whistle off some golf, ain't that right?"

"Why, yes, that's not a bad idea."

I touch my Zeiss-Ikon sunglasses lightly. I smile calmly at the cowboy. I'm beginning to realize that there is an advantage in knowing the approximate date of your death.

• Thirty-Four •

Nobody wants to die. I don't want to die. I'm not going to die. I'm supposed to be waiting up on the hill, but what's the difference? If those damn Azydians know anything, they know I'm here and need their help. Desperately.

Immediately they showed me my bachelor apartment, featuring a studio-with-bedroom, a bar-type kitchenette with two tall barstools, and a narrow, tiled bathroom in midnight blue. I pass out on a foldout bed. It's a long, deep sleep in which I resemble a deep sea ray stirring up the muddy bottom of my subconscious that hasn't been cleaned out in ages. So I sleep in the murky waters of my own fear. But it can't be fear of death, because I'm not going to die. Christ may have quit, but Azydia won't!

A telephone rings at the bottom of zero-visibility, rings again, and again, until I reach for the surface and catch it. It's somebody I don't know.

"Almost noon, Anton. Time to get up. We wanna show you the place."

"I'm at Mulatto Point, right?"

"You got it."

"You're a Pointer, right?"

"Right again."

"I'll be up in a minute. Give me five, okay?"

He clicks off and I sit up. The place looks like a standard motel. There's a television set. The venetian blinds are down, but what passes for light oozes in on the sides. I reach for my Zeiss-Ikons and put them on. The environment softens tolerably.

I waddle over to the blinds and peek out. An open mall, three bungalows with mine completing a suburban

174

circle. Looks as if there are two or three units in each bungalow, which makes it eight to twelve places like my own. Neat! I let the blinds go.

Right above the bed is what looks like an oxygen grate and below it, within reach, a knob with calibrations to regulate the flow. I try it and it works. Oxygen is tasteless and odorless, but after a while you develop an extra sense for it. This stuff is higrade, government purity. Great!

I sit down again on the Mulatto Point bed which is large and firm. I must have been exhausted to sleep this long. I pull on my light brown Desert Brothers slacks, my shirt which could stand a little fresh as a flower in just one hour martinizing. I stand barefoot, in a momentary relapse of drowsiness, when the door opens and a Pointer, smartly uniformed, pokes in his head.

"Ready, Anton?"

"In a jiffy, sir!"

I pull on my basketball boots, grab the Palm Beach windbreaker and we're off in a standard electric golfcart at least twenty years old, a vintage buggy. The young man who pilots it is dressed in wine-red, like the cowboy, but his hair is darker and shorter. He chews gum. And he squints as if we were going fast.

"We're a little late, Anton, so I'll leave out some of the sights. Here's a map."

He hands me a brochure whose cover and back, when folded out, make a map of the entire Mulatto Point facility.

"Boy," I marvel, "this is nothing like Creole County Jail!"

"No comparison," agrees the young man.

He makes a sharp right hand turn and drives across a closely cropped lawn which must be part of one of the golf courses.

"We're taking a shortcut," he explains. "This is Number One golf course, 18 holes. We'll catch up with them at the Academy of Music!"

There is something strange in the way he says "Academy of Music." Just a slight hesitation before he said it. And then a flickering of the eyelid on my side after he says it. Nor can it be that they have an academy of music here. It's a euphemism. Academy of Music is a euphemism for Sound Institute which is a euphemism for death. Maybe there are more euphemisms here. What about "golf course?" What does golf course stand for?

"Okay," I smile, "what does golf course stand for?"

"Most mules don't like to play golf this time of day!" he grins.

"You mean this is actually a golf course, for playing golf?"

"Read the book," he tells me. "It's all in the book."

We pass an idyllic looking scene, a small, man-made lake surrounded by rhododendron bushes, a slope of first class lawn, and a green which is marked Number 7 in yellow and black. A triangular plastic flag on a long pole is stuck in the Number 7 hole. I see the ball coming before he does. I see it just after it has passed its apex, curving down on us. It makes the green and rolls to a position some twenty feet from the hole, but the terrain does not permit me to see the player. We pass it and leave it behind, and a minute later we're off the course, on a graveled thoroughfare which winds its way toward what is euphemistically known as the Academy of Music. But on the Number One golf course they seem actually to be playing at the game of golf. Fantastic!

The so-called Academy of Music turns out actually to be the Sounding Center, housing the Sound Chamber. We join a group of maybe twenty newly arrived like myself, most of them in yellow coveralls, but some still wearing ordinary clothes. The young Pointer leaves without a word, and I join my fellow mulattos of whom some are actually dark of skin. We all follow a Pointer, crowd into a creaky elevator and get off after a short ride.

We are led along a number of criss-crossing corridors. I have the feeling that we are in a hospital, because from time to time Pointers pass us, wearing wine-red smocks like doctors and paying no attention to us. We enter a circular room with rows of seats sloping down toward the center at a steep angle. This room holds maybe two- to three-hundred people and is almost filled up, though I cannot imagine that all of these men are newcomers. Many of them do not seem to be interested in their surroundings at all. They lounge in bored attitudes, much as I saw in the county jail. They've been here for some time.

Below us is a circular area with what looks like a dentist's chair in its center. At either end of this elongated chair stand two machines that look like old-fashioned traffic lights, each with three circular windows, except that these windows are at the height of the chair. There is also a wire cage with a medium size dog in it. The dog seems to be sleeping.

We have barely sat down when two men and one woman in wine-red smocks walk out onto the circular stage below and the woman starts talking to the audience.

"Most of you have seen this demonstration before," she says, enunciating each word clearly in a slightly affected, nasal voice. "For those of you who haven't, let me explain. This demonstration is designed to acquaint you with the apparatus which will be used to implement your sentence. More precisely: we are about to show you how you will die. Today, as on most days, we will use a dog for this purpose. Dogs are not especially sensitive to music, but most people like some form of music. The devices you see at the head and footend of this chair are called soundboards. They are in effect no more than highly sophisticated amplifiers. They operate in principle like this!"

She walks to one of the soundboards, the one at the footend, and touches it as if it were a prize in one of the guessing game shows that went out in the Seventies.

"A certain tune is piped into this device from our central tape library which has available recordings of almost all the music ever recorded. And, let me assure you, what we don't have we can get. You will see in a moment why this is important. Now, this soundboard here compresses the music by speeding it up and drawing it out. It works in the way a spinning wheel is used on raw wool. The thread of sound that emerges is then further compressed and refined until it is so thin and so sharp that, with the proper equipment, it could be broadcast *through* the earth, to the opposite side!"

This, no doubt, is a noteworthy technological accomplishment, and she is justly proud of it, but the pause she provides for its appreciation by us is wasted. In fact, across from where I sit, a man who looks like an old-timer and reminds me a little of Pearl stifles a long yawn. And the newcomers are so engrossed in the show that they do not respond at all. So she continues.

"Three of such threads are manufactured in this soundboard and beamed across to the other soundboard. One thread above, one in the middle, one below. They are spaced precisely to your particular requirements, and they are aimed at your brain, your heart, and at your genitals, that is, at your abdomen. They will pass through you at a speed approximating the speed of light. You will feel nothing. We have established proof that death in every sense of that term occurs in less than one-hundredth of a second. In other words, for ninety-nine parts of your last living second you will be alive, and at the beginning of the next second you will be dead. But, just to reassure you, whatever minimal pain may occur even in that tiny fraction of a second will be eased by using a tune that you yourself choose. More precisely: you will be executed by a compressed distillate of your own favorite music. There is no question that this is one of the most humane ways to die in the world today, and the State of California is proud of this accomplishment. Thank you."

I can't believe what I have just heard. The new-comers around me sit stunned. Their eyes are glazed. I'm not going to die like this! This is not merely progressive, it's silly! Who thought of this, who invented this? Music is meant to elevate us, isn't it? Is *this* what it's come to? Apparently the answer to all these questions is: yes, but here we are!

Already the dog is taken out of its cage, strapped in the seat. The seat is adjusted to an almost perpendicular position. The soundboards are wheeled into position and fixed at the proper angles. The animal yawns, just as the man on the bleachers across from me yawned. Its narrow tongue curls, its fangs show. It does not struggle or snap at its executioners. Looks just like a mutt to me, skinny and unaware, and dirty! But that's no reason to kill it. This cannot be permitted. What has this mutt done to the world to deserve sounding? But what can I do! Regardless of what I can do or can't do, I get up, I stand.

178

Heads turn, a sea of faces blurs. I'm looking down on the execution platform, words come out of my mouth. I don't know what I'm saying, I'm stalling for time.

"I have a question," I call out loudly.

The woman in the wine-red smock looks up at me.

"Yes, what is it," she answers, confident of being able to explain, to make me sit down.

"Yes," I say loudly. "My question is, what music are you using to kill this poor mutt?"

There is a gasping moment of utter silence, then insane, howling laughter shakes the amphitheater. The woman is caught off balance. She confers with her assistants. Already she is regaining her composure. As the laughter subsides, she is ready for me. I can see her cold eyes protruding, drilling up to me, sending out threads of hate if anything even thinner than those musical stillettos that are used here.

"We will be using Beethoven's Fifth," she says. "Animals, and especially dogs, are generally unaffected by it, and that's about the best we can hope to achieve under the circumstances."

"It's not fair!"

There is more laughter and applause in my direction. But the newcomers around me are not at all pleased. Some of them gesticulate to make me sit down. I don't want to sit down. I want to keep standing up.

"What is your name?" asks the woman.

"Al Anton, ma'am, much obliged!"

"Anton, sit down!"

There is loud booing mixed with laughter and some sounds of approval in my immediate vicinity. The dog has begun to whine, feeling the excitement. What can I do? I look around and feel helpless.

"If you don't want to watch," she says, "leave!"

So I turn around and leave. I walk up the aisle, out the door, and down the corridors. I find the elevator and the exit and start walking along the gravel path. I find myself on Number One golf course, while the dog must already be dead. The seagulls at least have a chance. Only the dumbest get caught. That goes for fish, too. And for people. I must be one of the dumbest to be here! And where am I, walking along aimlessly. A low hill rises and

I make its crest, looking around. A palm grove blocks my view toward the mountain and the rest of the golf course. To my right, below, is an unmarked green, fronted by a sandtrap cunningly built into another even more obstructive little hill. Certainly that awful mutt is dead by now and everybody that much wiser for it. Why do the old-timers go? To learn, to get used to the idea. Very clever!

It seems to be another near-maximum day and I'm out of breath, so I sit down, surveying the area. In the distance, that which now passes for distance, about half a mile or so, lies the exit road through basalt gap. The peripheral parklands block out the view to the gravity gate, but here and there I can make out the moat. It's Mulatto Point, alright, much as I remember it. Wait a minute! When they built this place the construction road ran right through the middle, not far from here, maybe over there, behind those palms. There were no palms there then, of course. But the golf course was in the making. Bianca and I would park and walk away from the lights, turn, walk around the hill and . . . wait just a *minute!* This is it! It was here that. Yes, below, in the sandtrap.

"Mamma mia," she sighed appreciatively, "bene, bene!" Then her Italian temperament finally erupted.

"O mamma mia!"

She took me defiantly, as if I were a stallion, when I was just a kid ready to be transformed into a stallion. She held her breath and kept me trapped. I could not move. She clenched her teeth and drew back her lips, she did. I fought back. I held her down.

"O mamma mamma mamma mia!"

I could barely bear to look at her as her face broke out of Italy and flooded Europe and went all the way into the Vaucluse, the dry and desperate fist of France. Down there, in the sandtrap. That's where my daughter comes from. She thought she'd be clever. She insisted we call her Vox. But to me she will always be Anne.

I run down the hill, across the green. I stumble down the steep side into the sandtrap. Somebody has idled here. A Mulatto on his lonely walk has stopped and stooped to draw a message. Time has passed. Dew has fallen. Poisonous sunshine has rested on the sand. Fog has filled the trap. But still the message crumbles on to reach me: W - A - I, and a T whose crossbar is only half intact. A T that looks like the gallows, but is still what it was meant to be: the T in the word WAIT.

• Thirty-Five •

"Anton?"

"Yes." I turn. It's the wine-red witch from the demonstration room.

"Go away," I tell her, "you like to kill."

"Why are you afraid? What are you afraid of?"

"Go away," I tell her again. "We have nothing to do with each other."

I start walking away. She keeps up with me.

"Go away," I tell her.

She's Bianca's height. Her eyes aren't bulging now, they aren't sending out death rays.

"You're afraid of me," she says. "Why? No, don't tell me. I'll tell you. You're celibate; you're afraid I will seduce you!"

I can't help laughing at that.

"You enjoyed killing that little mutt!"

"I didn't kill it," she says. "You saved it, it's alive. By the way, it's a female."

"Wouldn't you know!"

She looks up at me from the side as we walk along.

"Why didn't you kill her?"

"I couldn't let you get away with walking out. It wouldn't have been good for the morale of our men."

"Our men?"

"Well . . ."

"Are they *all* yours?"

"Oh, come on. I don't like killing. But if I have to kill a dog to keep a man from going crazy, what choice do I have? I don't like to kill. I don't kill men."

"You sure aren't killing me, lady!"

She laughs unexpectedly, the bitch.

"What are you going to do with her?" she asks.

"With whom?"

"*Whom?*"

"Okay, with who then?"

"With the dog. When you save somebody's life, you're responsible for them, you know."

"That was last century, sweetheart!"

We walk along some more. Suddenly she cuts in in front of me and stops me. She looks right into my eyes with those evil, beady beepers of hers.

"You are coming with me now," she says, "we're going to sit down and have a coffee, or a cocktail, or a glass of champagne, or whatever you like, and we're going to have a long talk!"

"Wrong," I tell her stubbornly.

"Well, a short talk then."

I must admit that she drives one hell of a bargain. I shake my head and raise my left eyebrow as high as I can to give my left eye maximum exposure and if possible to catch what light there remains in this miserable day. I want it to glitter dangerously. This only amuses her.

"I like the way you lose," she says.

"Go home and give that mutt some water and a bowlful of mush!"

She takes my arm and makes me take a narrow footpath just wide enough for two. It leads across the lawn toward a low bungalow-style building whose neon signs are already on, glowing pale before the impending dusk that may be the last on earth. "Point of Order" is the name of the joint. Thank heaven neon never went out of style.

"Are you doing this professionally?" I ask blithely before we enter. She turns her shoulder, holding her hips back and makes a movement that looks like a girl swivelling through a hoop.

"Short talk is free," she croons and in we go.

• Thirty-Six •

The champagne made me strong against my fear of dying. I began to talk wildly to Wilhelmina, the demonstrator.

"I would never make love to a woman who likes to kill," I said.

"You don't have to. I was talking of orgasmic release, which is neither necessarily the cause of nor necessarily an effect of love. You like to relax, don't you?"

"If I get any more relaxed, I'll bubble away."

She was fondling my knee under the table. The table stood in a booth, but at such an angle that occupants of other booths in the joint could, if they wanted to, see what we were doing. It didn't seem to bother her.

"Gee," she said, "it's hard to get a little affection out of you. Your mother must have been a very cold woman!"

"Nobody knows," I said.

She carefully refilled my glass. There was a frosty film on it. It looked cool, endlessly inviting. I drank more champagne.

"I used to know a girl like you. Long time ago. She was very young. We did this once, what we're doing now. She asked me to put my finger in there and get it all wet."

"How interesting! And how did she ask you to do that?"

"By spreading her legs and rubbing up against me, just as you're doing now."

"Well, did you?"

"She had eaten some pills. I could feel that it was just her body. It was a young, juicy body. She had no mind. So I did the good thing. I did it."

"I'm not that young," said Wilhelmina, "I'm not that juicy. But I have something else she didn't have."

"Oh yeah?"

"Yeah," she smiled. "I'm the last!"

She raised her glass coquettishly and wet both lips slowly before tasting the champagne with the tip of her tongue. Then she sipped it, tilting the glass suddenly when she came to the end.

"Merde alors," I couldn't help saying. "Cheval d'amour!"

"What's a cheval d'amour?"

"Oh—nothing. A love horse, you know."

"I'm a love horse."

"Yes you are."

"I'll show you."

"Sure," I said, "you want me to put you out to pasture?"

"Shut your mouth and lend me your hand," she said.

I put my hand there, but I didn't do anything with it. A few couples were dancing. She had told me that the girls were Pointers. I had asked her if there were female prisoners. She had looked at me in honest surprise.

"Where've you been," she had marveled. "We don't execute women in the U.S.!"

Now she gets up and pulls me along. It's not easy to dance to this music. The beat is everywhere at once and there is no melody. The result is jumpy nothing. But Wilhelmina is enjoying herself. We heat up a little, and even though the music is canned she applauds between dances. Then we're cheek to cheek again.

"It's kind of hot in here," she says. "Let's you and me. . . ."

I stubbornly dance on.

"Your place or mine?" she whispers.

I don't pay any attention to her. I'm concentrating on Bianca. She must be over fifty now, oh no! Really. To be fifty on Azydia. Apparently, so she told me, it takes them no time at all to get here. And Anne is a young woman, twenty, no, let me see, twenty-two.

"Did you know that you're very attractive sexually," asked Wilhelmina.

"In the animal sense, sweetheart?"

184

"You get it," she pouts happily. "Let's get out of here!"

But there is still champagne in the bottle, so we return to the table. She has a diploma, she tells me. In Mandalic Psychiatry. She explains to me that Mandalic Psychiatry is the intellectual meeting of East and West, with the East represented by the lotus-heart symbolism of the mandala, and the West by the Freud-Jung-Erhardt-Papst tradition of intellectual enlightenment. She tells me that she can see straight into my little lotus-heart. She tells me it's unfolding at this very moment in the non-material plane where such phenomena take place. I try to be deliberately rude to her.

"If you keep up the honey talk, I'll develop hives, ma'm!"

She thinks this is uproariously funny.

"You're a throwback," she tells me, "a savage. You jumped twenty years of human evolution. There are millions like you, but the astonishing thing in your case is that you are intelligent, witty, perceptive, and very sensitive under that crusty exterior. You like to be thought of as a roughneck. You like to talk rough to conceal your soft core."

"Which reminds me," I'm quick to take advantage, "let go of my hand with your thighs."

It was not a halfbad bottle of champagne, but it's no use holding her off. I'll have to give up or go along. And I don't like to give up to a girl like Wilhelmina. So I go along.

We walk through a park, leaving the shadows of the Academy of Music to the left. These threads of music kill soundlessly, painlessly. There must be some way of beating the moat. Pearl might know. Why don't they organize a relief-party! Wilhelmina is carrying a small cylinder and we take sips along the way. A majestic grove of redwoods receives us. These trees were here long before recorded music. The landscape architects who designed Mulatto Point reverently incorporated them in their layout. Now Wilhelmina carelessly unbuttons her wine-red blouse and reveals pale, combative breasts. But she does not stop. We walk out of the grove, toward a group of buildings very much like the one where I live. Bianca lay in the sand, dissolved, her face wet like a young girl's.

"O, Alfons, what . . . what are you doing to me? You naughty boy you! So sweet forever!"

"They can't do that, can they," I had chanted.

"No, no, o yes they can't!"

I was not jealous. She wanted a baby. I was a young elephant among giant anemones in a subterranean forest. I had fought with Titiane's new lover, too, and he had routed me. But we had not fought to the death. It was a defeat, but I did not become his slave.

Wilhelmina's apartment looks like mine and mine like hers. And she wasted no time with lighting. She stripped off her clothes. I took off mine, more slowly, but I kept on my Zeiss-Ikons.

"Light a candle," I said, "in memory of Missy Montstream!"

She lit a candle.

"I think Missy Montstream is dead," I said.

"Look at *this!*" she commanded.

It was indeed remarkable. Wilhelmina was maybe my age, and she was ripe. What was most substantial of her was just now passing the point of no return. From now on this thing would keep her on earth. It hung heavy like a threat of meat and balloons. I'm drunk and I haven't been drunk in years! She shows me cleaving champagne lips, inner linings of dark flesh and bushy skin. She pulls up her legs, spreads her thighs and embraces her knees. And then she pulls and compresses. She must be enormously strong and if just now, in this position, I were to strike her it would have the impact of a feather. She is so compact and of such solid certainty! Reckless like a baboon, she spits on one thumb and starts provoking her clitoris.

"Come on, Anton," she spittles, "turn me on!"

She takes a hold of me and starts working on me as if a film had been speeded up. Here are all the movements and incantations of love, but greatly accelerated. And barely have I grown respectable under her hands, when she stuffs me in with frantic haste.

"Come on," she whispers, "you can do it. I know you can. Come on, Anton!"

This is an impossible spectacle, Wilhelmina on top of me, pivoting, making me inspect her quivering behind! How can I avoid it! If I close my eyes, I'll be in danger.

"You goddamn celibate," she curses, "you fucking holdout!"

"Wilhelmina!"

"Don't you Wilhelmina me, you mule! Do something, move!"

It is as if I'm the stage, a clearing with a belated dance around the May Pole. What has happened to our traditions! What *is* this! She is *crazy!*

"Can't you act like a normal man, at least!"

She's off and on her back, those massive pillars drawn back, marble-smooth, waiting for a herculean thrust.

"Straight on, Anton, straight on, Anton!"

I tilt myself leisurely to a squatting position.

"Come on, hurry!"

"You're all nerves, sweetheart," I tell her, but she pulls me down and I can't help falling into her. Give up or give in, Alfons Anton. How far this is from loving embrace, how far from Titiane! And if I started giving it to her "straight on," that will drive away the Azydians for sure. How sad this is, how pathetic! My mind is elsewhere though badly needed here. Miss Montstream is dead. I still have her glasses on to diffuse the glacial glare. Seventeen dead Germans with broken bones and frozen eyeballs, perfectly preserved, possess this fiendish woman. But she's got me good. She uses me as a wave uses a rudder. She swells and sinks away and swells again, slapping flesh in between. An astral jockey on a pogo-stick! Now it all goes haywire, but I'm holding on, I'm holding steady. This is where Anton breaks Wilhelmina. And she is through the gate. Her eyelids are fluttering, her neck pulse is beating, and where row upon row of fleshy abdominal musculature marched triumphantly toward victory, there are now pools and pockets of trembling skin, while Alfons Anton, certain and firm, feels her eddying about his determination. In other words: the wine-red bitch has come!

•Thirty-Seven•

I wish I had my cards! I wish I had my Chevy! I wish I had Titiane! I wish my daughter was here! Wishing, that's all California is good for, or ever was! Wishing and old cars.

I've shown some interest in the golf buggies they use to get around with, and the kid who first took me to the Academy of Music now and then lets me ride his. I guess they're instructed to go along with the inmates therapeutic fantasies. He's been very nice.

It's called a Playcoaster and is powered by a six-battery electric engine. It seats two, with plenty of room for golfing equipment behind the seats. It provides a smooth, shock-free ride and is capable of speeds up to thirty-five miles per hour. The kid has painted it a utilitarian green and slanted the sun-roof forward, making it at once more practical and more daring looking.

I've been here for ten days now and can handle the buggy almost as well as he can. He's taught me all I know and I've been a willing and adaptable pupil. Wilhelmina has insisted on placing the mutt in my care. She's an ugly little creature, with long hair of orange brown color. I gave her a bath and I share my meals with her. I call her Freedom, just to be nasty. When Wilhelmina comes to see me, we lock Freedom in the bathroom. Sometimes we have to run the shower to drown out her whimpering. I guess you have no choice in the quality of creature you save from death.

The news from Washington is encouraging in some ways. The Speaker of the House has passed away and an academic-intellectual junta, led by those who dared to attack the Christ, has declared a national State of Suspension. The democratic processes have been temporarily suspended, pending establishment of some sort of New Order. In the meantime all death sentences have been set aside until further notice. The rumor is that the junta will stay in power and a revision of many sentences can be expected. On the other hand there is an even stronger suspicion that the new masters of the United States of America will try to economize at the bottom of the social ladder, which is definitely Mulatto Point, and that they will do this by reducing the inmate population, and that this can be done only by speeding up the execution schedule.

It is interesting to note how the appearance and departure of the Messenger from Space is now presented to the people. Every day the local TV station broadcasts new instalments of authoritative opinion, all of which has viewed the Christ phenomenon unfavorably. The Saviour is pictured as a demented, power-hungry super-creature from Outer Space that came to earth for as yet nebulous but no doubt destructive purposes. His attempt to indoctrinate the people, and His regally authoritarian behaviour are called subversion on a global scale. He is charged with the murder of President Chin, and no attempt seems to be in progress to determine who the actual killers were. It is said that Chin was killed by paranormal means and the bloody wire found near his almost decapitated body is no more than manufactured evidence to make the gruesome deed look terrestrial. President Chin's last, blood-spattered address to the people of the United States, in his own natural handwriting and signed indisputably by himself, is brought forth as evidence against the Christ. The lines: "I feel that I am ready to be judged. Every moment that now passes is for me a gift, a precious grant of time," especially are construed as knowledge on the President's part of his impending execution by the Visitor from Space. Finally, the Christ's sudden withdrawal is interpreted as flight from the growing, righteous anger of Americans who were beginning to see that they were being deceived in some fraudulent, interplanetary scheme too murky and complex to be fully understood. All these broadcasts end with a tinny rendition of the national anthem and it has been announced that a new contempo-

189

rary verse has been commissioned to be composed by the American Poet Laureate, soon to be delivered and sung by the New Tabernacle Choir of Ogden, Utah. Try as I might, the world into which I have been forced to descend bores me. Freedom is a mangy mutt. Wilhelmina has a butt like the combined respectability of her Dutch ancestors: two enormous sacks of mashed potatoes flung almost nightly against the gates of my pent-up passions. So far, nothing! I derive a certain amount of pleasure from watching her convulsive performance on my body, but no more. Not that I am consciously withholding. It's not a matter of pride, either. The best way of explaining it might be to say that spermal release just doesn't seem to be in the cards for me. Which reminds me!

In just ten days the fierce demonstrator at the sound-boards has started purring like a kitten. She has obtained a transfer and now works as a clerk in the office that handles the bureaucratic detail of dispatching the bodies of those who are executed each day. She types up tags and vital statistics folders. Everytime I look at Freedom it seems to me that I should have kept my mouth shut that day.

I still have not made up my mind to play golf, but I have acquired a Number Seven iron in the golf shop which, in conjunction with my outfit, has earned me the nickname The Pro. When a man is condemned to death, his true personality emerges. Mulatto Point is full of nuts. The human personality in all its crazy variety bares itself, sometimes without shame, always without guilt or embarrassment. But how mundane our aspirations really turn out to be! There are at least a dozen or two inmates of every imaginary socially enviable position: baseball players with high batting averages, boxing champions in their daily workout routine, senators, sheriffs, even financiers whose secret fantasies pre-date the Class Riots of the Eighties. And, of course, an enormous assortment of saints and holy men who spend their days in religious poses cluttering up the hills and vales of Number Three golf course which has become their special domain. These are men who killed for profit or in the grip of alcoholic demons. They are already on the "other side," behaving like ghosts and angels. They glide rather than walk, dispensing effeminate smiles of forgiveness and love as they pass. For them the three threads of sound that will dispatch them are no more than a cloth line on which to hang the empty, useless garment of their bodies. Even so, they have heard of me. They know me. And their meditative mumblings turn to frantic buzz when The Pro walks through, swinging his club.

I can feel that this is the lull before the storm. I am spending a sweet honeymoon, not with Wilhelmina, but with life. With the rest of my life. There have been a couple of Maximum Days during which I lie, usually naked, in the oxygen-saturated comfort of my bachelor apartment, watching TV, or trying to get used to the new music. It isn't easy. Everywhere, pieces seem to be missing. My ears get numb, I have to switch off. But every once in a while the semblance of a tune emerges, though I still have great trouble coping with the titles. In fact, I have trouble understanding the names. There is one, particularly offensive number called, I think, "CanIliveanotherdaylikethis," or maybe it's "Can'tIliveanotherwaylikehis," or even "Cantilevereddaylikethis." If I can break through with this particular piece I've got it made.

I replay some of the episodes of my past, but find that the most recent past is more attractive. Once in a while some memory breaks open in me, as if a secret cave deep inside had suddenly collapsed, releasing a flood of pungent pictures. My fight with Titiane's lover, for example. I've relived that three, four times now, and I have no idea why. There is nothing particularly significant about this episode. Or maybe what is significant about it hasn't come out yet. It's always the same. He accuses me of killing her deliberately. I try to reason with him. I offer to take him to the place of the accident. He becomes angrier and angrier. I realize that I can't avoid the fight and strike.

He is enormous, just as I remember him that night of Bianca's return. He moves like a huge, black animal. I can't feel his blows, but I know that they are exhausting me. It isn't hard for me to hit him either, and once, in one flashy move, I think I've solved his style, broken through, he seems helpless. But the moment passes, the tide turns. My left eye is closed. I can now taste blood. I can barely see him, my arms are getting heavy. Then he

191

lets off. I know I haven't done much damage to him. And I turn and run, turn and run, turn and run. Silly!

Then, punctual as the deadly weather, Wilhelmina arrives. I know that all our conversations are merely preliminary. Still, I try to get something out of her. I try to use her. I say quickly, when she opens the door: "There must be a way of getting out of here!"

"Yes," she says, "there is. Krotentoter is out. He's been suspended. It was on the news this afternoon!"

"You're kidding!"

"They're reviewing his record. That means your sentence will be reconsidered. There may be a new trial. You may even be pardoned. A whole new system is coming in, Al, and they need you. The Sadoos are a nuisance to the new people in Washington. They'll be put to work."

"Doing what?"

"Digging ditches. Repairing freeways. Anything. If you don't watch out, you'll be a hero!"

Enthusiastically she steps out of her clothes.

"Aren't you being a little too optimistic, Wilhelmina?"

"Aren't you the man who's been waiting two decades for a Flying Saucer?"

"Is it really true about Krotentoter?"

"Yes, true. He's been suspended. He's under house arrest, I think."

"But why?"

"Nobody knows. Maybe they think he's too strong. He's had his eyes on the governor's office. And he was known to be pro-Chin!"

She has taken off her smock, and her trousers, as usual. Shoes as well. Her shirt divides her in the middle. She will overwhelm me routinely with her lower half. In the reflection of the wine-red shirt the otherwise blonde hair of her pubis sends out rusty glints.

I tried to get up to turn on the TV. This was important. But she pushed me back. Again it was time for us. Again she descended on me like a warm flock of naked geese.

"This is good news, Wilhelmina!"

"Let go of it this time, Al," she murmurs intensely.

"I'll try."

"Don't try," she starts to churn, "just don't hold it back."

"Krotentoter is really out?"

"Shut up and relax!"

I myself can't understand why we've made no seminal contact. She is all I can ask for: seductive, helpful, energetic, big, dedicated, orgasmic in the extreme, in fact, irritatingly so. And I have always considered myself a normal, healthy male. But there is also something else. There is a strange, hot wet lick on my face, a familiar sniffle and whine. It's Freedom!

"Damn that dog," growls Wilhelmina, her eyes still rolling.

"Let *me* take her out," I offer.

"Oh no you don't. You just lie there till our relationship gets better. And don't you dare move!"

She's off me like lightning. Freedom senses danger and escapes into the kitchen where she knows she can't be locked in because of food on the table. The threatening woosh of Wilhelmina's massive carriage is right behind her, while I'm left to contemplate the glistening, dipping thing that got me into all this trouble in the first place.

There's a crash and howl in the kitchen. Wilhelmina emerges with Freedom by the scruff. She dumps her in the bathroom and slams the door shut. It has taken only thirty seconds in time, but already there is slack in my stack. When she lets herself down, it kinks a little.

"Easy," I caution her, "gently!"

"One day . . . ," she snorts. "One day . . . !"

"Yeah," I say, getting hold of her Dutch breasts, "I know. One day you're gonna kill that damn dog!"

And when that day comes, no Alfons Anton will be there to stay the heavy hand of fate.

•Thirty-Eight•

Anne was born. I attended the ceremony in Creole General Hospital. It was a little embarrassing, the doctors didn't know what to say to me. They couldn't treat the father like a kid, and they couldn't treat the kid like a father.

I was equipped with face-mask and camouflage green smock, disposable, made of compressed paper. The dull tiles, the flecked metal machinery, the wrinkled smocks, and now the blood on rubber gloves and aprons made a slaughterhouse out of the delivery room. Babies can't see. They are born blindly into slaughterhouses.

Little Vox was healthy, strong, weighed almost ten pounds. Bianca disappeared when she was six months old. She herself had no idea when it would happen, and she instructed me not to try to follow her. There were no farewells, no kisses, no embraces, no tears. It was then, I believe, that Pops went crazy.

The flying saucer story had always been tenuous at best. I was naive enough to think that I had to stick with it. I thought that the truth would serve me well. Nevertheless there was an investigation. I was questioned by Tim. Psychiatric consultation was recommended. It was determined and broken to me gently that I had the makings of a schizoid personality and that I would be well advised to let go of my fantasies of flying saucers. But even though my version of Bianca's departure was rejected, I was cleared of suspicion. Besides, no bodies were found. Mother and child had vanished. It was extraordinary but not unique. Tim informed me at the time that there were twenty-nine cases of this nature in Creole County alone. I remember wondering if all the husbands

194

and lovers had been promised Azydia. Or other distant worlds.

In the old days a man made up his mind to leave and went down to the Greyhound station, or got on his horse. And the woman waved tearful goodbye as the child clung to her skirts. The modern version of this traditional parting contained these elements only in principle. Bianca and the baby went up, at least I think they did. Instead of the Greyhound, a shimmering vehicle out of notime swept them away. Still a teenager, I began my long wait.

Waiting is something that gives you strength and permanency. Even though I had fathered a child, I understood that that was not the flower I was destined to bring into the world. Or, maybe it was the flower, but not the fruit. The fruit of my wait was a ticket for a ride in space and time.

Waiting made me grow into a tree when all around me people grew into bushes. This was so because they followed their impulses in everywhich direction, and they let themselves be cropped by fear and ambition. By Christmas of 1977 the world had faded for me. From 1978 on it no longer interested me. I was growing up without encumbrance.

I have a terrible feeling, which is that I will die at Mulatto Point. It's as if I'm facing a firing squad made up of a single soldier with only one bullet in his rifle. What chance do I have? The soldier is Fate, and Fate scores perfectly! He stands close, maybe twenty feet. My hands are bound. He is aiming directly at my forehead. Think, Alfons Anton, and if thinking doesn't help, stop thinking, let your body take care of its own survival, for Azydia is far. Far as a teenage dream.

• Thirty-Nine •

On the thirteenth day of my incarceration at Mulatto Point Penitentiary I am informed that the deadline for my execution has been lifted indefinitely, pending re-investigation in the wake of Judge Krishna Bavan Krotentoter's suspension.

Wilhelmina has only seven corpses to process and manages to get off early. We spend the afternoon celebrating. She has bought three bottles of champagne and, waiting out the heat of this June day in the cool, oxygen saturated comfort of my studio apartment, we are confidently making plans for the future. I don't object that she includes herself. We shall see what we shall see!

"Now that the pressure is off," she flirts, "I know you'll be able to get release. I want to feel it, the most beautiful and most powerful fountain on earth!"

"Yeah," I say, out of my California champagne dream.

"You know something, Monsieur Anton, you should get married!"

"Savez-vous quelque chose, Mademoiselle," I reply, purposefully in the fat creole patois of the county, "je suis déja!"

"Yes," she says, "why not me, why not?"

"Ah oui."

"We could visit France."

"Honeymoon in the trenches of Verdun, sure."

She wraps her inescapable thighs around one of my legs.

"A change is as good as a rest. It would do you a world of good, I know. You would come back a new man."

I'm thinking about Azydia, and about the world. My

father is buried in France, a decency unexpected. He rests a stone's throw from an ancient abbey in the arid soil of the Vaucluse, near a village of ruins and old women called Le Vieux Opede. Are there ruins on Azydia?

"Give up on Outer Space," she smiles, generating a little friction with her thighs. She dips a coquettish index finger in her glass and cools my navel with champagne. We drink on. She leans forward and blows on my pubic hair as if to ruffle the hair of a child sleeping in the afternoon. It is a motherly gesture. She is *so* proud of me. It's such a miracle, isn't it? Every evening, every night, the cozy little sleeper rises and turns into a stallion. I'm so *reliable*. Our heads and faces and brains, and even our mouths have nothing to do with this. There are really four of us, aren't there: two above and two below. Always the same conversations, too.

"Tomorrow I'll get Freedom a toy," she promises.

"That'll be good."

Freedom hears her name, twitches one ear but keeps her eyes closed. I take her for walks. She rides with me on the Playcoaster. She sits proudly, with her little paws on the dashboard above the golf-ball tray. She likes to have the wind blow the hair out of her face, so I push the Playcoaster to capacity to please her.

It's really a little early, but the champagne is good, and I'm just beginning to realize that my premonition of death at Mulatto Point is probably a common fantasy among inmates. After all, they've *told* you that they'll kill you. And you know that they mean it. So why shouldn't you believe them? But there are other forces at work in the world, too. Who could have predicted this turn of events! It's no use speculating about the future. I raise my glass.

"Well, Wilhelmina, I guess maybe I'll never know!"

She purses her wet lips and frowns in mock astonishment at the movement in my lap.

"The gentleman bestirs himself?"

Another nod from below, and another.

"You flatter me, sir," she smiles, emptying the rest of the first bottle into my glass. Wilhelmina is fine, actually! What am I waiting for, tomorrow? She deserves more than the vessel, she deserves what's in it, too. It's a little early, still, but I can't help myself. Now the show includes me and we slide around each other in perfect choreography after all these dress rehearsals.

"Oh Alfons, darling," she moans, "O I love you so!"

"I love you too, Wilhelmina!"

"Oh this is so good. You are so good to me."

"I love you!"

"Yes, yes, and I love *you!*"

I close my eyes, observing nothing. We ride a single horse. I see nothing, I know nothing. The horse has wings, and a pointed head of beautifully cast steel, and it flies us into the ground, into the earth, through the fires of hell. Once again the precious distillate of life flows and joins the river. We are locked into each other's arms and sleep overtakes me.

When I wake it is dark outside. Wilhelmina is still sleeping. I open the blinds. It's a night of the full moon, but a heavy fog has crept in from the bay and enveloped Mulatto Point. It looks milky in the lights around our compound, but I know that its true color is brownish yellow. This is a dangerous fog, and besides, Freedom is nowhere to be found. But the door is closed. Maybe Wilhelmina let her out earlier, before sundown. She is just getting used to her new home and usually stays close to the door. I want to go back to bed, but there's no choice. I put on my outfit, even my Zeiss-Ikons which protect my eyes. I know the terrain. Quietly I sneak out of the house.

The fog is thicker than I expected, and I go back in to get my oxygen cylinder and a surgical mask. Wilhelmina stirs in sleep and I stand petrified for a moment, holding breath and pose. I see myself in this stance: aha, already the considerate husband! I tiptoe out and don my mask, secure the oxygen cylinder. Then I pad down the narrow street, keeping a sharp lookout for Freedom.

Only five minutes outside and I need oxygen. While inhaling I realize that my search for the dog is wild. Visibility is extremely limited and getting more so every moment. No use working in a straight line, I'll have to work in circles around the house. So I quietly walk back, around the house, and back into the street. No sign of Freedom. This could be an immense job, and Mulatto

Point, after all, is not a desert. I decide then to take the Playcoaster.

A short walk gets me to one of the staff compounds with its park of carts. The Playcoaster starts up and I let myself out easily, driving at low speed back to my place. No sign of Freedom along the way, but the terrible fog is getting thicker. I drive with one hand and handle the oxygen equipment with the other. A tour of the golf courses may be in order. Freedom may have lost her way, but more likely the smoggy soup of fog is getting to her. I stop for a moment, straining my ears, but there is no sound of her.

The familiar landscape, the greens and traps, hills and ornamental lakes, the groves and roughs and fairways are changing as I drive along. Far distance and middle distance have been swallowed and with it all points of reference that might guide me on a moonlit night. The nasty fog covers all. I can't see more than ten feet ahead. The Playcoaster's lights bounce off and lose themselves. I am gliding in dripping, eerie silence in an ocean of fog.

I have walked these lawns long enough not to lose my way, and by my calculations I'm somewhere near where Number One golf course adjoins Number Two, by the Ninth Hole. Sure enough: there's the pole and the flag, limp and damp, passing silently to my right. It is swallowed up by fog the moment I see it. This is a useless search! If Freedom has passed out somewhere, or if she's sleeping, I could drive by her close enough to touch and not notice her. And still the soup is thickening, forcing me to proceed at slower than walking speed. On the other hand, as long as I keep driving, the damn dog may hear me and come running. Even though she must be stupid not to have sensed her impending execution, I hope her instincts are keen enough to know that the low-pitched whine of the Playcoaster means man. And that man means rescue and company, safety, warmth and food.

I cut across Number Two course, onto Number Three. Progress is becoming extremely difficult. I don't want to get stuck in a sand trap or drive into a water hole. I stop and sit quietly, inhaling fresh oxygen. I let the silence descend. What on earth am I *doing* out here?

199

Where *am* I? What is this: it's ridiculous! The dog may already be back there, whining Wilhelmina out of bed. Maybe I should get out and walk back.

I push my sunglasses up on my forehead and adjust the surgical mask. Visibility is not improved by this. I stretch out my arm in front of me and my hand literally disappears, and that *is* a strange phenomenon. I'm going to give it one more try!

The engine does not immediately come on. I try again. Another false start. Then, at last, it's alive. This has not happened before. I guess the old Playcoaster is finally getting senile. I proceed at snail's pace, my face stuck far forward, trying to pierce the thick moon fog. A slice and tilt. A silvery shark's fin rips into the cart, the wing of a gigantic metal bird dips low, the tilted sun-roof sliced clean off, severed by a monstrous, airborne scythe. The buggy's on two wheels, tumbling, and I'm thrown. The picture of the blade that nearly sliced me in half flashes again and again in my mind as I roll on the ground. Around me all hell breaks loose.

What *was* that thing, what *is* it? There's no time to think about it. All impressions are chased back into my subconscious by a burst of automatic weapons' fire coming from my right. I try to melt into the ground. I'm the hands on a clock with my feet pointing to six and my head to noon or midnight, and they are firing from approximately two. Now another burst of fire from five o'clock on this insane dial. Then, so low it almost sears my hair, a streak of flares coming from the left, from nine. I'm caught in crossfire! But who is firing? And then I know: this is a prison break!

Low as a snake I crawl forward, trying to reach cover. There are opposing parties in this firefight, and they are using automatic weapons, explosive ammunition, and every once in a while there is the hiss and splat of a laser gun, so fast and eerie. As the fire dies away I crawl some more. There's a helicopter above, it seems to be circling. A tremendous explosion, a shockwave of air hits me. The fog turns luminous as a thousand candles are lit above. They're dropping flares! To my right at two o'clock the stooped shadow of a man runs in strange, dreamlike movements, drawn out unnaturally by the descending flares. He falls. The firing rises to a peak. Suddenly, down at six o'clock, Pearl's voice breaks through the night.

"We know where you are, Krotentoter. Give up!"

"Pearl," I scream stupidly. "Pearl, over here!"

I've given away my position. Bullets come whistling in bunches, passing over me in formation. There must be at least three machine-guns and a couple of lasers. More flares from above. A shadow runs at me. There's a burst of fire from Pearl's direction. The shadow falls, but in a strange, jerky way. He's been hit.

"Alfons!" It's the voice of Freddy.

"Over here, kid!" More bullets and laser hiss from my right.

"I'm Mike Junior," he screams, "Mike Voronov's son!"

"Yeah," I scream back, "I thought you were!"

"Stay where you are, Al," Pearl yells, "we're gonna get you out of this. Scott is here, too. Krotentoter is out to get you personally, but I think I just got *him!*"

And now Judge Krishna Krotentoter's voice, colder and thicker than the fog.

"Anton's gonna die! I sentenced him to death, he dies tonight! Do you hear me, Anton?"

Krotentoter's party spits fire. Most of it comes my way, the rest goes to Pearl and Mike and Scott. But I notice that they are firing behind me, too, assuming maybe that I'm trying to crawl back toward Pearl's party. A veritable sheet of flames goes up to my left, at nine o'clock. That's where the Pointers are. More fire from ahead, too. They are surrounding us, and we'll all be cooked in this deadly stew. How on earth did Pearl get across the moat!

I've reached the edge of a green, I crawl on, and now I feel sand. I let myself down, sliding slowly into the sandtrap amid the cacophony of gunfire. It can't be! It feels familiar. It's the trap where Bianca and I . . . and now the picture of the slicing scythe again. It's them, yes, it's the Azydians! Bianca is here. They've come to pick me up. It was their ship that sent the Playcoaster flying, they're hovering above!

A laser hisses by, melts sand not two feet from my head. They're here to pick me up, they're close, I can feel it. It's now or never, Alfons Anton, now or never!

Up I jump like a bunny in one tremendous leap and howl, a mad muscular effort. You save me now or a crazy man is cut down on earth! I get almost to the top, slip, fall, a burst of gunfire wooshes by. My fall has saved me, but I'm up again between bullets, bounding out of the sandtrap, screaming with all I have:

"Biancaaaaaa! Azydiaaaaaaaah!"

I leap as no kangaroo ever leapt. They are boundless dream leaps, I'm invincible, I know not where I'm running. I must be out on the fairway, zigzagging, and then I'm hit, in the face, blood gushes, the mask dangles, my glasses are gone. I sway and stumble. All connections are cut. I'm caught in a column of light. There is music, no, sound. A tone, a single note, a one-note melody. A hit from a thousand years hence. Colors cascade down upon me, the thunderous fire grows distant. I wipe my bloody face and sway transfixed as they are coming down upon me. I pass into the rainbow. No, no, the pain, the blood, oh no Bianca, I am dying, let me go! Too late! A man has waited and is dying, leave him be!

I'm dying and yet I am at rest, my eyes are open, staring. It is Bianca, yes, the young Bianca. I try to speak. Two men are at her side. Strange men, too gentle to be human, too tall. Their hands are clouds of mercy above my face. My blood is scarlet vapor, rising. I breathe again, their hands descend and vaporize more blood. Then less, and less.

"Bianca, my face, my nose!"

It's *not* Bianca, it is Anne! Her voice is familiar, her English slow, a porous harmony of tentative words.

"Fa-ther! Dad-dy!"

I try to smile and I succeed.

"Freedom!" I whisper. "Where is the dog?"

"Free-dom is safe!"

Again there is that tone, the one-note melody. I close my eyes. I want to listen. The shock subsides. My body lives. Fate was the firing squad. Fate missed. My nose is gone, that's all!

"They got me in the nose," I moan. My daughter smiles.

"Azydians have no no-ses, Fa-ther!"

It must have been that I turned my head. I ran and turned my head just when Fate fired. Maybe it was Krotentoter. I ran and turned my nose out of time.

There is no ambiguity, no weight. I'm sandy, I raise

one hand. Anne shimmers silver, green and gold. I miss my playing cards. I have to laugh but mustn't laugh. I've paid and now I know the price of this ticket: my playing cards and my nose. And a pair of Zeiss-Ikon sunglasses, Everest.

Rainbow colors shiver through metallic skin inside the small, domed chamber where I lie. These mild and insubstantial strangers are Azydians! They have no noses, but they seem to smile.

"Come closer, Anne!"

She puts my hand to her cheek. Her face is close to mine.

"Where's Bianca?"

"Wai-ting, Fa-ther."

"But why, for heaven's sake? Why wait so *long?*"

"Azydia owed the world a ba-by, Fa-ther."

"A baby! What, whose baby?"

"*Your* baby," smiles my daughter Anne. "With Wil-hel-mi-na. Azydia had to wait until you made another ba-by! Ano-ther ba-by for this world! A ba-by to replace me!"

THE BEST IN SCIENCE FICTION
AND FANTASY FROM
AVON BOOKS

URSULA K. LE GUIN

The Lathe of Heaven	47480	1.75
The Dispossessed	44057	2.25

ISAAC ASIMOV

Foundation	44057	1.95
Foundation and Empire	42689	1.95
Second Foundation	45351	1.95
The Foundation Trilogy (Large Format)	26930	4.95

ROGER ZELAZNY

Doorways in the Sand	32086	1.50
Creatures of Light and Darkness	35956	1.50
Lord of Light	44834	2.25
The Doors of His Face The Lamps of His Mouth	38182	1.50
The Guns of Avalon	31112	1.50
Nine Princes in Amber	36756	1.50
Sign of the Unicorn	30973	1.50
The Hand of Oberon	33324	1.50

Include 50¢ per copy for postage and handling, allow 4-6 weeks for delivery.

Avon Books, Mail Order Dept.
224 W. 57th St., N.Y., N.Y. 10019

SCIENCE FICTION AND FANTASY
FROM AVON ▲ BOOKS

INTIMACY . . .
BEYOND ECSTASY . . .
BEYOND TIME . . .

MINDBRIDGE

BY NEBULA AND HUGO AWARD WINNER

JOE HALDEMAN

"FANTASTIC . . . A MINDBLITZ
. . . BRINGS OUT ALL THE TERROR WE REPRESS AT
THE POSSIBILITY OF HOW EASILY WE MIGHT BE
POSSESSED BY A STRONGER POWER."
Los Angeles Times

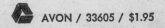 AVON / 33605 / $1.95

MIND 7-79